WYOMING RANCH PROMISE

AMIE DENMAN

Recycling programs for this product may not exist in your area.

ISBN-13: 978-1-335-60516-0

Wyoming Ranch Promise

For questions and comments about the quality of this book, please contact us at CustomerService@Harlequin.com.

Harlequin Enterprises ULC
22 Adelaide St. West, 41st Floor
Toronto, Ontario M5H 4E3, Canada
www.Harlequin.com

HarperCollins Publishers
Macken House, 39/40 Mayor Street Upper,
Dublin 1, D01 C9W8, Ireland
www.HarperCollins.com

Printed in U.S.A.

1 2 3 4 5 6 7 8 9 10 HDC 28 27 26 25

Beck noticed it was getting dark.

"We should talk about business," he said. "Before the sun goes down. I don't want you driving across the ranch in the dark."

"The SUV has headlights," Nora replied.

"Animals don't share the road well, and the roads aren't what you're used to."

Nora laughed. "I drove a rental car in Rome. *Rome*," she emphasized. "The hundreds of scooters were scarier than wild animals, and the traffic circles were like the Wild West."

Beck laughed.

"Okay, maybe not the real Wild West," she said. "I suppose you know more about that than I do."

"Maybe a little," he said. "I could teach you."

The moment he said it, he wished he could take it back. Nora wasn't a tourist, and he didn't want or need to spend time showing her his world. She didn't need to know how much he loved it—why he loved it and how it was part of his skin and bones.

"I'd like that."

Dear Reader,

Thank you for reading *Wyoming Ranch Promise*. I hope you'll love your visit to Remedy Creek, Wyoming, a small town with a reputation for healing. The lure of the American West with its wide-open spaces, scenery and (of course) cowboys was my inspiration for this book. The mountains, plains and starry skies are the perfect backdrop for romance.

This is the first book in my Remedy Creek miniseries, and you'll meet Beck Duncan, who's trying to run the large family ranch and the luxury ranch resort his brother left behind...while also coping with guilt over his brother's death. Nora Myers knows how to turn around a failing resort property, but she has a lot to learn about ranch life. I love a fish-out-of-water story, and being vulnerable is sometimes the first step toward falling in love.

I hope you feel transported to a luxury ranch resort and fall in love with Remedy Creek. I had so much fun writing *Wyoming Ranch Promise*, and I can't wait for you to read the next book in the series.

Happy reading,

Amie

Amie Denman is the author of over fifty contemporary romances. A devoted traveler, she loves reading and writing books you could take on vacation. Amie lives on the shores of Lake Erie with her husband, sons, extended family and numerous pets. She loves playing outside, running and paddleboarding. Her favorite indoor activities are reading and writing (of course!), sewing and crocheting, and playing her antique Steinway grand piano.

Books by Amie Denman

Harlequin Heartwarming

Meet Me at Niagara Falls

Falling for Her Fake Fiancé
Falling for Her Ranger
Christmas with the Single Dad
Second Chance with the Firefighter

Return to Christmas Island

I'll Be Home for Christmas
Home for the Holidays
A Merry Little Christmas
Last Summer on Christmas Island
Under the Mistletoe

Cape Pursuit Firefighters

In Love with the Firefighter
The Firefighter's Vow
A Home for the Firefighter

Visit the Author Profile page at Harlequin.com for more titles.

CHAPTER ONE

BECK DUNCAN KNEW what an albatross was. He'd read the classics in college, even though he'd bucked his parents about going. What good were stories of epic wars and ancient mariners to someone destined to run the family ranch? But still, he'd read those stories and then tucked them away when he came home to his real future at Remedy Mountain Ranch. Some of those stories about heroes and battling obstacles had stuck with him, though he couldn't help but think those ancient characters would be disappointed in him over the past year.

"I'm no Hercules," he said aloud, and his horse pricked his ears at the name. "Not talking to you, Herc."

Beck halted his horse on a high trail that gave him a clear view of his own personal albatross down in the valley: Remedy Mountain Lodge, his brother's dream. The August sun had been up for three hours and heat radiated from the trail. He and Bryan had gone out early on mornings like this from the time they were old enough to seat a horse to check on cattle, ride fences and evaluate the grass and water sources.

He'd always believed his brother loved ranching, until push came to shove and Bryan had invested his half of their inheritance into the one-hundred-room resort with a mostly empty parking lot shimmering in the heat below. All those empty spaces felt like a poke in the eye to Beck and a stain on his brother's memory.

"Gotta face it," he said to his horse.

Hercules tossed his head, and Beck would have sworn he was getting side-eye from the seven-year-old roan. He nudged the horse toward a switchback trail winding down the mountain. It would take a good half hour to safely reach the bottom and make his way to the grand front entrance of the Lodge, and he had plenty to think about on the way.

The summer heat siphoned off his energy and patience, and by the time Beck dismounted at the Lodge's hitching rail shaded by a tall tree, he was formulating an escape plan. He didn't want to go to this meeting. He didn't want any part in this.

He filled a water bucket for Hercules and patted the horse's neck. "I won't be long," he said.

Dust from an approaching vehicle swirled in the sun up the valley, and Beck stood under the front portico, steeling his nerves as if for attack. The hired gun from the hotel management agency—insisted upon by his family lawyer, who warned him the Lodge was sinking and taking the whole ranch with it—would have a lot of questions, and he was in no mood to answer them. He hadn't even bothered to review the information the company emailed about the "hospitality management consultant," some guy named John something, who'd be swooping in for six weeks to turn around the failing business.

His failing business now—sitting squarely on a set of shoulders meant for ranching, not offering concierge service to visitors who only wanted the fun parts of Western life, not the reality.

"Morning, boss," Allie, a perky gal at least ten years younger than Beck, said as she came out the front door. A whoosh of air-conditioning came along with her. She wore jeans, a plaid shirt and a hotel name tag, with her brown hair in braids. She was just out of college, and he'd hired her for the summer to manage the front desk, even though there weren't many guests to check in. No doubt she needed to be looking for a more permanent job, since her degree was in biology, not hospitality.

He was letting everyone down.

"Howdy," he said quietly, not wanting to engage in conversation. If the valley floor could open up and quietly swallow Remedy Mountain

Lodge, he might be able to start breathing for the first time since last October.

"Today's the big day," Allie said.

"Uh-huh."

"I think this is our person."

Beck wanted to remark that it could be a carload of guests who'd heard of the Lodge and shown up to stay a week, but since he'd done exactly zero advertising and guests were usually people who accidentally stumbled on the place while they were in the nearby town of Remedy Creek for some other reason, he doubted that SUV was bringing paying guests.

The black car, covered in dust, stopped under the portico, and Beck took a deep breath, the kind he'd take before leaping into a cold mountain stream in the early spring. It was the kind of breath he knew could be his last for a while.

No one got out of the car at first, and Allie sidled closer to him. "Do you…think we should open the door for him…or something?" she whispered.

Beck had to take another deep breath. His patience couldn't be stretched thinner. There were miles of range he should be riding, a whole ranch and a dozen ranch employees under his supervision. The SUV's windows were tinted, but Beck could see the silhouette of someone who was on their phone, probably finishing up some important business call with another struggling hotel property. This company existed for a reason, which told him he wasn't the only failure out there in the hospitality business.

Not that it made him feel any better.

"We don't offer butler service at this hotel. If this guy is going to tell us how to manage the Lodge, I bet he can open his own car door."

Finally, the back door opened and two red high-heeled shoes emerged followed by two long legs. Beck let out a sigh of relief. This was obviously not the man from the management company. Even a temporary reprieve was welcome.

The slender blonde with long wavy hair studied Beck for a minute, and then reached back into the car. She tucked a messenger bag under her left arm and walked toward him, right hand extended. He had no idea how she crossed the flagstones so quickly in those ridiculous shoes without even a teeter.

"I'm Nora Myers from Total Hospitality Management."

Beck was so surprised he didn't even offer his hand in return. "What happened to the other guy they were sending?"

The blonde's smile faltered, and she said in a more businesslike tone, "There was a last-minute change. I'll be your on-site consultant for the next six weeks."

Beck was silent, absorbing this information.

"I believe you are Beck Duncan?" the newcomer—Nora—said. "I saw your picture online when I was researching this assignment."

Assignment. Remedy Mountain Lodge was an assignment for this lady. *Please write a 500-word essay on how the brother of the original owner has no idea how to run the place and discuss a plan to kill the echo in the Lodge hallways and clear the dust from the empty cabins.*

"Mr.….Duncan?" the blonde prodded.

He blinked a few times, then finally completed the handshake she offered.

"Nora Myers," she repeated as if she didn't believe he'd been listening.

He had to look like a wooden replica of a cowboy, but that was how being at the Lodge made him feel—as if he'd frozen in time that awful night last October that took his brother.

"You'll…want to settle in," he said. He wanted to get back on his horse and hightail it out of there. "This is Allie. She'll show you around and direct you to your room."

He turned on his boot heel and took a huge step, only to have his movement arrested.

"I'm ready to get to work right away," Nora said. "If someone can get my luggage from the rideshare so he can get back to the airport."

Finally. Something useful to do that he understood. The back hatch was up on the SUV, and Beck strode over and retrieved the two suitcases that the rideshare driver handed out.

"I didn't mean for you to—" Nora began.

Did she think they had bellhops? Hadn't she noticed the empty parking lot?

"I don't mind," Beck said. He strode through the front door, deposited the suitcases next to the desk, and then continued straight out a side door that led to the hitching post where Hercules waited under a tree.

"WHAT WAS THAT?" Nora asked the girl with braids who looked as shocked as she did as they watched Beck Duncan make his escape. She couldn't believe the owner of the place could act as if she was there to wash the windows. If that was how he treated guests, it was no wonder his Lodge needed her company's services.

Speaking of guests, where were they? She took a moment to inspect the lobby with its high ceilings, impressive stone fireplace and huge paintings of the American West adorning the walls. Comfortable-looking leather armchairs and couches upholstered in shades of green and tan sat in inviting groups. But those seats were empty.

"That was Beck," Allie said with a shrug. "He never comes here."

"How can he never come here? He owns this place, doesn't he?"

"Yes," Allie said.

Nora had the impression there was a lot more story behind that one word, but she was hardly going to get to the bottom of the resort's issues by interrogating a college-age girl with braids and cowboy boots.

Beck had also been wearing cowboy boots. And a hat, and he'd stood with a very cowboy-like posture. Maybe it was the attire, but he'd been almost half a foot taller than her.

Nora straightened her spine. She would be successful turning around this resort just as she had plenty of others, and she simply wasn't letting a grumpy cowboy stand in his own way or hers. She started down the hall toward the door he'd disappeared through. Her heels clicked on the flagstone floor, and her pencil skirt made it hard for her to take the long strides she needed to catch up with Beck.

He was headed for a horse—an actual horse—tied up under a shade tree. Was he seriously planning to escape her on horseback? Sure, she knew this was a Western resort with a working ranch theme, and she'd read something about it being located on property that once belonged to the family ranch…but was this guy really some kind of a cowboy?

"Hey," she called. "Beck Duncan."

She noticed a hitch in his stride as if she'd interrupted his movement but not arrested it. He was still headed for the brown horse that now had its head up, watching Beck approach.

"I feel like I'm in a movie," she grumbled to herself as she trekked through the grass to catch up with Beck. The red heels she'd slipped on in the car so she'd look professional when she arrived were now an anchor dragging her down. She was pretty sure she was going to lose one in the grass, and then she'd look ridiculous chasing down a person she was supposed to be partnering with to save his resort.

The shoes had been terrific on the streets of Paris, New York and Los Angeles—cities and hotel properties where her gorgeous, expensive wardrobe was appreciated. During the long ride from the airport filled with rustic scenery and unforgiving terrain, she'd begun regretting the silk and linen in her suitcase.

Beck halted when he got to the horse, untied the reins as if he'd done it ten thousand times and swung a leg over the saddle. Just like that, his scowl was about ten feet in the air.

Nora stopped, pulled off her shoes and trotted the final few feet to the shade tree.

"We need a meeting," she said. "That's the process. A sit-down. You and me." She pointed to him and then back to herself. "We make a plan together to determine how I can best serve your property and your needs."

She was relying on almost ten years of hospitality experience to help her find the right language and moderate her tone. Maybe they'd just gotten off on the wrong foot. Maybe the guy had some kind of cowboy emergency, or he'd misunderstood exactly who she was and why she was there. He'd approved a substantial budget she could use at her discretion for hiring and making changes, but he also needed to participate.

"I'm busy," Beck said.

"I was under the impression you knew I was arriving today. You were there to greet me."

He pulled his cowboy hat a little lower, shading his eyes.

"Which," she continued, "would indicate to me that you're ready to discuss the challenges and opportunities of Remedy Mountain Lodge and how we can ensure a quality and profitable guest experience going forward."

She could tell she had his attention. He sat in the saddle and stared at her for a full ten seconds. Of course he wanted to be successful and make a profit; she just needed to persuade him that she was the person to help him with her years of experience and—

"Not today," he said. He made some sound to

his horse, which turned and began trotting away with a cowboy in the saddle who didn't glance back at her.

Nora's shoulders sank and she stood there in the valley ringed by mountains, clutching her city heels in one hand and wondering how on earth she was going to manage this assignment and restore her company's faith in her.

CHAPTER TWO

BECK STARED HARD at the silver-haired woman who made breakfast for his ranch hands, cleaned his house and office, and did so many other tasks he wouldn't even know how to write a job description if she ever quit or retired. Judy had been on the ranch so long she was practically an institution. She'd known his parents and worked for them until they passed, and her own son had worked on the ranch since he was a teenager. Unfortunately, that son, Mitch, was just one more person leaving the ranch. Leaving Beck high and dry.

Judy stared right back at him. "It's true, I'm sorry to say. But I did warn you it was coming. Mitch turned thirty last week and he thinks his clock is ticking. He always wanted a shot at the rodeo, and if moving to Cody is his chance, I couldn't talk him out of it, though heaven knows you need him here." Her lip trembled. "And I'll miss him."

"We all will," Beck said. He put a comforting

hand on Judy's shoulder and tried to focus on her feelings as a parent instead of his own panic at losing his assistant ranch manager.

"I hope you'll leave the door open for him in case he comes crawling back, hat in hand," Judy said.

"Of course."

"In the meantime, I put the word out in town that there's an opening here. You pay decent and I cook a mean breakfast, so between us we might find someone soon."

Beck tried to breathe. Soon was a relative term. It could mean a few days or a few weeks, and then there would be training time on top of that. Meanwhile, the cattle would continue to need someone to move them to better pasture and water, the horses would need care, trails would need to be maintained, fences fixed. There was a never-ending chore list on a large ranch with cattle, sheep and hay production.

"Thank you," he said at last.

"And how is the new manager at the Lodge?" Judy asked.

Beck paused. He had no idea how the pretty lady—Nora—was. He hadn't asked. And he hadn't returned her phone calls. She'd likely acquired his number from the property's paperwork, since he was technically the owner of the Lodge, cabins and the vast acres surrounding it.

But he was just…well, giving himself a moment before he reopened the wound of the Lodge. His brother's death had left the place orphaned, and Beck knew it was his responsibility to step in and save Bryan's legacy.

But he had so many other responsibilities. So many people depended on him.

"I'm meeting with her soon," he said, unwilling to admit to Judy that dealing with the Lodge problem meant dredging up a wagonload of guilt over Bryan's passing. Judy might understand, but Nora Myers would not. She was there to do a job.

Jody crossed her arms over her red apron. Breakfast was over and she already had dishes soaking in the ranch house sink. Beck knew she'd transition next to lunch preparation for the workers who came in around one o'clock. Only a few of the twenty hands lived on the ranch, in a bunkhouse not far from Beck's house. Most of them lived in nearby Remedy Creek and only stayed over when the weather was bad.

"Well, I hope you meet with her soon," Judy said. "She's here to help you. An expert in hotel management, at least that's what I overheard when your lawyer was here a few weeks ago."

Beck raised an eyebrow.

"Of course I was too polite to listen to the whole conversation."

"I appreciate that," Beck said, not believing

a word of it but not actually minding. Judy had been his parents' friend, and she'd also been his rock during the past year. He wouldn't have eaten a solid meal without her, and neither would the men who worked here, which would have meant losing more of them. Money talks, but sometimes a hot meal speaks louder.

His own parents had been older when he and his brother were born two years apart. His dad never kicked his smoking habit, and cancer took him just a year after Beck and Bryan lost their mother to a stroke. Ranch life was hard on people, and passing his thirty-second birthday reminded him every day that he needed good help.

Bryan would have been good help, but he was gone.

His phone rang, and when he saw the number he rejected the call with a stab of guilt.

"You're going to have to face her sooner or later," Judy said. "And the rest of it."

She didn't have to explain what she meant.

"I will, but right now I have work to do," Beck said. He nodded to Judy and crossed through the kitchen to the porch door. He needed fresh air. Outside, he leaned on a porch post and crossed one boot over the other. It was a fresh, clear Wyoming morning. His ranch—he had to remind himself that it was his, not his parents' or shared with his brother—comprised just over 20,000 acres. His grandparents had made a wise selection of the property with its varied terrain—mountains, flat lands, ample grazing. Most importantly, it had reliable fresh water running through it from Remedy Creek, which never ran dry. With good water for growing crops and watering the cattle and sheep, the Remedy Mountain Ranch had been going strong for decades.

He had to keep it that way, but he was the first generation of his family to run it alone. Some days he wondered why he tried so hard if the Duncan legacy was destined to die with him anyway. Wyoming's small population made it hard to find someone—especially a woman who wanted to tie herself to a guy with perpetual sunburn, dust baked into the wrinkles around his eyes, and a giant ranch to keep afloat that left no time for anything else.

A dust cloud, weirdly reminiscent of the one the black SUV rideshare had rolled in with the previous day, appeared in the direction of the Lodge and moved his way. It could be one of his ranch hands coming in late for breakfast, knowing Judy always saved something back for latecomers.

Just his luck, though, it probably wasn't. He squinted. As the vehicle approached, he recognized it as the one belonging to the Lodge. Bryan had purchased an SUV for guest convenience, but it had been used so little it probably hadn't even had its first oil change yet.

It could be any of the employees from the Lodge, but something told Beck it wasn't. He should have taken Nora's calls. It would have been easier to put her off over the phone than having to look her in the eye and admit that he didn't know anything about running a resort, had never wanted a resort, and now was stuck with it because the massive structure and outbuildings weren't going to sink into the valley. No, they were a permanent reminder of what he'd lost and the heavy guilt of failure. But he had a plan to ease that guilt, and Nora was a pivotal part of the plan.

He stood his ground on the porch and waited while the vehicle parked right in front of him. He saw the blond waves first, emerging like a pistol shot from the driver's seat. She was probably afraid he'd hop on a horse and elude her again. He'd lain awake cursing his cowardice last night.

"There you are," she said. She wore a smile and used a perky tone, but Beck doubted she was in the habit of having to ride herd on her clients and hunt them down like rabbits.

"I tried calling, but I must have an incorrect number," she continued politely, though they both knew his voicemail greeting clearly identified him. "So I thought we could meet in person. It's always better that way," she added.

Beck doubted that. He should have taken her calls. Looking at her eager face and pretty smile made him feel like the only kid in his class who hadn't done the homework. She wore a skirt and jacket again today—city clothes—but he noticed that her shoes didn't have high heels. He internally grimaced. Had she destroyed those red heels chasing after him yesterday?

"I have to check fences on our sheep pasture," he said, cursing himself for being a coward. "Can we do this another time?"

Her smile stayed in place but her eyes raked him. "I think it's best to get moving on this project," she said. "I don't want to waste time when you have empty rooms in your beautiful resort property."

He almost corrected her, almost said it wasn't his. He didn't view the Lodge as *his* resort property, even though it was. He didn't need anyone to tell him that his unwillingness to take responsibility for the Lodge was one of the reasons for its failure.

"Tomorrow," he said.

"I'm free all day today. I could sit down with you anytime, and, like I said, it seems a shame to waste time."

"Can't."

Nora tilted her head. “Mr. Duncan, while I’m here for six weeks, I work for you, but you’re paying me by the day and I want to—”

“I know,” Beck said.

“And I brought a list I’ve drawn up. Mostly the usual questions, but I added a few yesterday after I started looking around and talking to employees and guests.”

He could only imagine what questions she’d come up with after some digging. People who worked at the ranch and Lodge were loyal, but he wouldn’t blame them if they’d been truthful about Beck’s lack of interest in the Lodge. He suspected they all knew why. They’d know about his grief over his brother’s death, even though they might not know about his guilt. Or the reason for it.

“I don’t mean to scare you,” she added quickly, her eyes still searching his face.

Did he look scared? Beck never backed down from danger on the ranch, and he was brave when it came to the daily threats of wild animals and bad weather. Those were the easy things to face.

“I do this for a living,” Nora continued, “and I travel all over the world working with hotels and resorts that aren’t…living up to their potential.”

Beck shoved off the post. He didn’t want to talk about potential, and he sure didn’t want to compare anything on his ranch to fancy hotels in big cities. If Nora’s goal was to hold Remedy

Mountain Lodge up against hotels in Paris and Milan and New York, she was going to be disappointed. She could add her name to the list of people who were disappointed in him.

"Like I said, I have fences to mend," Beck replied. "We'll talk tomorrow."

Nora studied him for a minute and then pulled out her phone. Her finger hovered over the screen. "I'll send you a calendar invite. What time?"

He used the calendar feature on his phone all the time to keep track of things and set reminders, but he didn't want to see this meeting pop up. He knew the sooner the Lodge got on its feet, the better. He'd face it, of course. He had to. Just not today.

Maybe not tomorrow either.

"I'll let you know," he said.

"SO, YOU'RE TELLING ME there isn't an actual system for taking reservations?" Nora asked.

The front desk employee with the braids—Allie, according to her name tag—chewed her lip. "Not really. I think there used to be one, but no one paid for the software updates, so it doesn't exactly work. We take phone calls and walk-ins, though."

Nora breathed in the scent of the lobby. It smelled clean, and not in the way that scented cleaners and chemicals make a place smell clean.

It was fresh, like air and trees and sunshine. She remembered a hotel in the Virgin Islands that had that freshness that seemed to seep in through the windows and doors. It was nice, but she loved the scents and sounds of cities, with the excitement of hundreds of people coming through the lobbies, thousands of guests a week—including celebrities, bejeweled women, men with finely tailored suits.

Those were the kinds of places where her work was noticed, and making those resorts shine had catapulted her to the list of top consultants in her company, a spot she was scrambling to regain.

Allie was currently sweeping some dust and leaves out the door where Beck had made his exit yesterday. A whole day had gone by, and Nora had not even started her usual checklist: meet with owner; examine financial records; extensive property tour; meet with heads of front desk, housekeeping, food and beverage, and maintenance; develop a plan based on a ten-point system she'd helped her company develop and was now in place at luxurious properties around the world.

"Can you show me the system, even if it isn't currently working?" Nora asked.

"Okay," Allie agreed. She put down the broom and dusted her hands on her jeans and then jiggled the mouse on the counter. "I guess Bryan

Duncan put this in place before he…before, you know."

"I don't exactly know," Nora said. People at the Lodge seemed unwilling to say much. Was it loyalty to the resort? Maybe they hadn't decided to trust her yet. Sometimes it took a while. "I understand that he is deceased, but I don't know the circumstances. I'm assuming his brother is his heir and was not involved in planning or running the Lodge."

Allie looked down. "I wasn't here at the time. I was still in college. This is a summer job for me."

It sounded like the kid wasn't planning on sticking around past fall. When fall came, Nora hoped she'd be at a resort where her hard work would get attention. There was an upcoming job at a prestigious hotel in Barcelona that had suffered lately after being handed down to a third generation. It was her kind of challenge in her kind of place—sophisticated, cultured, European old-world charm. And very *on the radar*. Unlike this quiet lodge tucked between mountains in a state less populous than the Sahara Desert.

Cowboy charm with antlers in the chandeliers overhead was not going to offer her the ladder she somehow needed these days at her company if she wanted to move up. The Barcelona job was scheduled to start in two months, which meant she had to turn this place around fast and get out of Dodge.

She just had to keep the cowboy owner from sidestepping her attempts to help. The man looked like he'd just ambled out of a Western movie, but he could be the handsomest cowboy in the West and it wouldn't fill the rooms in his hotel without some decent management.

"Here it is," Allie said, nodding toward the computer screen, "but we keep getting this pop-up warning saying this version is out of date and we should contact our administrator."

"Who's the tech contact for the Lodge?" Nora asked.

"One of the housekeepers has a son who's good with tech. Tristan's been here a few times to help."

No tech person. Now, that was something Nora had only heard once before at a quaint, family-run French hotel that was one of her first big turnaround projects. She thought of that place on the Riviera all the time, especially when she saw wisteria in bloom. She swallowed. She'd turned it around the first time, when she was young and eager, but her visit there six weeks ago when it had new owners hadn't turned out so well, and she still stung from the fallout.

"Do you think your tech genius is available?" Nora asked.

"I'll ask Marcy if she can bring him to work tomorrow."

"How old is Tristan?"

Allie shrugged. "At least twelve, I think. Maybe thirteen."

Nora nodded, trying to maintain a professional expression, but *come on.* The resort had a junior high kid in charge of a system with credit card and personal information? "I'm glad you've learned to improvise with phone reservations," she said as pleasantly as possible. Although Allie was clearly temporary, she seemed competent, and Nora never made an enemy among hotel employees. They didn't get paid enough to put up with criticism or take the fall for problems that should have been solved by their employers.

"Is there anything else you want to know?" Allie asked. "I'm off in an hour and we don't have any check-ins coming that I know of, so I could finish showing you around if you want. You haven't seen the riding stable."

The previous day, Nora had wandered the halls and toured the banquet room, dining room, kitchen and pool area. Then she'd sat down in the office with a nameplate on the door that said Bryan Duncan. She'd asked to take a look at the files, and Allie had shrugged and waved her on. The computer spent about fifteen minutes running updates as if it hadn't even been booted up in months, and then she started trying to get a handle on the many ways in which Remedy Mountain Lodge wasn't thriving.

Like a ship with no captain, the beautiful resort was foundering, and it was only a matter of time before it sank entirely. She knew her company's services had been engaged and paid for through an attorney's office, and she assumed that the attorney was working for Beck Duncan.

The cowboy.

An idea occurred to her. In other assignments, she'd had to meet owners halfway. Meet them where they felt comfortable. On many occasions, that meant the hotel bar or an off-site restaurant. She'd brushed up on her dancing skills to win the trust of a hotelier in Rio. Practiced her French to prove her worth to a hotel on the Seine. Cheerfully downed a pint of heavy beer in Germany to demonstrate her knowledge of the local customs during an assignment in Berlin that spanned Oktoberfest.

There was one good way she could fit in while she was collecting dust in Wyoming. She could saddle up.

"Great suggestion," she told Allie. "I'd love to see the riding stable."

Allie's expression brightened. "Do you ride?"

"Not yet, but I have the feeling this is the perfect place to start."

Nora followed Allie through a lobby door that led to a patio area. Flagstones and comfortable chairs anchored the space with a large firepit in the middle. Nora pictured firelight dancing there while stars hung overhead. She'd seen those stars from the balcony of the hotel room she'd been assigned. The room itself was pure luxury with a king-size bed, soaking tub, exquisite linens and decor that *said* Wyoming without *screaming* it. Someone—presumably the late Bryan Duncan—had good taste. The balcony overlooked a flat plain, and mountains rose into the night sky beyond.

The stars had been incredible. Even on Caribbean islands and mountain retreats in Europe, she'd never seen stars that bright or imagined there could be so many. If that many stars had always been there in the night sky, she'd never been in a place where she could see them.

For a moment, she wondered if she'd been missing out her entire life.

But morning had brought her back to reality when she called for room service and no one picked up. The continental breakfast she found off the lobby would have been outclassed by a roadside motel's. Though she'd had a nice conversation with a woman named Judy who worked at Beck's ranch house and said Nora wasn't likely to see Beck because he took a Sunday morning ride up a nearby mountain.

The mountains and the stars were beautiful, but this hotel in Wyoming needed work. Her hard work *and* the cooperation of the owner.

"What made you to want to learn to ride?" Allie asked as they approached a stable at the end of a pathway that wound through native grasses and flowers.

"Beck Duncan is a busy man, and I thought riding might be a good way to catch up with him."

When in Rome… Nora thought.

CHAPTER THREE

TODAY WAS THE day he was going to face the Lodge office, behind the door that still bore Bryan's name. Beck rode to the lonely family cemetery on a hill shaded by pines way up behind the main ranch house. His brother's name was engraved there, too. As Beck paused by the graves of his grandparents, parents and brother, his horse pawed the ground delicately, as if suggesting they move on.

Moving on was a hard thing. He couldn't escape the memories of his parents and brother. Not with them all around him on the ranch. For a brief time during the winter, Beck had considered moving off the ranch. Selling the place and starting over somewhere else captured his imagination for a few days, but he'd held those thoughts deep inside him as he'd gone about his daily tasks with the people who'd worked at the ranch for years.

He was glad he'd never said the words aloud.

Just thinking them had made him feel like he was betraying his family.

No, Beck would never leave the land he loved, where the memories of people he loved lived in every mountain, tree and sunset. But he had to do something, no matter how painful it was going to be.

"I'm done being a coward," he said.

Beck would be embarrassed if his brother could look down from the wide Wyoming sky and see him running away from the pretty blonde lady with her impractical clothes and her tough questions.

Starting down the mountain, he was surprised to see a lone rider coming across the clearing that led to the Lodge. The person riding the horse looked as if she was trying to balance on a swaying ladder. Beck sometimes saw beginning riders around, total greenhorns who were guests at the Lodge.

Those beginners, though, were never alone. This rider wore a helmet—an excellent idea for novices—but he'd bet there was wavy blond hair underneath. She was riding directly toward him, which suggested she had inside information about his whereabouts.

Judy.

His housekeeper and all-around helper knew his Sunday morning ride typically included a cemetery visit, and Judy had also been called in to help with breakfast at the Lodge because two food workers hadn't shown up.

Beck connected the dots quickly and decided to take matters into his own hands. Nora was lucky he'd already ridden the tough part of the mountain and come out on the side nearest the Lodge where the terrain was flat and friendly to a new rider. Still, it was reckless of her. A novice rider alone was dangerous, and he didn't want anything to happen to Nora. He had enough on his conscience. He turned Hercules toward the approaching rider to meet her halfway. As Nora approached—and he was now certain it was her as the distance between them closed—Beck slowed his mount. Nora's horse paused to eat some grass and then trotted forward.

Beck gave the reins a small tug and Hercules stopped. He and Herc had been together for over six years, but Beck had been a good rider for a lot longer. He was thirty-two now and didn't remember a time when he couldn't ride. It was as natural as buttoning his shirt or pulling on his boots.

"Whoa, horse. Stop," Nora called as she approached Beck. Her horse slowed to a walk and strolled right on past Beck. "Wait, I said whoa," Nora said. "Hey."

Beck suppressed a grin and turned Hercules

to come alongside Nora's horse. He reached over and grabbed the reins. The horse stopped.

"How did you do that?" Nora asked. "I did everything the guy at the stable told me to do."

"Experience," Beck said.

Their horses were side by side, plenty close enough for him to see hair escaping Nora's helmet, a shimmer of sweat on her forehead and an exasperated expression on her face. Not at all the cool, in-command person who had rolled up to the Lodge the day before yesterday.

"Well," she said. "I have experience with other things."

"I'm sure you do."

She tilted her head and looked as if she were about to tell him exactly what those things were, but then she rolled her shoulders and forced a smile.

"I came out here to meet with you."

"I figured."

"Because we have a lot to talk about if you want my help turning the Remedy Mountain Lodge into a world-class destination."

Beck reminded himself of his earlier resolution to face this problem head-on and get it resolved fast. Would Bryan have described the Lodge as world-class? What the heck did that even mean? "If you're trying to make this place like a fancy, big-city hotel, you've got the wrong idea."

Nora wiped her brow. "I'm not trying to turn it into anything. But at the bare minimum, I'd prefer that someone answers the phone when I call for room service and the hallways aren't a ghost town."

Beck sucked in a breath. He hated to admit it, but the very few times he'd walked through the Lodge after his brother's death, it had also felt like a ghost town to him. His brother's ghost had plenty of room to wander in those empty hallways.

"Okay," he said neutrally. "What do you suggest?"

Nora gave a half chuckle. "I have plenty of suggestions, but it's not quite as simple as a list of things I can rattle off." She swatted a fly that had landed on her cheek and almost lost her balance. She righted herself, but her cheeks were flushed pink with either exertion, heat or frustration. "Especially under these circumstances," she added.

Beck had solved a lot of problems on horseback and had had about ten books worth of conversations with people while riding the range. For him, saddling up was a problem-solving exercise. If Nora Myers wanted to know his world, the ranch world, and tell him how to fix the Lodge, she ought to learn how to think on the back of a horse.

But she couldn't learn his world overnight, just

like he couldn't learn the hotel world. Life wasn't that easy.

"We can take a shady trail back toward the Lodge," he suggested. "Your horse will follow my horse's lead."

"How do you know?"

"The stable horses for the Lodge are all docile and easy to manage, accustomed to greenhorns. They'll sense an alpha horse like Hercules here."

Nora stared at him, and from her expression, he'd offended her somehow. He reviewed his language. *Greenhorn, docile, alpha.* Sometimes he cursed his parents for making him spend four good years of his young life at college, and sometimes it enriched his thoughts as he rode by himself. Days like this, his education chided him for expressing himself poorly.

"I just mean horses are sensitive and react to their situations," he said. "You can lead if you want to."

"You named your horse Hercules?" Nora asked, surprising Beck.

Beck shrugged. "He's never had to slay a lion or a hydra, but ranch life is tough and demanding."

Nora gave him a smile. "My horse's name is Daisy."

"See what I mean about the stable horses?" Beck asked, unable to resist a smile in return.

Nora was pretty, especially when she smiled, and it had been a long time since Beck had talked with a woman out on horseback. Or anywhere. Ranch life took too much of his time. He used to go into town with his brother sometimes, and they'd dance with the locals or tourists. Bryan had had a serious relationship going with a woman who managed a restaurant in town until… Well, Beck should have done a better job of checking on Riley, but he hadn't. On the occasions when he was in Remedy Creek, he saw Riley at her family's restaurant but avoided any serious conversation, keeping his head down and pulling his grief over him like a blanket.

Nora had been tugging on the edge of that blanket from the moment she'd arrived.

"Do you encounter a lot of Lodge guests riding on the trails?" Nora asked.

Another tug.

"No," Beck said.

"Why not?"

He blew out a breath and turned Hercules toward a shady trail. Daisy followed just as he'd predicted and then plodded alongside him. "You know why not," Beck said to Nora. "You've seen the place's books, right?"

"Some," Nora said. "There was no security on the office computer so I could see bookings and transactions from October to roughly March, but then there's been a lot of paper recordkeeping since then."

"Okay," Beck said. He didn't know what he was supposed to say to that. He was decent with computers and used specialized software written for ranch management. He worked with his tax accountant and his attorney and kept the ranch up-to-date. When the accountant had tried to get a handle on the Lodge records, Beck had washed his hands of it and sent the poor guy to sort through whatever documentation he could find.

"I'm sorry about your brother," Nora said softly.

The quiet words jabbed him in the heart and he forced himself not to flinch. "Appreciate that," he said.

"I have the impression you're not closely involved in managing the Lodge."

Beck grunted and kept his eyes straight ahead. It was best to get this over with. He would tough out an hour with Nora and then hopefully she'd be able to figure it out and...well, fix up the Lodge enough to make it *look* like a viable venture.

Like a hard day's work, the only way out was going straight through it. And he was, ultimately, traveling that road alone. He'd had people in his life he'd loved and depended on, and they'd all left.

Beck faced the trail ahead and guided Hercules into a slow walk, determined to get to the Lodge and muscle through a meeting with Nora. But then he saw something move low in the brush.

NORA HAD BATTLED language and cultural barriers many times as she'd tried to help turn around hotel properties. Sometimes, she'd navigated strong regional political and economic obstacles. One time, she was working at a hotel in the Caribbean when a hurricane shut off power to the whole island and left them up to their knees in floodwater.

Seldom, though, had she encountered a hotel owner who seemed to have zero interest in fixing his own problems. It was baffling. Did he think he didn't have to communicate with her or participate in the turnaround? And what did he think was going to happen when she left? Because she was definitely leaving—in six weeks, tops. Wyoming was not her world and the voice in her head reminded her hourly that she would never climb back up in the company pecking order if she was stuck where no one could see her.

"Seriously, Mr. Duncan," she said, trying to sound cool and professional despite her aching legs and the sweat trickling down her back. "I think we need to talk about whatever is standing in the way of the Lodge's success, and from what I see so far—"

Beck made an almost imperceptible sound to his horse and reached out to touch Nora's horse, bringing them all to an abrupt halt.

"What?" Nora asked. Was he stopping them so they could finally have a conversation?

He held up a hand like a stop sign and focused on the trail ahead. Nora followed his gaze but saw nothing on the trail except rocks and some scrubby trees. Farther ahead, the trail turned toward the Lodge and there were actual shade trees. It was hot, and if Beck wasn't going to talk to her, she was ready to give up and return to the air-conditioned Lodge where maybe—if she was lucky—she could make sense of the financial records whether the cowboy owner wanted to help or not.

"What are we doing?" she asked. Her horse's head came up sharply and she felt the animal tense. Beck put a reassuring hand on Daisy's neck and murmured something calming.

He didn't take his eyes off the trail as he finally answered her question. "There's a rattlesnake ahead, and we're not going to startle him because their bite is bad news for horses."

Nora caught her breath. A real live rattlesnake? Her heart kicked into overdrive and she almost wished Beck would put a calming hand on her shoulder just as he was doing for her horse. Hercules was looking ahead but had gone still. Had the horse encountered rattlesnakes before?

No one had told her about rattlesnakes when she was assigned this job. Of course, no one had asked her to saddle up and chase down a rancher either.

"What do we do?" she whispered.

"Wait."

"That's it?"

Beck put a finger over his lips and glanced at her long enough to know she'd seen the gesture and then refocused on the trail ahead. Nora shaded her eyes and looked but didn't see the rattlesnake. Not that she was going to doubt Beck. She'd learned to trust locals on her many travels.

This time, though, she was sweating and the insides of her knees were aching because of the way they were forced around the saddle. She pictured the cool indoor pool at the Lodge. The lucky thing about the management's lack of interest was that she'd have that pool all to herself when she got back there.

She counted to ten, growing more restless with each number. She resolved to go to twenty-five, but it chafed her like that saddle. Nora was not a person who sat back and waited for things to happen. Remedy Mountain Lodge was not going to rise from its own little campfire of ashes unless somebody did something. And that somebody was her—if this snake ever let them by.

"Well?" she asked quietly.

"Stay here," Beck said.

Nora bristled at his authoritative tone while also wondering if she had any choice. Her horse was in charge of her movement.

Beck motioned to her horse and said something—Nora didn't catch what it was—and Daisy didn't budge when he clicked to Hercules and they went forward on the trail. She watched him ride ahead, irritated by the whole situation but also fascinated by his form in the saddle. He looked tall, even sitting down. His straight spine showed his core strength and confidence. He would be the star of a Pilates class—especially when the other women got a load of his face and shoulders.

Not that it mattered how handsome he was. Nora never got involved with the people at her hotel assignments. She knew better.

Beck stopped where a bush grew near the trail ahead, peered at the ground all around him, and then clicked and motioned to Nora. She was about to tell him she was there to fix his resort but not to be ordered around, but Daisy took the matter out of her hands by trotting toward Beck and Hercules.

The horse clearly trusted Beck because they spoke the same language, which reminded Nora how much of an outsider she was.

"Girl," Nora said to the horse, "it's not going to be easy fitting in here."

CHAPTER FOUR

HE CONSIDERED GALLOPING. At least trotting. A slow walk back to the Lodge alongside Nora gave her way too much time to get under his skin. Not that he should let her. She was a person hired to do a job he couldn't—or wouldn't—do. Just like he kept Judy on the payroll to run his ranch house kitchen. But while Judy sometimes asked him tough questions, she knew where the line was and didn't cross it.

Nora didn't know his lines, and he suspected she'd cross them anyway because she was clearly determined. Her spunk was the reason he couldn't hurry their ride to the Lodge. It would be irresponsible to push a beginning rider beyond her comfort level, no matter how tame old Daisy was.

"I like to start at the beginning," Nora was saying. Beck glanced over and noticed her clinging to the saddle horn and leaning forward, probably trying to take the pressure off her legs and backside. He didn't remember being a beginner. He'd been too young, and when you're a child you're a beginner at everything. Being an adult and trying to learn something new or—worse yet—start over on something is a whole lot harder.

"Okay," Beck said, acknowledging her but not encouraging her.

"Back to the planning stage, then. Most of the projects I take on are older, some historic, with lots of history."

"That's interesting," Beck said. "I'd like to hear about those."

Nora glanced over, looking surprised, possibly because it was the first time he'd shown much interest in anything she had to say. Beck hoped she didn't figure out he just wanted to give her something to talk about that wasn't his brother's Lodge, something that wasn't personal.

"Oh," she said. "Well. For example, one of my favorite turnaround projects was a villa on the Riviera."

He nodded.

"In France," she added.

"That's usually the one people mean when they say 'the Riviera,'" Beck said. Sure, he was a working rancher in Wyoming, but he wasn't a caveman. Still, he didn't like coming across as defensive and grouchy. Nora was just trying to do her job and he had asked about other hotel properties. "Although I guess you might have meant the part of it that's actually in Monaco," he conceded. "Or the Italian or Turkish Riviera."

Nora gave him a small smile and he wondered if she was impressed he knew something about European geography or if it was because he'd rescinded a testy comment. It wouldn't be the worst thing in the world to have a positive working relationship with her. It was in his best interest to get that albatross off his back so he could finally lighten his guilt and steer past his grief.

"It was a small family-owned villa on its third generation. They had all kinds of good intentions, but they were struggling with the balance between keeping a historic feel and offering modern amenities."

"Couldn't they do both?" Beck asked.

"Yes. But it's subtle. One time I was on the road to somewhere else and I stayed in a place in Michigan that was super proud of being a historic hotel dating back to 1883, but the hallways and rooms had been remodeled and it looked like any bland, neutral Airbnb that could be anywhere. It was really disappointing."

"But did it have modern amenities?" Beck asked.

"Weirdly, only some. Like a fancy coffee maker in the room and a bidet in the bathroom, but then the historic porch floor sagged, and it was built right over their laundry so you sucked in all the laundry smell and humidity."

"Did you help them out?"

Nora shook her head. "I wasn't assigned to the hotel, just an anonymous critic in room 103 who'd stopped for the night. I didn't say a word and didn't leave a review. Finding balance is hard, but honestly I think it could be a real strength of your Lodge."

Beck tried not to flinch when she called it his Lodge. It was within view, but they still had at least ten minutes on their ride before they got there. He hoped to keep Nora talking about other properties because it allowed him to keep hiding from his own. Plus, he was finding it interesting hearing her talk. When was the last time he'd had a decent conversation with someone new?

"So, what did you do to turn around the French Riviera villa on its third generation?" he asked.

"We did a deep soul-search."

Beck sucked in a breath. He did not want a deep soul-search.

"I asked them what they truly loved about their villa." She smiled as she spoke. "It took almost a whole case of wine because we had the whole family on the patio. The beautiful Mediterranean Sea was out there in the darkness, but the string of lights and the candles on the table illuminating all those faces—some as young as three and as old as eighty—took all my attention. I'll never forget it. You can't believe some of the stories I heard," she said with a laugh. "But we got to the bottom of it before the wine was gone. We really discovered what the villa meant to them and what they hoped it would mean to their visitors in the future."

Beck could almost picture it. The wine, the extended family, the laughter. It sounded so appealing it was almost physically painful. He had no family. Everyone he'd loved was gone. Who was he even keeping this ranch alive for?

"I was back there earlier this year," Nora said softly.

"Was it still going strong?"

Her expression became wistful, but then she straightened in the saddle and gave him a direct look. "We should talk about what you love about the Lodge."

Beck felt his heart lurch. "I can't."

"You can't think of anything you love about it?"

He swallowed. He didn't love it. It had caused a rift between him and his brother. If it weren't for that place, his brother might be right here, on horseback next to him, riding the range.

"It's harder than most people think to quantify the strengths of their property because they're often too close to it," Nora said matter-of-factly, as if she was running a business meeting. "If it would help, we could gather a small group of people who were influential in planning the Lodge and creating its vision."

"Can't do that either," Beck said.

"But—"

Maybe if he said the words aloud it would both satisfy her curiosity and tell her that she was basically free to do whatever she wanted to fatten the place up for a potential buyer. He didn't need to know the details or participate.

"It was entirely my brother's baby. No one else's."

"But this ranch is also yours, right? Surely you were involved in the decisions and building."

"The ranch part is mine, the Lodge's land was his. That's how we divided things when our… when we inherited everything."

"But now that Bryan is gone," she said softly, "I assume you are sole owner of both the Lodge and the ranch."

He nodded. Sole owner. All alone. Just him and the ghosts of his parents and brother, rambling around on 20,000 acres of Wyoming. Man, it sounded so bad when he looked at it that way, which was probably why he avoided thinking about it. He just kept his hat on, his butt in the saddle, and his cows fed and watered. What else could he do?

"You know how I said balance was hard, like blending the old and the new, and some places really get it right and some struggle?" Nora asked.

Beck nodded. He hoped she was going to tell a story about some resort in London or Mexico City.

"The Lodge's challenge is blending rustic with elegant, a luxury feeling with a ranchy feeling."

"Ranchy," Beck said.

"You know what I mean."

"Do I?" he asked, risking a small smile. He almost wanted to hear what Nora Myers thought ranchy meant. "Have you ever been to a ranch before?"

She hesitated. "No, not exactly."

He didn't say anything as Hercules navigated stepping through a small stream and over smooth rocks. Daisy walked alongside, just a few steps back, and Beck kept a close eye on Nora. Her posture told him she was hurting. She'd been in the saddle for well over an hour, and that was a long time for first-timers. Even though he didn't want to hurry back to the Lodge and face a business meeting with her, he wanted to help her off that horse, maybe even rub some of the tension he suspected had gathered between her shoulder blades. He admired her determination and the way she blended her business attitude with something softer. Like the hotels she helped balance the old and new, the ranchy and the luxurious.

"I've been to the zoo," she said. "And a farm during apple picking season. And I spent two months on a vineyard in Napa Valley helping them with their resort. It was similar."

Beck chuckled.

"Okay, not that similar. They didn't have horses, and it was greener, and it was, well… California," she admitted.

They rode under a line of shade trees that also provided a windbreak for the Lodge, and when they came out from under the trees, the Lodge's windows sparkled in the morning sun. Nora's horse picked up its pace and headed straight for the barn, and now it was Hercules who followed, probably hoping for some shade, water and feed.

Outside the barn door, Beck swung a leg over and hopped down from the saddle, then quickly took Daisy's halter so Nora could dismount. Nora's face contorted as she tried to mimic Beck's easy swing and dismount, and Beck let go of the tame horse's halter to hold up both hands to Nora. "Can I help you down?"

She hesitated. Nora was clearly a woman who handled things herself, but she was out of her element here. Finally, she nodded and he put both hands on her waist to ease her to the ground.

"You might be sore later," he said, keeping

his hands at her waist just long enough to make sure she was steady before taking a step back to give her space.

"I'm sore right now," she said with a rueful grin. "But I've survived killer sunburns in Dubai and a bedbug infestation at an island resort that shall remain anonymous."

Beck smiled. It was sort of nice hearing her stories, but he wondered what a well-traveled woman like Nora thought about being stuck on a ranch in Wyoming for six weeks.

"I'll take your horse inside and make sure she gets a rubdown and water," Beck said.

"And then you're coming inside for a meeting?"

He nodded. "In a minute."

As he watched her take a few clearly painful steps toward the Lodge, Beck admired her dedication but decided he didn't want to get too accustomed to Nora's smile and spunk. She'd be gone before October and he'd have to face the one-year anniversary of the Lodge's opening alone.

THEY WERE SITTING on the shaded flagstone patio tucked between the main Lodge building and the two wings that formed three sides of a square. Outdoors, at Beck's request. Nora had enjoyed three minutes of blissful air-conditioning when she'd popped into the kitchen to request a pitcher of something cold and some light snacks. She hadn't specified what the drink and food should be. It was part of an experiment on her part to see what the kitchen staff would come up with. It would be a test of their creativity and service. Of course, she expected they would do their best since the request involved the owner.

"I don't have a lot of time to talk," Beck said as he sat on the edge of a deep chair with a thick cushion. She wanted to suggest he sink into that big cushion and get comfortable, but his vibe could best be described as "flight risk."

"It's Sunday," Nora said.

"Ranches don't observe weekends."

She sighed. Even if Beck refused to settle into the comfy chair, her own body was thanking her after that long, hot ride and the hard saddle. Seriously, why couldn't saddles have cushions? That hot tub was going to be amazing later, too. But first, she really had to nail Beck down on some details.

"Hospitality doesn't either," she said. "I guess we have that in common." She opened the laptop she'd grabbed on her way back from the kitchen. "Let's start with the beginning. What was the driving vision and motivation for the Lodge?"

Beck scooted even closer to the edge of his chair. Any more and he'd either have to stand up or fall out of it. "You're asking the wrong person," he said.

"There's no one else to ask," she said. "I read the mission statement on the website, but those seldom tell the whole story. What inspired your brother?"

Beck let out a long sigh and inched back just a little. "Vacation," he said. "Our parents didn't take vacations. It's tough to get away from the ranch. But they insisted that Bryan and I got away. They practically kicked us off the ranch and made us go."

Nora crossed one leg over the other and set her laptop on the table beside her. "Where did you go?"

"A lot of places. The first one was when I was eighteen and Bryan was sixteen. It was the summer before I went off to college."

"Where did you go to college?" she asked.

"Wyoming State. Far enough, but not too far."

She nodded. The questioning was going better than she expected. "And you studied…?"

"I majored in business. It was a practical choice."

The way he said it almost begged her next question and she couldn't resist. "What was your minor?"

Beck put his hat on the table next to his chair and ran his fingers through his hair. The hat had pressed his dark hair close to his scalp, and when he ruffled it back up, he suddenly looked younger. Nora could almost picture him at eighteen, heading off to college.

"Classics," he said. "Winters are long and there's a lot of time indoors to read. Internet isn't reliable, but my mom had a big shelf of books she read in college."

"You like reading?" Nora asked, enjoying the glimpse down another trail inside the gruff cowboy.

"I don't mind it," he said. He stared at her as if he was daring her to comment, but she decided to get back to business. There was no reason to get to know Beck very well. She'd be gone in six weeks, back where people could see and appreciate her efforts, back to climbing the company ladder, hopefully fresh from a big success here.

"So you went on vacation with Bryan and he was inspired. Where did you go?"

"The first year we went to Yellowstone. Stayed in the big lodge there."

"Ah," Nora said.

"Have you been there?" he asked.

"No," she admitted. She'd seen pictures. It was beautiful, historic, truly grand and from another era. It was on her list for someday when she had time to choose her destinations and vacations.

For the past ten years, she'd only gone where her job took her.

"The next year we went to San Francisco. Bryan wanted to see the ocean and the Golden Gate Bridge. I wanted to see Muir Woods and the redwoods."

Nora could picture it, the two brothers traveling together, making their plans. "Did you stay in a historic lodge there?"

Beck shook his head. "Little family-run place close to the ocean. Tiny bathroom and twin beds, but a great view."

"Where did you go the next year?" she asked, enthralled by the idea of traveling with a sibling every summer. She had never been on vacation with her family, not even when she and her brothers were kids. And now? They were adults and there was no way they'd take off on an adventure.

"We got braver," Beck said. "Went all the way across the county to Niagara Falls. There was a drought on the ranch that year, and I'll never forget the look on Bryan's face when we saw all that water just rushing over the falls, no end in sight. He turned eighteen while we were there."

Nora was genuinely astonished. These travel stories were not what she'd expected from Beck. His expression lost some of its guardedness, and she hoped he'd go on talking. Knowing about the travel experiences of a hotel owner was often very helpful to her as she assisted them in improving their own hotels.

"Do you have brothers and sisters?" Beck asked, the question hitting her out of the wide blue Wyoming sky.

"Two brothers." She wasn't here to talk about herself, though. "Where was your next trip?" she asked.

Beck tilted his head. "Do you ever travel with your brothers?"

No one, in all the places she'd been, had ever asked her about her family or anything personal. She usually liked it that way. Remain anonymous, do a job, get attention only for the work, and then use those accolades to continue improving her chances for promotion. It was far safer to keep her personal life out of her work.

"We're all very busy," she said. She risked a glance at Beck and found him studying her as if he saw right inside her.

"Cruise," he said. "That was our next trip. The whole Caribbean thing with the private island, pools and waterslides on the boat, expensive drinks and a stop at Nassau. It was hot and there were too many people crammed in one small place. I think the whole population of Wyoming could have fit on that ship."

"Cruises aren't for everyone," Nora said. "Definitely not my specialty area."

Beck gazed off toward the mountains. "Our last trip was after my senior year of college. We went to Europe."

"Really?" Nora blurted. She hadn't missed that he'd said it was their last trip, but she was surprised by how far they'd gone. She glanced over at the Lodge, trying to put her finger on something. The Lodge was almost exactly what a person would expect from a ranch-inspired resort, but there was an elegance about it. Had Bryan Duncan been inspired a little bit by each of his trips? Why was Europe their last one?

"It was one of those see-everything-in-ten-days trips across Europe. London Bridge, Eiffel Tower, castles in Germany, the Vatican," he said, still gazing off toward the mountains as if he was remembering it all. Suddenly he turned his gaze back to her. "Monaco. That's on the French Riviera, you know," he said with a hint of a smile.

Nora smiled back. "I've heard. Did you like that trip?"

He shrugged. "Bryan did."

"Is that what inspired him to build this place?"

Beck nodded. "I was anxious to come home and get to work now that I was done with college. Bryan's heart wasn't in ranching after that. And our parents died a few years later, so..."

Nora scooted to the edge of her seat, desperate to hear what came after "so."

But Beck stood and picked up his hat. "That should answer your question about the vision for this place," he said. "My brother's vision." The way he said it made it clear what Nora already suspected. Beck wanted nothing to do with the Lodge. He put on his hat and started to walk away.

Nora jumped up. "Wait," she said. "If you don't want the Lodge, why don't you just sell it?"

Beck's shoulders stiffened and he kept his back to her. Finally, he turned his head just enough to say, "Come to the ranch house tomorrow for supper. You can show me your plans then."

CHAPTER FIVE

NORA'S DAY—DAY THREE—had provided no clarity about the operation of Remedy Mountain Lodge. It was Monday, Allie's day off, and no one else seemed to know much about running the front desk. Nora had been in the office making a list of questions that had come up when six guests arrived to check in. They were three retired couples traveling together and they'd only discovered Remedy Mountain Lodge because they'd called Wellness Springs, the spa in town, and asked specifically if there was any place in the area they could stay.

That was another challenge Nora wanted to address with Beck. The Lodge needed a more robust website with better search engine optimization and key words for discoverability. They also needed advertisements in regional magazines, perhaps a relationship with a travel influencer. How on earth did Beck expect anyone to find the place otherwise?

And it would be a shame if no one did. It was

a beautifully appointed resort. The mattresses were soft and the sheets luxurious. Although they were water-savers, the showerheads were also a delight. Nora had relaxed her aching muscles in the shower after yesterday's ride, and then she'd soaked in the hot tub and fallen into a deep, refreshing sleep.

She'd awakened ready to take on this project, but then challenges had blown across her path like errant tumbleweeds. Breakfast—no one answering her call for room service again—had been another spread of muffins and coffee on a table off the lobby. Sure, the view from the floor-to-ceiling windows had made up for the lack of a hot breakfast, and the few pastry choices were exceptionally tasty despite their simplicity. But then she'd gone back to her room to get her laptop, and her key card hadn't worked. And the hallway lights in her wing were off.

When she stalked back to the front desk, she found six people in front of it and no one behind it. Nora glanced around and then greeted the guests herself with the professional smile she'd cultivated over ten years in hospitality. She was glad she was dressed for business, not trail riding, today.

"Sorry we're so early," a tall woman with short gray hair said. "We know our rooms won't be ready, but we hoped to just drop our luggage with you and do some hiking and exploring for the morning."

"Of course," Nora said. Where was everyone? "Let me just get some luggage tags." She started opening desk drawers, feeling a little foolish searching while the travelers stood there and watched. This was embarrassing and looked bad for the Lodge. Why weren't the simplest things attended to?

She knew the answer, of course. The building was beautiful and—miraculously—clean, probably owing to the personal pride of the people who worked there. Honestly, the housekeeping staff had very little to do except clean the public areas and keep polishing the woodwork. At least the skeleton staff was still being paid by Beck's accountant who worked out of an office in Remedy Creek. Nora appreciated the fact that hotel associates showed up, but no one was really in charge, and the Lodge was drifting along on good intentions. It couldn't last much longer.

"We just rearranged the desk," she said with a smile. "Pardon my fumbling."

"We're on vacation," one of the men said, and Nora couldn't decide if he meant he had no patience for someone wasting his valuable downtime or if he meant he didn't mind waiting because he had all day. Wasting guests' time at the desk was a serious no-no in hotel management. The first impression lasts.

To her great relief, Nora swept her hand into an open shelf below the computer and found a stack of luggage tags in the back. She put them on the desk and then began searching for a pen.

"Here you go," the tall lady said, producing a felt-tip marker from her purse. She smiled at Nora, clearly sympathetic to Nora's bungling efforts. Nora felt her face burn. This was not the kind of hospitality she was accustomed to offering, and she was not a hapless newbie in the hotel world. She'd streamlined front desk operations at some of the finest resorts in the world.

"We travel a lot," the lady said, indicating her group. "Since we retired. And I'm always prepared."

"Her packing is a work of art," one of the other women said. "She makes videos and has a big Facebook following of people who geek out about savvy travel tips."

Nora felt the breakfast muffin rising in her throat, but she smiled at the woman as if that was the best news she'd ever heard. "Let's get those bags tagged, and we'll find you some coffee before you head out to explore. We also have a pool you can enjoy while you wait for your room."

She could have told them that there were dozens of rooms available—surely they had noticed the empty spaces in the parking lot—but she didn't want to admit how under-booked the place was. So she guided the group to the breakfast area, then went to double-check the group's three rooms for herself. If there were travel tip videos going on Facebook, Nora would make sure they were positive ones—not cautionary tales.

Next, she did a walk-through of the whole hotel, paying attention to everything a guest would see. The Pool Closed for Cleaning sign she'd noticed last evening was still outside the pool door. A pickup truck that was clearly someone's older personal vehicle was parked on the lawn near some shrubs. An older woman with a housekeeper's apron stood chatting with a young man who was trimming the shrubs. She handed him a muffin and coffee from the breakfast spread in the lobby and then gave him a big hug.

Not professional. Any guest could have seen that. Not that there were many guests around this early, except for early checkouts, which reminded Nora she should go see if anyone was covering the front desk.

Did she have to run everything herself around here?

Nora waited inside the door near the shrubs, hoping the woman would come inside and she could give her a quick reminder about professional behavior in public-facing places. Nora leaned backward, trying to see down the long hallway to the lobby and hoping no one was waiting to check out. She counted to ten and then started over. The housekeeper came through the door when Nora got to eight.

"Well, hello," the woman said, glancing over Nora's shirtdress and low heels. "Can I help you, pretty lady?"

Nora glanced at the woman's name tag. Nancy. She'd intended to tell Nancy to be more professional in her interactions, but it was hard to argue with a warm smile and being called pretty lady. Most people didn't even notice her. She was in the background making things work.

"I—I'm Nora Myers," she said, expecting her name to ring a bell. It was a small staff. Certainly word had spread about her arrival and why she was there.

"What a beautiful name. I had a sister-in-law named Nora, bless her memory," Nancy said, putting a hand on her heart.

"That's…very nice. I noticed you outside talking with the groundskeeper—"

"My grandson Harvey. I took him a little breakfast. He doesn't eat enough, and I worry about him." Nancy smiled. "You look like you could use some breakfast, too. Can I walk you to the lobby and show you where to find muffins and coffee?"

"No, I…work here."

"You do?"

"Yes, well, sort of. I'm a consultant with a hospitality management company. We come in and help hotel properties that are struggling."

Nancy's smile sank on both ends. "I did hear someone was coming to whip us into shape. I've been off the past two days." She extended a hand. "I'm Nancy Phillips, the housekeeping manager."

Nora's first reaction was surprise that the housekeeping manager had the weekend off. That was usually a busy time in hotels. But she didn't say anything, instead taking Nancy's hand. It was strong and calloused, the hand of a woman who worked hard.

"I wanted to talk to you about…" Nora pointed outside but her words trailed off. Was she really going to begin her relationship with the housekeeping manager by berating her for taking muffins to her grandson and hugging him? There were plenty of muffins and very few guests to eat them.

"I'll pay for the muffins I took to Harvey, of course," Nancy said.

Nora shook her head. "That's not what I was going to say. I wonder if perhaps we should have a nice break area where hotel staff can eat."

Nancy's guarded expression relaxed a little.

"And give hugs to grandkids when they need

it," Nora said. She was rewarded with a warm smile.

"We do have a staff room, but it's usually empty," Nancy said. "We don't have a large staff, but we all know each other and we do our best. We've been trying to just figure things out ever since Mr. Duncan…well, you know."

Everyone assumed she knew. Nora had found Bryan Duncan's obituary online, but there were no details on his death, just that he died as a result of an accident on the ranch. She was tempted to ask Nancy, but Nora was still trying to meet the staff—who seemed to work intermittently—and find out how to move the hotel forward. Dwelling on a past tragedy wasn't going to help.

"Who do you report to?" Nora asked instead.

"Myself," Nancy said.

Nora had been up late working on a flowchart with roles and responsibilities, trying to put names of the few employees she'd met in the appropriate places. Her next nightmare was job descriptions and training, but only after figuring out how the Lodge was, miraculously, running at all with no leadership.

"And how many people are on your housekeeping staff?"

Nancy looked pensive and turned her left hand palm up. She began touching her fingers as she went through the names. "Joan comes in on the weekends and she usually brings her daughter with her, and there's Neil—he's our maintenance guy—who's pretty much here whenever we need him. Emily and Maria, they're part-time, mostly switching off with each other, and we have Laura every day, except when she has to take her dad for physical therapy."

Nora had worked in small resorts that were mostly family-run, and she'd heard a roster like this before. But there was no way a one-hundred-room hotel could scale up to full occupancy with such a small staff.

"Do you think we need more housekeepers?" Nora asked. Over the years, she'd found out a lot by talking to employees. Of course, their perspective didn't always reflect the overall goals of the property, but they had good insight. And she had to begin somewhere. Starting at the top had not been productive—yet. She'd gotten a terse dinner invitation to the ranch house from Beck Duncan, and she wanted to go armed with more information and some concrete suggestions. At some resorts, cleanliness and reputation were challenges, some places struggled with transportation and parking, some needed remodeling and redecorating.

What did Remedy Mountain Lodge need to pull itself together and be profitable? Obviously guests and a marketing plan, but those things would—hopefully—mean she needed to hire and train more staff. Quickly if she wanted to be done in less than six weeks and get back on the road.

"More staff? Heavens, no," Nancy said. "Sometimes we barely have enough cleaning to fill up our days. What we need is more guests, and I hope you're here to tell us how to get them."

LATE ON MONDAY AFTERNOON, Beck was out by the horse barn when he got the call. Within minutes, he and Judy were in his truck with Beck shoving the gas pedal to the floor. One of the hazards of running a huge ranch was how far away he might be when someone needed him. Sometimes minutes could mean the difference between life or death. The road that ran through this part of the ranch had once been smooth, even paved in some parts, but time and nature had given it deep ruts. Some sections had been washed out by heavy rains in last fall's brutal October, leaving potholes, and Beck hadn't addressed all of them.

It was one of many things he'd let go since then as he'd struggled to find his way forward alone. And now he regretted it with every bump that slowed him down. A horse would be better at covering the distance, but he didn't know the extent of his ranch hand's injuries. He couldn't put an injured man in a saddle.

"The ambulance will meet us at the house if

we can get him that far. It'll save time," Judy said from the passenger seat. She had a huge first aid kit tucked between her legs. "I just talked to the dispatcher from the sheriff's office."

Beck considered the location of the injured man—reported by Wyatt who had found him—and the trajectory back toward the ranch house. It was late afternoon, and no one had seen Allen since lunch. Beck didn't like anyone working alone. Animals could be unpredictable, and falls and accidents were a constant risk on a working ranch. He knew a man who'd lost a leg from being gored on a neighboring ranch and a woman who nearly died in a tractor rollover.

The ranch hand who'd called Beck ten minutes ago had been rattled, and Beck hoped Allen wasn't as badly injured as the hand thought. A rut in the road jolted the truck, but Beck pushed on going fast. Time could make all the difference.

He focused on the road ahead and finally saw a horse just off to the side. Someone—Wyatt—was waving a red bandanna to get his attention. Beck parked and got out with Judy at his heels. Just as he'd feared, Allen was on the ground, his face twisted with pain. Wyatt had tried splinting the leg with sturdy sticks and some rope, but Beck could see the leg was at an unnatural angle.

"Steady, Allen," he said, dropping to his knees and putting a hand on the young man's shoulder.

Judy unpacked her bag and got out a portable splint. Many of the ranch hands were trained in first aid, since medical help could be far away depending on their location on the thousands of acres. Judy and Wyatt went to work with the better splint. Beck dug a bottle of water out of the medical bag and encouraged Allen to drink.

"What happened?" Beck asked, hoping to distract Allen while Judy splinted his leg.

"Bull," Allen said. "Mean one. He came at my horse and pinned me. I tried to shake him off and circle around, but then he got my horse and we both went down."

Beck didn't ask what happened to the horse, but he knew it wouldn't be good. The poor horse was almost certainly injured and running loose. He'd organize a search for it and do what he could later, but for now he was responsible for an injured human. He just hoped Allen would stand a better chance at walking again if they moved him carefully. It would be a slow, painstaking drive back to the ranch house, and then a long road to recovery for Allen.

"Sorry about this, boss," Allen said. "I know you're shorthanded."

"We'll make do. The only thing I care about right now is getting you to a hospital."

CHAPTER SIX

When Beck pulled up to the ranch house with an injured man lying across the back seat, he noticed two things right away: the ambulance waiting to make the journey to a level two hospital an hour away and the black SUV belonging to the Lodge with Nora Myers standing next to it, talking to the first responders.

Just what he needed. He'd forgotten he'd invited her for supper. His plan had been to meet her on neutral ground, or at least ground that didn't belong to the resort. Truthfully, there was no neutral place anywhere on the Remedy Mountain Ranch. Almost every square foot of every acre reminded him of the people he'd loved and lost—especially and most recently his brother. But the ranch house, at least, was his domain and, usually, a respite from facing his failure to run the Lodge.

Today, he felt as if he was failing to do everything, including keeping his people safe.

Nora broke off from the first responders and

went to stand by her vehicle, clearly trying to stay out of the way. Beck got out and opened the rear door. Allen looked gray and his face showed his pain but also his grit. It was a mask a lot of people who worked in the tough and dangerous ranch world wore.

"It'll be okay, Allen," Beck said as the ambulance crew approached with a stretcher and bags of equipment. "They'll get you over to the hospital and you're going to be okay."

"Sure, boss," Allen said through gritted teeth.

Beck was aware of Nora watching from beside her vehicle, but he didn't look her way. He kept all his focus on communicating with the medical personnel and helping them transfer Allen to the ambulance.

"I'll call your dad and your sister," Beck said. "If it's okay with you, I'll let them know what happened and where you'll be."

"Appreciate that," Allen said. His voice was weak, and Beck was relieved when the ambulance drove away. Everyone who worked for him was his responsibility, but Beck trusted the two men from the fire station in Remedy Creek. They'd take good care of Allen, and Beck could at least breathe now that the man's care was out of his hands.

Judy patted Beck on the shoulder as she walked past and went into the ranch house. It was supper-time, and Beck knew Judy would pull something from the freezer to heat for the crew who stayed to eat. They'd also have questions and want updates on Allen. It was going to be a busy evening, but first he had to make those calls.

"Can I help?"

The voice at his elbow startled Beck. He'd been watching the ambulance disappear around a bend at the end of the long driveway and hadn't noticed Nora approaching him.

He shook his head.

Nora moved in front of him and gave him a sympathetic look. "The first responders told me a little bit about the accident while we waited for you," Nora said. "I know you've had a rough afternoon. We can reschedule our meeting."

Beck's first reaction was relief at not having to have this difficult conversation tonight, but he'd had some time to think on the slow drive in from the range with Allen lying on the back seat. Everything that happened on his property was his responsibility. No matter how painful it was, no matter how much he wished he could share the burden with someone else, it was all still his. There was no point in hiding from it. And the sooner he dealt with the Lodge and got it off his mind and heart, the more he could focus on what really needed his time—the ranch.

"We don't have to reschedule," he said. "Judy will fix you something, if you don't mind eating with five or six of my ranch hands. I need to make some calls and then we can talk afterward."

"But you have to eat, too."

"Maybe later." He doubted he could work up an appetite, not with the image of Allen's twisted leg fresh in his mind. "I'll show you where the kitchen is."

He turned and started walking but then paused and waited for Nora. He wasn't running from her anymore. Shame at the way he'd escaped on horseback that first day punched him. He took responsibility for everything at the ranch. It was time he included the Lodge. Nora glanced at him with a hint of surprise and then walked alongside him. They mounted the three low steps onto the wide porch of the ranch house. Beck held open the door and followed her inside.

"Wow," she said. Her face showed her approval of the large, comfortable living room spreading out on their right. Beck had inherited the leather couch, but he'd added two upholstered chairs facing the massive stone fireplace. He'd also installed bookshelves on both sides of the fireplace and filled them with a selection of his favorites and also quite a few books he intended to read, maybe in the winter, maybe if things ever slowed down.

"Do you want to sit here until dinner is ready or—"

"I could help with dinner," Nora said, surprising him. "I love cooking, but I don't want to get in Judy's way."

"I don't mind," Judy called through the kitchen doorway to their left.

Beck smiled. Of course, Judy heard everything that happened inside these walls.

"This way," he said to Nora. He ushered her through the dining room with its long table and ten chairs and then into the bright, modern kitchen.

"I'm trying to hurry something onto the table," Judy said over her shoulder while she stirred a pot on the stove. "I could use some help if you don't mind." That smell was persuading him he could eat after all—but not until he'd made those phone calls.

"I'd love to," Nora said. She took an apron from a hook, and that was when Beck noticed for the first time what Nora was wearing. Actually, what she was not wearing. No skirt and matching jacket, nothing that looked dry-clean-only. Nora wore jeans and a green shirt that looked comfortable and…soft. The color contrasted with her blond ponytail. He glanced at her feet. No boots—she probably didn't have any—but she wore sneakers. For the first time since she'd arrived, Nora looked as if she could possibly fit in at Remedy Creek.

Not that she needed to bother. She'd be gone just as soon as she could, and he might as well take her help and get her out the door and off the ranch. Then he could focus on somehow moving forward each day. Talking with Nora about the trips he'd gone on with Bryan had stirred up a lot of memories, and those memories got in the way. He needed to put the past behind him, and the sooner she finished her assignment and left him in peace, the better.

"I'll be in my office," he said gruffly and then strode back through the dining room, across the living room and into his study, closing the door behind him.

"I'M SORRY YOU had a hard afternoon," Nora said as she sliced bread to go with the emergency chili Judy had pulled from the freezer.

"I've had harder," Judy said. "It's okay to cut those slices thick. We don't have any dainty eaters coming to the table."

"Got it," Nora said. She cut the homemade bread into slices twice as thick as her experience told her to, then covered them with a clean kitchen towel. "That chili smells wonderful."

Judy glanced over and smiled. “Thanks. It freezes well. We were going to have roast chicken, but I never got it in the oven. I don’t think anyone will complain, though. Chili is a favorite here. I got the recipe from Beck’s mother. That woman could save the devil’s soul with her cooking, God rest her.”

“I believe Beck’s father has also passed away,” Nora said cautiously. She didn’t want to pump Beck’s employees for information about his personal life. It was really none of her business, but she was trying to understand how things worked around the ranch. And why some things did not work.

“It’s just Beck left now,” Judy said.

Maybe it was Judy’s tone or the words themselves, but Nora suddenly felt a wave of empathy for Beck. Was he lonely? If there was a woman in the picture, she suspected Judy would know about it, but that was absolutely not Nora’s business. Although someone as handsome as Beck who clearly cared about the people who worked for him…well, certainly some local woman might be interested. The man had to have good relationships with local people; that was the only thing that would explain why a skeleton staff continued to work at the Lodge even though the place was flailing without any direct leadership. People were doing the best they could anyway and seemingly taking pride in their work.

That kind of loyalty was hard to find and nearly impossible to manufacture. She could work wonders with a small, loyal staff like the one at the Lodge, but she needed Beck's help to get the place going.

Judy left the stove and began pulling items out of the fridge. "Can you cut up some vegetables and make a salad?" she asked.

"Of course," Nora said. The kitchen was well organized, stocked and practical, and she quickly found another cutting board and a clean knife and went to work.

"You've done that before," Judy observed.

Nora looked up and smiled and then returned to concentrating on her work. "My little secret is that I love hotels and front desks and lobbies and valet parking and all the things, but I usually sneak into kitchens and try to befriend and learn from the culinary staff. They are the people who can truly make or break a good hotel stay. There are guests who'll put up with slow elevators, crowded pools and lumpy pillows, but no one wants bad coffee and mediocre meals."

"Can't argue with that," Judy said.

Nora didn't add that the hotel kitchens she sometimes invaded were often staffed by five-star chefs and the restaurants had waiting lists as long as her arm. She didn't intrude on those kitchens anywhere near the dinner service, although she did enjoy dining in places like that, often with the hotel owners and managers.

She was a long way from those opulent dining rooms with their exclusive menus and world-class service, but they'd be waiting for her as soon as she turned Remedy Mountain Lodge around and extracted herself from obscurity.

Still, she'd been pleasantly surprised at the planning and execution of the Lodge's kitchen—even though it was hardly being used. She'd wandered through it, making notes the day before. It was large with commercial appliances that wouldn't be out of place in the four-star hotels she'd worked in. Beck had mentioned that he and his brother had toured Europe. Had Bryan Duncan been inspired by those travels?

"I noticed the Lodge has a fantastic kitchen. I love the design and the chef's quality appliances," Nora said.

"But," Judy said.

Nora looked up and saw Judy's expression. She looked not as if she expected an argument but as if she knew Nora was holding back some criticism.

"I haven't met any of the kitchen staff," Nora said with a shrug. "Not yet."

"Right now, you're looking at one," Judy said.

"You can't help in that kitchen and run this one, too."

"You've got that right," Judy agreed.

Nora bit her lip for a minute and continued slicing carrots. She wasn't sure how wise it was to get into this conversation with someone who worked for Beck on the ranch, not just at the hotel. Her plan was to talk to him before she did anything. However, she suspected that Judy wouldn't be surprised by anything Nora had to say to Beck.

Nora had been the one to be surprised, though, when Beck had declined to take a rain check on tonight's meeting. What had changed? Three days ago, he was galloping away. Yesterday, he'd put on his hat and left when her questions got tough.

"There aren't a lot of guests to cook for right now," Nora said, "but it seems to me we have a classic case of which came first, the chicken or the egg. If we hire staff and improve our offerings at the Lodge, it will increase business."

"You don't have to sell me on anything," Judy said. She nodded toward the door leading toward the rest of the house. "And I wish you the best of luck getting through to Beck Duncan."

CHAPTER SEVEN

Beck was the last person to the table, and only his growling belly got him there at all. The questions came immediately, and he had to retell the story of Allen's injury and relay the very brief message he'd gotten from Allen's family members who met him at the hospital. They wouldn't know much until they heard from the surgeon, but Allen was alert and hating all the attention, according to his sister.

Nora sat in Allen's empty seat, and it was a relief to have someone there instead of staring at the empty chair. Beck had passed his brother's empty room far too many times, and even keeping the door shut didn't help. He knew Bryan's clothes were still in the dresser and closet and his model of the Eiffel Tower was still on his desk next to the picture of Riley, the woman he'd been dating when he died.

Everyone ate in silence after Beck had told them what he knew about Allen, so Judy filled in the conversation.

"I hear you rode one of the Lodge's stable horses," she said to Nora.

Beck noticed interested glances in Nora's direction. Of course, there could be other reasons for that interest. They seldom had guests for dinner, especially beautiful strangers.

Nora smiled. "Should I confess that I'm saddle sore?"

"After only one ride?" Wyatt asked.

"It was a long ride," Nora protested. "Over an hour."

Beck saw the smiles all around. His ranch hands, himself included, were accustomed to rides that lasted all day and into the next.

"When are you going out again?" Jay asked.

"Oh, I don't know," Nora said. "I have to wait for the cushioned saddle I ordered online to arrive."

Everyone laughed, and then the conversation became less awkward. Jay told a funny story about a horse he swore could read minds and understand English, and Nora talked about a parade in London where some of the horses got loose and caused a panic. Beck ate his chili and grabbed a slice of thick bread from the cutting board after he made sure everyone else already had one. He didn't say much, but it was nice listening to the conversation. He caught Judy giving him an assessing glance a few times, probably making sure he was eating, being the mother hen she was.

One by one, the ranch hands said good-night and left until it was just Judy, Nora and Beck. Nora got up and began rinsing the dishes the men had scraped and left in a neat stack by the sink—just like Judy had trained them to do.

"I've got this," Judy said, bumping her hip against Nora's at the sink. "You and Beck have things to talk about. Thanks for your help getting dinner on the table, but you go on now."

"Are you sure?" Nora said. "I don't mind."

"You go on now, but thanks anyway," Judy said.

"We can talk on the porch," Beck said. "Through here." He didn't want to be confined in the house, and he always felt better outdoors, as if he could feel his brother's spirit roaming free on the land. It was better than the empty chair by the fireplace and the boot tray by the front door with only his own boots.

"Okay," Nora agreed. She wiped her hands and went through the door Beck indicated, which led straight from the dining room and kitchen onto the porch. The long porch took up the entire side of the house and there was also a door in the middle and another one that led into his office on the far end.

"This is nice," Nora said. She took a chair facing the sunset. This time of year, Beck knew they'd have a view until the sun dipped below a mountain, but even then the pink and orange colors would light the valley where the ranch house sat amid barns and pastures.

"Thank you for helping Judy with dinner," he said. "She had a tough afternoon."

"It was my pleasure. As I told Judy, I like cooking and usually find a way to get into the kitchens at whatever hotel I'm assigned to."

Beck nodded, trying to picture those fancy kitchens in hotels around the world. He and Bryan had stayed in some nice places on their Europe trip, and he wondered if their paths had ever come close to crossing Nora's.

"How long have you been in the hotel business?" he asked.

"Ten years. Since I was nineteen and started working in an Atlanta hotel. That hotel was actually a client of the company I work for now, and that's how I got involved in this work."

So she was only a few years younger than him.

"Sounds like hotels are your calling," he said, glad to be talking about her instead of the failing Lodge, at least for the time being. It was a nice break, talking to someone on the porch instead of being alone with his memories. Of course, he'd be alone with them in six weeks when she left, though, but it would be September, and the fall season was always busy on the ranch. He'd get through it.

"I like the work, and I get to travel," she said. "Are you from Atlanta?"

"Yes."

She didn't elaborate, and he was tempted to pry. Wasn't she sitting right there on the porch of the house where he grew up? She was in his business, literally. But her life was not his business, even if the pink rays of the sunset did light her face in a gentle way, almost as if they wanted her to belong.

He cleared his throat. "We should talk about the Lodge," he said. "Before night falls. I don't want you driving across the ranch in the dark."

"The SUV has headlights."

"Animals don't share the road well, and the roads aren't what you're used to."

Nora laughed. "I drove a rental car in Rome. *Rome*," she emphasized. "The hundreds of scooters were scarier than wild animals, and the traffic circles were like the Wild West."

Beck laughed.

"Okay, maybe not the real Wild West," she said. "I suppose you know more about that than I do."

"Maybe a little," he said. "I could teach you."

The moment he said it, he wished he could take it back. Nora wasn't a tourist, and he didn't want or need to spend time showing her his world. She didn't have to know how much he loved it—why he loved it and how it was part of his skin and bones.

"I'd like that," she said.

"You would?"

She gave a little shrug. "It might help me do my job if I knew more about—"

"Ranchy things?" he asked, unable to resist a smile.

"Exactly." She laughed and a shaft of gold from the sunset washed over both of them for a moment before it disappeared behind a mountain, and suddenly he was aware of the darkness. Light from the kitchen spilled onto the porch. She got a tablet out of the large purse she'd picked up before they walked onto the porch. "I have a list of questions so far and also some documents I'm hoping you can review with me so I can really get started."

"Tomorrow," he said. "We can talk tomorrow. You should get back to the Lodge now. It should only take ten minutes, but it's later than I realized and getting darker by the minute. Supper was late and ate into our time. You'll be safe if you get going soon."

She tilted her head and gave him a quizzical look. "Rome," she reminded him. "Traffic circles and scooters."

"This isn't Rome. You need to listen to me on this one." He could feel his chest getting tight just thinking about the roads at night.

"But—"

"I'll pick you up," he said abruptly, hoping to end the argument. "Ten o'clock tomorrow."

Making a definite plan had the desired effect, and Nora nodded. "Do I need to wear anything special?"

"We're going into Remedy Creek."

"Swimming?"

"The town. I think you should see it. We'll have lunch. You can meet some people and start to get a feel for the area."

Nora gave him a half smile. "Smart idea. It's good to foster a relationship with the locals, especially since I'm going to have to start hiring more staff."

Beck stood and offered her a hand to help her up. He held her hand a moment in the fading light, but then Nora pulled it slowly away.

"You can…text me when you get back to the Lodge, just so I know you didn't get lost," he said.

Nora looked surprised, and Beck felt foolish. He was sure hotel owners in New York or Brussels would never make such a personal request. But it was his land, his responsibility.

"It's that Wyoming hospitality thing?"

"It is here."

"Okay." Nora gave him a long look. "I'll text you tonight, and I'll see you in the morning."

She stepped off the porch and got in the Lodge's car, but as he watched her drive away, he wondered if she had hard days, too. She'd been a lot of places after she left Atlanta and he wished he'd asked her if she ever went home to visit. He couldn't imagine leaving the ranch and putting his feet up on other porches.

He was here to stay, and that meant he needed her help even though she wasn't going to approve of the way he planned to resolve the issue of the Lodge's future.

"YOU CAN GO shopping and get some boots while you're in town," Allie said from behind the front desk. "There are two places in Remedy Creek I can recommend."

"I don't need boots," Nora said. "I'm not a cowgirl, and most of my work is indoors."

Allie grinned. "Maybe you *want* boots. Just because they look good and it helps you fit in."

Nora thought her beautiful shoe wardrobe looked good, and they definitely fit in all over the world. She was a short-timer here. Did she really need a wardrobe revamp?

"I might look at a new pair of jeans," she conceded, not wanting to offend Allie, who seemed to have a different pair of jeans and flannel shirt every day. Nora had been working on a plan to standardize a front desk uniform. Something like black pants and vest with a white shirt. Something that made it clear to guests that they had arrived at a well-managed resort, not a rodeo.

"That's a start," Allie said. "Are you wearing that to go into Remedy Creek?"

Nora glanced down at her tan linen pants, white, sueded silk blouse, and matching navy-blue belt and loafers. She wore her hair secured in a low bun, just in case Beck was one of those people who drove with the windows down. She hardly knew Beck Duncan, but she'd entrusted herself to tour guides she didn't know in plenty of places. This was a business trip so she could investigate the environment. It just happened to be a business trip with a handsome cowboy who owned a massive ranch and cared for the people who worked for him.

He'd even cared about her getting back to the Lodge safely the night before. Practically threw her out so she'd beat the darkness, and she'd seen him in the rearview mirror, watching her until he was out of sight. Not many men she'd met in her travels had been so…well, protective.

He'd even answered her text with a Thank you when she'd let him know she'd arrived safely back at the Lodge.

Beck Duncan had appealing characteristics,

but the appeal for Nora had always been doing her job well and being rewarded. Moving up, moving forward. Until her recent stumble—something she wasn't going to dwell on but was going to learn from.

She'd do an excellent job at Remedy Mountain Lodge and then reclaim her spot on the climb, getting always higher and farther away from the Atlanta apartment where she'd grown up. Maybe if she'd grown up under the wide Wyoming skies with plenty of room to roam, she wouldn't feel so compelled to keep moving.

Beck was certainly determined to stay, even though he seemed to have no family and no time for a personal life.

"Yes, I'm wearing this. I'll be meeting people and I want to make a good impression," she said, hoping Allie would take a hint about dressing up for work.

"You'll make an impression," Allie said.

Something about the way the girl said that made Nora wonder if she should borrow a flannel shirt.

"I hope to make some connections that will help us hire more staff."

"You can put an ad in the local paper that comes out twice a week," Allie said. "I think most people read it. I have the app on my phone."

"Has anyone already tried placing ads?"

"Not that I know of. I found out about this job from my mom who's friends with Nancy in housekeeping. But I don't think there's a sense of urgency. We're not overrun with guests and we're managing okay with the staff we have," Allie said.

Nora smiled at the young woman, but she had her own opinions on whether or not the Lodge was "managing." No one seemed to be managing it at all, but she was finally getting cooperation from Beck so she could change that.

"Your ride is here," Allie said, nodding toward the front portico where a gray pickup waited.

Nora headed for the lobby door, expecting to just go out and get in the truck, but Beck was already out of the truck and opening the side door for her. He wore his usual apparel. Plaid shirt in a cool summer-weight fabric, buttons down the front. Jeans, belt, boots. He wasn't wearing the hat, but his hair was pressed down on the sides as if he'd put it on right out of the shower. As Nora stepped close enough to get in the truck, she smelled his soap and tried to identify it. Personal products were among the amenities that made a difference to guests in high-end hotels, and she liked choosing local products if possible, and always ones with a pleasing but light fragrance. Beck's smell was just right, and she was tempted to ask him what shower soap he used—

"Are you sure you want to wear that?" he asked.

Nora tried not to show her annoyance. Why did people not appreciate her cultivated outfits?

"I'm sure."

Beck nodded. "Okay."

"We're going to an actual town with shops and restaurants and businesses, right?"

"Yes."

"Okay," Nora said. "I should be fine." Surely not everyone in the area dressed like Beck and Allie and…well, everyone else on the ranch. But that was the ranch. She'd researched Remedy Creek online the previous night and found numerous small and medium-sized businesses, including Wellness Springs—which seemed to be a nice spa built on the grounds of the natural spring that had begun Remedy Creek's reputation as a place of healing and well-being. It was tucked behind a main street that looked like a picture out of an Old West travel brochure.

She got in and Beck closed her door. The truck seemed new, and the interior was clean with nice leather seats. The windows were up and the air-conditioning on. She knew it was only a ten-minute drive into Remedy Creek, and it was going to be a comfortable one.

Beck got in and tugged on his seat belt. The truck's large cab suddenly seemed smaller.

They'd been alone together on horseback and on his porch, but the confined space made her more aware of him as a man, not just a client or a rancher. She had no idea what he thought of being in an enclosed space with her, but he had been the one to suggest this trip together.

"Are you hungry?" he asked.

"For breakfast or lunch?"

"Does it matter?"

Nora tilted her head and glanced over at him. From the corner of her eye, she saw his hat on the back seat. "What time did you have breakfast this morning?"

"Five. Like always this time of year."

Ah, ranch life. He was literally up before the sun. That didn't happen everywhere she went.

"What about you?" he asked, surprising her. Beck was a pretty reticent guy so far, and she expected to have to be the one asking questions and moving the conversation along.

"I got a muffin around nine," she said.

"That all?"

Nora watched the Lodge grow smaller in the side mirror as Beck drove down the long approach road.

"Have you ever eaten breakfast at the Lodge?" she asked.

"No."

"I didn't think so. It could use improvement."

"Oh."

"Lunch and dinner aren't bad if you don't mind a limited menu. I suppose guests only staying a few nights would be okay, but I'm here for six weeks and I don't think I can get food delivery out here."

Beck was silent a few minutes, and Nora regretted complaining about the food offerings at the Lodge. It was her job to recognize the shortcomings, but it was also her job to suggest ways to improve. She'd already drawn up a plan including a full breakfast, an expanded lunch and dinner menu, options for room service, and potential boxed lunches for taking on picnics and trail rides. Of course, all these ideas required more staff, and she hoped her visit to Remedy Creek would enlighten her on how to acquire that staff—including a general manager. Good leadership was essential, but it was going to be a tall order attracting the kind of talent the Lodge needed and deserved. Could that person be found locally?

"The pizza place behind the post office delivers sometimes when they have enough help."

"Have you ever had a pizza delivered at the ranch house?" Nora asked. Somehow, she couldn't picture it.

"No. I considered it once on Judy's day off,

but she'd be insulted if I didn't heat up what she left in the fridge."

"Has she worked for the ranch a long time?"

"All my life."

"I love that loyalty," Nora said. "You don't find that just anywhere."

"Not even at the villa on the French Riviera you mentioned?" Beck asked with a hint of a smile.

Nora laughed, surprised he'd been paying close attention to that story. She had no intention of telling him the whole story about that place and how she'd failed. "A beautiful location and a loyal staff are essential to a hotel's success."

"And a good breakfast," Beck added.

"Nonnegotiable," Nora agreed.

"Have you ever thought of owning your own hotel?"

"No," Nora sputtered.

"Why not?"

In truth, she *had* thought about it over the years. How could she not? There was always that voice in her head saying if this was my hotel, I'd do this or that. The idea of owning a big piece of property and calling all the shots was tempting, but dangerous. Giving your heart to one place made you vulnerable because things could change fast. If no place was home, at least you couldn't lose your home. She'd been there.

Beck glanced over, clearly waiting for her answer.

“No way do I have that kind of capital,” Nora said, pulling her thoughts from the apartment building in Atlanta where she’d taken her first steps. “Plus, it’s more fun going to new places all the time and telling other people what they have to do. I get to be the expert, but I don’t have to stay and do all the hard work.”

“I’m ready for you to tell me what I have to do to make the Lodge live up to…well, be what it should be.”

She guessed he was about to say live up to Bryan Duncan’s hopes and dreams. It had to be so hard for Beck, missing his brother and facing the sinking resort. Other hotels she’d rescued had become special to her, but she was starting to think it would be personally satisfying to turn around the Lodge. She’d never known Bryan, but she saw his vision everywhere and respected it. The quiet cowboy next to her and his need for her help was tugging at her heartstrings.

Which was dangerous. She’d learned the hard way that getting too close to hotel owners or falling in love personally with the hotel led to decisions that came from her heart, not her head. And sometimes those decisions were big mistakes. She was going to redeem herself in her own eyes and her company's estimation with this assignment.

"But not until after we get something to eat," Beck added.

Nora watched the Wyoming landscape—gorgeous trees, mountains and ravines with racing water—flash past as they neared the small Western town with a reputation for healing.

CHAPTER EIGHT

"YOU HAVE FOOD choices in Remedy Creek," Beck said as he pulled into the public parking lot between the library and the post office. He'd taken note of Nora's shoes when he picked her up. Not the high heels. Not practical, either, but at least these looked like shoes an average person could probably wander a few blocks in. "All of them are a short walk because, as you can see, downtown isn't that big."

"I'd love to hear my options."

Beck backed into a parking space between a truck similar to his and a small car with California license plates. Tourists came to Remedy Creek all the time to visit Wellness Springs, which was why his brother had been certain a resort on their ranch would pan out. And it should have. Beck felt the familiar wave of guilt. If he'd taken any interest in the place, it wouldn't resemble a ghost town now. He needed to let Nora do her job.

"There's a bakery with good coffee and also the fancy stuff."

She laughed. "You don't think good coffee and fancy stuff are the same thing?"

Beck smiled but continued, "There's also a family restaurant which is probably the nicest one in town. The FarmHouse. If you want to go out for a birthday dinner or impress someone, you'd go there. And they have good meatloaf on Wednesdays."

"Then we're in luck since it's Wednesday," Nora said.

Beck added it up in his head. Nora had been here less than a week, and she'd already gotten under his external layer. As a person who moved somewhere new every month or two, though, she was accustomed to acting fast and acclimating herself. He wasn't sure he could do that.

"There's also a diner only open for breakfast and lunch. Huge plates of food, good prices. If you like diner food."

"Doesn't everyone?" she asked.

"And there are two bars, one for the fancier wine crowd and one that's more of a beer vibe. Both of them serve bar food." Beck couldn't remember the last time he'd used a word like *fancy*, but he'd done it twice now in the space of a few minutes. Being with Nora seemed to awaken a side of him he usually kept quiet—an imaginative mind that he allowed to wander only in the evenings, when he picked up a book he'd enjoyed in college or a new one he'd ordered online.

As soon as Beck turned off the truck, the lack of air-conditioning blowing out the vents made the cab seem hot and crowded. He opened his door, though the August heat provided no relief. "Your choice," he said.

Nora shook her head and gathered up her purse. "You're the local. Wherever I go, I trust the hotel staff's recommendations."

He almost objected and said he wasn't hotel staff. He didn't have a single thing to do with the running of the place. Hadn't been inside a guest room since the night of the grand opening when his brother had proudly walked a tour group through that included a lot of locals who were excited for Bryan and the Lodge.

They got out, Beck grabbing his hat from the back seat out of long habit.

"Well?" she asked.

He put on his hat to cut the sun's glare. "I'm going to say the FarmHouse family restaurant," he said.

"The birthday dinner location?" she asked with a smile. "The one with meat loaf Wednesday?"

"It's always cool in there," he said. For a moment, he wondered when Nora's birthday was. Did she celebrate it alone every year wherever she was in the world? He wondered if she got lonely, traveling like that.

Of course, a person could be lonely right at home in the place where he was born. That was probably why he found himself talking to Nora. She'd be gone, though, in less than six weeks.

They crossed the small parking lot and started down the sidewalk past the post office.

"Am I getting the tour on the way to the restaurant?" she asked.

The family restaurant was directly across the street and Beck was hungry, but a lap of the main street would only take ten minutes. He ignored the aroma of bacon and nodded.

"This is the post office," he said. "There're also delivery lockers in the back, so if you order anything online, you can pick it up there. It works pretty well out here where delivery trucks would have a long way to go to get to some houses." He pointed to the next building, a sign overhanging the sidewalk indicating it was a bank. "ATM here, and there's also one in the grocery store on the back street in case this one isn't working."

"Good to know," Nora said.

"Here's the Saddle Bar," he said. A neon sign with a beer mug and the name of a popular brew flashed by the front door.

"Fancy wine or beer vibe?" she asked with a grin.

He laughed. "The other bar is called Sunset Rosé." He pointed across the street where there were sidewalk tables and flower planters giving an almost Parisian café feel to the place.

"Wine bar, got it," Nora said. "I like a good glass of rosé, so we may have to pop in there while I'm in town."

"You can come into town using the Lodge's SUV anytime you want," he said.

Her smile faded, and he realized quickly that he sounded like he didn't want to take the time to have a drink with her.

"Although it might sound good later if we get thirsty after talking to people," he amended quickly. "That's one of your goals for today, right? Meet people and get a feel for the locals."

"Yes. If I can build a few relationships, we might find additional staff which we need to scale up."

"I know basically everyone in town," he said.

"Have you talked to anyone about coming to work at the Lodge?"

She probably already knew the answer to that question. He'd been wearing blinders, but he wasn't a horse frightened or distracted by the world around him. He needed to open his eyes and see everything, even the things that hurt.

"Coming up is the Farm & Home store where you can get almost anything you want."

"Can I get a farm?" she asked. "How about a home?"

Beck blew out a sigh but couldn't resist a smile. "Maybe it's not exactly as advertised."

"Few things are," she said. "Which makes it even better when something turns out to be the real thing." She paused and turned toward him, piercing him with a serious gaze. "I believe Remedy Mountain Lodge could be the real thing, an authentic and luxurious Western getaway. We will get there, and it will be spectacular."

Beck couldn't breathe. The last time he'd heard someone speak passionately about the Lodge had been his brother's speech at the grand opening. Bryan's expression had been pure joy and pride as he welcomed over a hundred people, mostly locals, some reporters and a few guests who'd heard about the place online. Bryan had led tours himself, poured champagne and smiled for picture after picture.

Beck had been there at the grand opening, in the corner of the room, doubt dampening his smile as he thought about the division of the ranchland and the impact on the size of the herd, the resources taken up by the resort. The fact that his own brother didn't want to be a rancher like the generations before them. Bryan's dream diverged from Beck's so hard it hurt, and that was why he'd left early that night. He didn't want to argue with his brother—again—and ruin the party, but, in his heart, he didn't think he'd ever understand why Bryan wanted something different from the land.

He'd had ten months to regret his attitude and beat himself up for leaving early that night, his parting words—his *final* words—to Bryan seared into his memory. *I hope you're happy, if this is what you want to do with our family's land.*

"Hey," Nora said. "Don't worry. This is what I do. By the time I leave town, you won't need me anymore and you also won't be able to find a parking space at that gorgeous hotel of yours."

Beck was fairly certain it was her standard pep talk for distressed hoteliers, but he wasn't like all of those other people. He wanted the Lodge to struggle back to life only because it was a necessary step toward getting it off his back.

"Going in?"

Beck glanced up and saw a man he knew, holding open the door of Farm & Home with a questioning expression. The guy probably wondered why Beck was standing on the street with a beautiful woman no one in town had ever seen before. He'd be getting a lot of questions about that, but it was unavoidable. Talk would die down when Nora left.

"Do you want to go in?" Beck asked Nora.

"Maybe later. You've got to be starving by now. How much farther to the restaurant?"

Beck pointed down the street in the direction they'd come from. "It's back there."

Nora laughed and put a hand over her mouth. "You didn't have to go so far out of your way to give me a tour." She put a hand on his elbow. "Let's eat."

Beck tried to remember the last time a woman had touched him—not including Judy who sometimes gave him a maternal hug he didn't try to dodge. Nora was not only beautiful and determined but her hand on his elbow reminded him that he was a human and needed connection with someone.

"We…have to cross the street," Beck stammered, hoping Nora would drop her hand. He found it hard to think when she was so close to him. There was no choice but to resist her, though. She was there to do a job, and she would leave as soon as she could. Why torture himself by caring about someone who was just going to be gone anyway, just like everyone else he had loved?

Nora turned and shaded her eyes, looking out for cars. She kept her hand on his elbow and tugged him across the street. They walked past a gas station that sat at the end, and Nora paused to look in the front windows of a gift shop. "Whoever runs this place has great taste," she said. "I love the window display."

"New owner," Beck said. "A woman who came for the healing spring but spent a lot of time at the wine bar." He pointed to the wine bar with the sidewalk seating next to the gift shop. "She ended up marrying the guy who runs Sunset Rosé and opening a gift shop next door."

"Romantic," Nora said.

Beck didn't comment on that and kept walking past the café tables on the sidewalk. "Next up is the real estate office, and then that diner I told you about that's only open for breakfast and lunch, and then a drugstore. The pharmacist sometimes acts as a local doctor in a pinch, giving advice and stuff like that."

They walked quickly down the block, and he gestured. "And here's the FarmHouse restaurant. Finally."

"Right across from where we parked," Nora said. "You should have told me it was right here. It would have saved you the walk and you'd be eating by now."

"You wanted a tour, and I wanted to show hospitality."

Nora grinned at that, and he held the door open for her, smiling despite his hunger. He'd never thought he could joke about hospitality, not after Bryan building the Lodge and then dying on opening day. Why did Nora make him feel as if he could loosen the tight reins on the past just enough to take a deep breath?

As soon as they stepped inside the restaurant, a woman greeted Beck with a long hug. "Window table or something in the back?" she asked. At least that was what she said, but Nora was pretty sure there was an underlying question. The woman—Riley according to her name tag—was giving Beck a long, inquisitive look, and Nora could guess why. She suspected people in town already knew there was a temporary manager at the Lodge, but maybe they didn't know she was young, not much younger than Beck.

"The sun's pretty bright out front today, Riley," Beck said.

"This way," the woman said. She grabbed two laminated menus and ushered them to a table in the back. "You'll have more privacy back here anyway, just in case you need it."

Did she sound offended? Nora couldn't decide. For all she knew, this was a past or present girlfriend of Beck's or maybe an old friend who felt he should explain his company.

"This okay?" Riley asked.

"Yes, thank you," Nora said. "I'm Nora Myers. I'm here for a while working with the team at Remedy Mountain Lodge."

Riley nodded. "I heard you were here, but I didn't know you would be so…"

Nora waited, worried now that this was someone with an interest in Beck who would see Nora as competition. Which of course she wasn't. Beck was attractive and admirable, sure, and he made her laugh. Even better, she made him laugh and she couldn't help noticing he always seemed a little surprised, as if he wasn't accustomed to finding anything funny. She liked being the person to bring out his very nice smile.

"Dressed up," Riley concluded, bringing Nora's attention back to the present. "We don't see much silk or linen here in Remedy Creek. Not that it doesn't look good on you."

"Thank you," Nora said. She wished she had listened to Allie and worn something more appropriate so she wouldn't look like such an outsider. "I confess I packed the wrong things, but I was planning to do some shopping while I'm in town today." She turned to Beck. "If you don't mind."

"Oh," Beck said, clearly caught off guard by the question. "No, not at all."

"Maybe you could point me in the right direction for my shopping trip," Nora said to Riley.

Riley smiled. "For one thing, don't listen to Beck about style. For another, you can shop at Farm & Home if you want to look like everyone else. But I think you'd do better with the boutique next door."

"Thank you," Nora said.

"Do you want the breakfast special?" she asked Beck. "It's on until noon. It's all the usual stuff you order on one big plate."

Beck looked to Nora. "I'll have whatever you're having," she said. This was a strategy she'd learned over the years. Not being a picky eater was helpful, of course, and she tried following the lead of a local person whenever she could.

Beck handed Riley back both menus. "Two specials. With coffee?" he asked, directing the question to Nora. She nodded and Beck added, "Two coffees."

"I didn't know if you thought it was too hot for coffee," he said after Riley left.

"It's nice and cool in here," Nora said. She looked around at the booths with thick vinyl seats in a shade of pine green. The booths rimmed the outer walls of the restaurant, and tables for two or four were scattered throughout the middle. Wide front windows offered a view of the street, but Nora liked the quieter light in the rear of the restaurant. It was easier to see Beck's face.

"Have you known Riley for a long time?" she asked.

Beck's expression sobered. "Yes."

"She must have a good memory for customers' orders."

"Her family owns the place, and they've been in business for years," Beck said.

Another server brought two glasses of ice water and placed them on the table.

"Are there a lot of family businesses here in Remedy Creek?" Nora asked. The Lodge had been sort of a family business, with the ranch next door owned by Beck, and she knew the two brothers had inherited the land. She wondered what that must be like, inheriting something of value from parents. Her father hadn't even left a life insurance policy when the accident happened.

Beck took a long drink, practically draining the water. "Are a lot of the hotels you work with inherited properties or run by families?" he asked.

Nora thought about it for a minute, a bit surprised by having her questions turned back on her. She couldn't decide if Beck was good at deflecting or if he was genuinely interested in her work.

"Some of them, but quite a few are owned by small corporations or partnerships and have new ownership trying to turn around a struggling property. Sometimes those failing hotels are great buys because they sell cheap but have great potential."

"Interesting," Beck commented.

"I often think the previous owners gave up too soon. If they had called in help like my company, they may not have had to sell. I hate seeing people give up and basically get forced out."

Beck drained the rest of his water and shifted in his seat. "Did you ever have a property you couldn't save?" he asked. "Someplace that was beyond your company's ability to rescue?"

She had been asked this question before by nervous hoteliers, and her standard answer was no. Her company had an excellent success rate, and her personal statistic was *almost* 100 percent. She always relayed this information and reassured the property owner they'd succeed, no doubt about it.

But she wasn't quick with her answer this time because that apartment building her parents had owned in Atlanta flashed into her mind. Maybe it was the talk of family businesses, or maybe Beck made her want to let her guard down. Of course, that failure hadn't been hers. She'd been eighteen when her father fell off the roof of that building, leaving her family without money, a home, a living. She'd been too young to know what to do.

She'd never been that vulnerable since.

"My success rate with Total Hospitality Management is very high," she said.

Beck tilted his head and studied her for a minute, but he didn't ask whatever question was lingering behind his eyes. She didn't want to talk about her second visit to the Riviera.

"Here you go," Riley said as she slid two huge plates onto the table.

Nora almost laughed aloud. The plates had eggs, ham, sausage gravy and biscuits, and a waffle sticking off the side. Riley pulled bottles of ketchup and mustard from her apron pockets and set them on Beck's side of the table. "You and your brother are the only people who've ever wanted mustard with breakfast," she said.

Beck reached up and squeezed her hand. "Thank you."

Nora noticed that Riley referred to Beck and his brother in the present tense, and she was almost sure she saw tears in Riley's eyes before she quickly turned around and walked away.

Beck met her gaze. He swallowed, his eyes momentarily bleak. "Riley was dating my brother when he passed last October."

"Oh," Nora said, all the breath leaving her body. "That must have been so hard…for all of you."

Beck closed his fingers around the mustard

bottle but didn't pick it up. "She took it hard," he said, looking at his plate instead of Nora.

"Had they been dating a long time?"

Beck continued staring at his food, and Nora was afraid she'd overstepped with the question. It was none of her business, and she didn't want to ruin his appetite or let his food get cold.

Finally, he looked up but his voice was so quiet she could hardly hear him. "Yeah, a long time. I never told her, but Bryan had a ring. He just hadn't given it to her yet."

Nora's heart felt as if it was being squeezed by an invisible fist. She knew what it was like to suddenly lose someone. She could feel that pain even after more than a decade. It was shocking that Beck had trusted her enough to share something so personal.

"What did you do with the ring?" she asked, her voice practically a whisper. She knew she shouldn't ask, but she couldn't stop herself.

"It's still in his room at the ranch house."

Nora wanted to cry. She wanted to go hug Riley and cry. Her meal smelled amazing, but she didn't think she'd be able to get one bite past the lump in her throat. When Bryan Duncan died, he'd left a very large void, and saving his hotel dream was only one small part she could play. She wanted to do more to help.

Beck's phone rang and he glanced at the screen and then said, "Sorry. I have to get this."

Nora nodded, glad for the distraction. She watched his expression lighten up in stages, a little at a time, as he said, "Okay, okay, yes, that's great news...Uh-huh, thanks for letting me know...Yes, okay, will do."

He put the phone back on the table and picked up his fork.

"Allen is going to be okay," he said. "The break is clean. They were leaning toward surgery today, but the surgeon thinks they can set it, and it will heal on its own. With some physical therapy, he should be able to do just about everything he did before."

The tension broke open in Nora's chest and she felt like laughing with relief.

Beck squeezed mustard all over his ham and started eating, and Nora wondered if this was typical for the hard life of a rancher—moments when breathing seemed impossible followed by bursts of joy that made moving on seem possible. It made her want to know Beck better, even though there was no reason for it and it would make it harder for her to do the job and leave. Like she always did. Before she started to open her heart.

CHAPTER NINE

WHEN RILEY RETURNED with the check, she lingered, and then said to Nora, "I have a lunch break right now, and I wonder if you'd like company shopping next door."

Nora hesitated, genuinely surprised at the gesture. She seldom made friends on the road, but she stayed so busy she didn't have time to be lonely. Around the holidays, she visited her mother who lived with her older brother, but she kept those visits short intentionally because her mother liked to relive the past and Nora did not.

"You look beautiful," Riley added. "But I hear you're going to be here for a while, and I thought you might like advice on clothes from a local perspective. It's okay if you'd rather not."

"No, I'd love that. Are you sure you have time?"

"It's a quiet weekday and I have a good staff. I can go next door for half an hour," Riley said. "Okay by you, Beck, if I steal your hotel consultant for a little bit?"

"Of course," Beck said. "I'm going to the drugstore to pick up a get-well card for everyone to sign for Allen."

Riley nodded. "Heard he's going to be okay."

"How did—" Beck began.

"News travels," Riley said. "I'll cash you out." She left with his credit card and Beck turned to Nora.

"Good luck shopping with Riley. She's brutally honest, but in a good way."

Nora laughed. "I do appreciate that in a person but thank you for the warning."

Nora usually thought of herself as being brutally honest, too, but she found herself being overly cautious in her evaluation of the Lodge's management shortcoming. Personal feelings had no place in hotel management. She knew this. She liked Beck and empathized with his feelings, and it was already getting in the way of her work and slowing her down. At this rate, she'd be lucky to get the Lodge on its feet and get out of Wyoming in six weeks, and that Barcelona job wouldn't wait.

She needed to keep her head in the game and build quick relationships in town so she could hire staff. What better way to connect with Remedy Creek businesses than to patronize one of them with a shopping trip?

Five minutes later, Riley stood in front of a

wall of giant shoeboxes containing women's Western boots in a variety of colors and styles. They were mostly white, brown or black, but there were a few pairs that came in red and even pink and purple. She couldn't imagine herself wearing any of them. Especially the ones with fringe, embroidery and shiny beads. Nora had hardly worn any kind of boots in the past decade since she'd started working for Total Hospitality Management. She chose her locations wisely based on the season and preferred warm climates. The more seniority she'd gained, the better choice of locations she'd had.

The few winter clothes she owned were in a storage locker owned by her company near its headquarters in Atlanta. She visited her possessions about as often as she visited her mother. She didn't feel guilty about the possessions, though.

"I don't know," she said to Riley. "I'm not sure any of these are really me."

"Try on a few. You might surprise yourself."

"Okay," Nora said. She considered buying a pair just to humor everyone, but the boots were definitely on the expensive side, well-made and genuine leather. If she was going to shell out her cash, she wanted to at least *like* the boots, even a little.

"But not with that outfit," Riley added. She turned to the clerk who she clearly knew, since they'd spent several minutes discussing the clerk's new niece already. "How about a pair of boot-cut jeans in her size?"

"Dark wash or faded?" the clerk, Sandy, asked.

Riley eyed Nora up and down and she and Sandy both said "dark wash" at the same time, much to Nora's relief. At least dark jeans looked dressier. Were people really expecting her to wear jeans and boots at work? She'd once worked at a national park's resort lodge in Maine and, despite most of the guests wearing hiking boots and apparel, Nora had dressed like a working professional.

"And a shirt or two," Riley added.

Nora looked down at her white silk blouse with its beautiful, covered buttons on cuffs just above the elbow. "Does it have to be flannel?" she asked.

Riley laughed. "It's okay if you're not ready for flannel. You've got time."

Nora sighed. She still had over five weeks, but that seemed like barely enough time to make a dent in the challenges at the Lodge. Beck was coming around, but they had still not had a serious conversation about her goals for the resort and how they were going to achieve them. She was supposed to be making connections with locals in town, though, and that was exactly what she was currently doing, so she cheerfully went into a dressing room and put on the clothes that Riley and Sandy slung over the top of the dressing room door.

The blue knit top and dark jeans weren't bad. She could see herself wearing the outfit on a casual date sometime—if she ever went on dates, which she didn't because she was always on a work trip and she did not date clients or anyone who worked at the hotel she was assisting. She did shop locally, but always alone.

Nora opened the dressing room door and revealed her outfit, which she thought looked very nice. She expected approval from Riley and Sandy, and then a quick checkout and exit. Was Beck chomping at the bit, waiting for her?

"Too loose," Sandy said, pointing to her jeans. "You have a nice body, and you should wear something with a closer fit."

"Same with the top," Riley agreed, and then she playfully pushed Nora back inside and closed the door. A moment later, the same clothes in a smaller size came over the door, and Nora resignedly wriggled into them. Although the breakfast special had been delicious, she really wished she hadn't eaten most of that giant plate of food. Beck was probably walking off his breakfast somewhere down the street, not stuffing himself into tight jeans that—admittedly—hugged her hips nicely and flared out at the bottom, making her look somehow taller. She evaluated herself in the mirror for a moment before opening the door.

"Better," Sandy said. She stood in the open doorway and pushed three boxes of boots into the dressing room with her own booted toe. "They'll be stiff, so just be prepared for that as you tug them on. They'll soften up and mold to you like those jeans if you wear them enough."

Sandy went off to greet another customer and Riley took her place in the doorway. Nora considered which boots to try first as she weighed what she wanted to say to Riley. She'd formed an idea over that giant plate of eggs and gravy, but it was risky because of Riley's personal relationship with the Lodge and Beck's family.

Nora reached for a dark brown pair of boots with no decorations aside from tasteful embroidery over the toes. "Riley," she began. "I wonder if I could ask your advice about a matter of food."

"Sure," Riley said. She squeezed onto the little bench in the dressing room with Nora. Riley smelled like coffee and toast. All the people Nora had met in Remedy Creek seemed somehow…comfortable. Except Beck. He acted as if something was chasing him.

"You know I'm helping Beck with some management strategies at the Lodge because it hasn't been…so it becomes a successful destination and…"

"Lives up to what Bryan wanted," Riley said. "You don't have to dance around it with me. I see what's happening out there. We all do. Beck can't get over losing his brother, but he can't live with that Lodge being an empty shell either."

Nora tugged on one boot and then straightened up and looked at Riley. "Beck told me that you and Bryan were dating."

Riley nodded. "For years. I knew all about his dreams for that place, saw all the plans, even gave him some practical advice on the kitchen. You should have seen how happy he was when it opened."

Riley struggled to smile, and Nora's heart hurt for her.

"It's beautiful," Nora said. "I can see his vision for it even though it's pretty empty."

"I haven't been out there in a while," Riley said.

Nora tugged on the other boot and then stood, shifting her weight and trying to wiggle her toes.

"They'll soften up, they just take some getting used to," Riley said. "Sort of like some of the people around here."

Nora looked herself over in the mirror from her casual top to flared jeans to boots. The outfit was unlike anything she owned and, to her surprise, she didn't dislike it. She even had a little tan contrasting with her blond hair.

"I know what you're thinking," Riley said.

"You do?"

"The boots are too tame." Riley held up a white pair with deep fringe dangling from a side seam. "These are the ones you want."

Nora was quite sure that was not true, but she was going along with the spirit of the shopping trip, so she sat down and tugged off the brown boots. She turned to face Riley and held out a hand for one of the white boots. "Riley, quite frankly, I could use your help at the Lodge."

She paused, watching Riley's face. The last thing she wanted to do was cause her pain, but Riley's expression was more interest than sorrow.

"Please say no if it's too much to ask, but would you consider helping me figure out a menu and better food service options? Trust me when I say your food is the best I've had this week."

"Except for Judy's chili at the ranch house," Riley said. "Like I said, news travels, and don't let Judy hear you saying her food wasn't good."

Nora smiled and pulled on the white boots. "Dinner at the ranch house was very good." Until Beck had practically thrown her out before dark. At least that quick exit had also come with an invitation for today. One step at a time.

She stood in the white boots and took a moment to balance on the high heels that wore a lot different than her high-heeled pumps. She walked out to the large mirror in the shop and Riley followed. Sandy finished with her other customer and gazed at Nora in the mirror.

"You look tall and confident in that outfit," Sandy said.

"Is that what I was going for? I thought I was just trying to fit in."

"Tall and confident never hurts," Riley said. "I think you should get the whole outfit."

"Maybe I will." Nora knew the boots were pricey, but the jeans and top weren't expensive, and honestly, she had money in the bank. She lived in hotels where her food was provided. Her travel was covered by the company, and she didn't own or rent a home or have a car. Most of her expenditures were on clothes, her armor preventing herself and anyone else from seeing her as the poor kid she'd once been. The one who lived with her mother for a full year on the charity of the new owner of the building her parents had once owned.

Sandy went into the stockroom at the back, leaving Riley and Nora alone again.

"And I'll think about what you asked," Riley said. "It's painful to think about Bryan and how he never got to run the hotel he'd dreamed up, but it's even worse to know it's sitting there like an empty promise. I'd want you to run this by Beck first, though. I wouldn't consider coming out to help unless it's what he really wants."

"Thank you," Nora said.

"One more thing."

Nora caught Riley's glance in the mirror.

"Do you know your hat size?"

"Is there such thing?" Nora asked.

Riley laughed. "There is in Wyoming." She picked up a white hat from a rack and handed it to Nora. "Give this one a try."

Nora put the hat on her head. It felt heavy, but it was a good fit. She evaluated herself in the full-length mirror. She looked like a city girl in cowboy clothes, but keeping a part of herself separate was the safest way to prevent herself from getting emotionally involved with her assignment and risking a mistake that could endanger her job.

CHAPTER TEN

BECK KILLED AT least half an hour downtown before settling onto the bench in front of the boutique. No way was he going in. What had motivated Riley to invite Nora for a shopping trip? Was she lonely? Did she feel sorry for Nora's fish-out-of-water appearance?

Maybe she was hungry for a connection to the Lodge. He cursed himself for not reaching out to her much in the past year, and he felt sick when he pictured her reaction to his plans for the place.

He was ashamed of its current state, but also ashamed of his plan to unload it. Selling his brother's dream made his ham and mustard churn in his stomach. Riley wouldn't understand. No one would. But he'd have to live with it.

When Nora emerged from the store, she had a big box the size of new boots and a huge shopping bag. A cowboy hat peeked over the top of the bag. Nora was back in her city clothes, though.

"You were in there a while," Beck said.

"Making connections. I met Sandy who owns the place. She has a great eye for retail. And also someone who works at Wellness Springs who told me all about their business. It was interesting hearing the history of Remedy Creek and its reputation for healing everything from saddle sores to broken hearts."

Beck laughed. "I don't know how much of that is exactly true, but you could decide for yourself."

"I didn't ride long enough to get actual saddle sores," she said. "I know my limits."

They stowed her purchases in his truck.

"Do you need to get back to the ranch or could we visit the winery?" Nora asked.

Of course he needed to get back to the ranch. The whole operation depended on him, and here he was lunching and shopping in town, right in the middle of the day. But this was the price he needed to pay to solve his problems.

"Let's do it," he said.

They walked over to the Sunset Rosé where Nora went inside and got two glasses of wine. When she returned and put the glasses on the table, Beck concealed a smile while she dusted off her chair before sitting.

"We need a kick start," Nora said after several sips of wine. "Something to plan for, something to talk about on social media, something to involve people and make them feel as if they're part of the Lodge's revival."

Beck sat back. Their trip into town had been relaxing, friendly even, but Nora's tone was all business now. "Tell me more," he said.

"I'm thinking of a party, a dinner we can sell tickets to, some kind of a great local menu, but upscale."

He remembered the grand opening party all too well, but it was too late to do that again. You can't pretend something is new when it isn't.

"What's the occasion?" he asked.

"We make one," she said. "It's almost September. Is there some kind of local event… I don't know, a festival maybe? For example, we did a kickoff party at a mansion turned resort on the New England coast because it was the wedding anniversary of the long-deceased Gilded Age couple who had built the mansion."

"I'll think about it," Beck said.

"I was talking to Riley, who obviously has great ideas about food, and I wondered if maybe I should ask her to get involved."

The thought of seeing Bryan's sweetheart at the Lodge took him right back to the grand opening. Memories like that were what he was trying to avoid, for himself and others.

"No," he said. "It's too soon to ask Riley to go out there. It'll be hard for her to see the place again and definitely too hard to get involved in a big event." An event of any kind would take Riley back to the grand opening, too, and the terrible end of that evening. He doubted she'd healed enough to handle it, and he wanted to protect her.

"But don't you think—" Nora began.

"No," Beck said.

Nora sipped her glass of chilled white wine. Her cheeks were flushed, and he assumed it was either the summer heat or the wine. He'd taken one sip from his glass and decided it wasn't for him. Beck seldom drank, preferring instead to keep a clear head. Since his brother's death, he'd had a few beers with his ranch hands. Most of them had become friends in the many years they worked there. But he drank with them only to be social and only because he didn't have to drive after, and their bunks were a short walk away from the ranch house. The company and the beer dulled his heartache temporarily, but it was waiting for him when he tried to close his eyes at night anyway.

"I can start somewhere else," Nora said, her tone cheerful and determined. He imagined he wasn't the first hotel owner to push back on her ideas. She'd only been there a week—how could she possibly know what was best for the Lodge?

"Okay," Beck said. "Let's hear your ideas."

Nora pushed her wineglass away and got out

her phone. She scrolled a minute and then began reading from a list.

"I've done an audit of your staff and determined you have great people who honestly don't have enough to do."

"Okay."

"But I'm recommending you double the size of the staff right away."

"What…what would more people do?" Beck asked. This advice sounded completely backward. He hired ranch hands for exactly the amount of work he needed them to do and operated on a slim margin of efficiency. His business degree and experience told him he was doing it right.

"We'll start training them now, and then they'll run the hotel when it comes up to capacity. After that, you'll need even more employees."

"What are these people going to do while we wait for this magical guest capacity?" Beck asked.

"First of all, we're not *going* to sit around and wait. We're going to scale with advertising, connections, outreach. When was the last time you updated the website or got ad placement on social media?"

"I—" He stopped. He knew the embarrassing answer to that question, and so did Nora. He felt his own face heat, but it wasn't the wine, and he was accustomed to summer in Wyoming.

"I'm sorry," Nora said. "That question sounded more like an accusation. I'm not here to dump on you or criticize your management of the Lodge."

"You can take off the kid gloves, Nora. We both know I haven't been managing the Lodge, and I don't think anyone else has either."

"I…know it was your brother's dream, not yours," Nora said cautiously. She leaned forward so her words couldn't be overheard by anyone on the street. "But I don't want you to feel discouraged or give up—"

"I'm not giving up," Beck said, his voice too loud. A man entering the Farm & Home across the street paused and looked over at him. Nora had unknowingly made a direct strike at his guilty spot. Selling the Lodge was selling out his brother. But what could he do? He couldn't run it and the ranch.

Nora smiled. "That's the passion I want to see in a hotel owner."

Irritation bubbled in his veins. He was irritated with himself for everything, but that didn't mean he had to take it out on the person he should be accepting help from. Nora was trying to do a job, just like he was. And he needed her. He could hardly sell a Lodge with empty rooms and no track record.

“Sorry,” he muttered.

“You have nothing to be sorry for,” Nora said.

Beck picked up his wineglass just to feel its coolness on his fingers. Nora had no idea how much he was sorry for and how he wished he could go back three years to when his brother first showed him the plans for the Lodge. He’d never supported the idea, but he couldn’t stop Bryan from doing what he wanted with his half of the inheritance. He’d gritted his teeth all through the construction when he should have been celebrating his brother’s vision. He should have stayed at the grand opening party and celebrated. Maybe if he’d been driving, he would have seen that flooded ravine in the dark. His brother wouldn’t have died, or at least not died alone.

Beck stood up and put cash on the table. “We should get back,” he said.

Nora left her half-empty glass on the table and stood, too. “Do I have your support for hiring and training a new group of employees?”

Beck put on his hat. “I brought you into town to meet people, didn’t I?”

“There’s a difference between going along with something because you feel you have no choice and actively supporting it.”

Her tone was pleasant, but her words packed a punch. Nora seemed to see inside him, and she wasn't going to take a quick look and back slowly away. No one had challenged him like this in a long time. Spending time with Nora was going to hurt, but he had to do it.

"I do believe in what you're planning," he said.

"I'm glad. I'll email you my entire list of recommendations and action steps."

He nodded. "I'll read it tonight. And I'll…try to help."

Nora glanced up at him. His shadow blocked the harsh afternoon sun from her face, and he saw his own reflection in her eyes, hat and all. He also saw a glimmer of hope in those eyes, and he wished for a moment he was worth her belief in him.

"I could teach you some ranchy things," he said, using her words from days ago. "If you're willing to meet me halfway."

ON SUNDAY MORNING, Nora pulled on a pair of jeans she'd brought with her and a shirt she intended to use for working out in the hotel gym. She laced up her sneakers and went down to the always-disappointing breakfast buffet off the lobby. She was the only guest getting a muffin and coffee, and it made her even more determined to advertise the Lodge's attributes far and wide.

What a shame, she thought as she sat in the

lobby and tried to see the place as a traveler. The furniture was comfortable, the view from the tall windows exquisite, and the air-conditioning nice and cold. It had to be costing Beck a fortune to maintain this place and keep it running with very little revenue coming in.

"Hey, Nora," Allie said, pulling up short on her way to the front desk. "Are you taking the day off?"

"No, I'm working," Nora said.

Allie smiled. The young woman wore her trademark jeans, flannel and braids. "I like your new look. This way I don't feel so underdressed at the front desk."

Nora offered Allie one of her muffins, and Allie took it and unwrapped it.

"Did anyone give you instructions on your uniform?" Nora asked.

"No, I just thought I should fit the theme."

"What's the theme?" Nora asked. This, like a vision and mission statement, was an important consideration. Did everyone have the same idea of what Remedy Mountain Lodge should be? Without its founder, what was the place?

"Um, Western. I think. You know, cowboys and ranchers, mountains, stuff like that."

"But there are expensive shampoos and body wash and luxury linens in the rooms."

"So, classy cowboy," Allie said.

They ate in silence for a moment.

"Did you know Bryan Duncan?" Nora asked.

Allie's expression shifted to serious. "I grew up around here, so I pretty much know everyone. The Duncan brothers are older than I am, but Bryan was in my older brother's class in school."

The girl looked so sad that Nora was sorry she'd brought it up. Bryan had left a large hole in a lot of hearts when he passed away. Nora smiled and lightened her tone. "Was Bryan a classy cowboy?"

Allie shrugged but still looked pensive. "Beck's the cowboy in the family. Bryan was always different, kind of like he wanted something more than being a working rancher. Which you can probably guess from this beautiful place."

Nora absorbed that. Beck had said something similar about his brother being inspired by their travels and European hotels. She wondered if the brothers had fought about the resort. If they had, where did that leave Beck when his brother had suddenly died?

"Speaking of Beck," Allie said. She pointed through the large lobby windows that offered a view of the stables and trails leading to the mountains. It was barely eight o'clock, but Beck was there on horseback. True to his word, he'd shown up to teach Nora more about the ranching world. He wore a plaid shirt and his big hat, and he held the reins of a second horse, saddled and waiting next to him.

Nora had expected a ride in the pickup truck, perhaps a guided tour of the ranch and a lecture on how it all operated. But there was no doubt who that empty saddle was for.

"It's rare to see him anywhere near the Lodge," Allie said. She glanced at Nora's clothing again. "Oh, I get it now. But you're going to need a hat and maybe some riding boots. Do you have any?"

Nora's heart sank. The fringy white ones she'd dropped big bucks on in town yesterday seemed more like dressy boots than working boots. She didn't want to ruin them. She wasn't even sure she intended to keep them and had carefully tucked the receipt into the box.

"It's okay if you don't. We have a closet full of loaner clothing for guests, hats and boots included. Bryan thought of everything." Allie pointed toward the door leading to a staff-only section of the hotel. "We'll find you something. Most of it has never been worn. Should I tell Beck to come inside and wait while we get you outfitted?"

Nora shook her head. "It's his hotel, he knows he can come inside." Beck clearly didn't feel comfortable spending time inside the Lodge, and she was pushing him enough already. He'd agreed to meet her halfway, and that was progress.

"We can be quick," Allie said, leading the way.

Nora followed her to a small room where there was a double rack, shirts on top and pants on the bottom. Women's clothing was on one end, men's on the other, and below them were plain brown riding boots lined up. A separate rack held a selection of cowboy hats in black, white and brown.

"Size?" Allie asked, pointing to the boots.

"Eight," Nora said.

Allie selected a pair and Nora sat on a bench in the room and tried them on.

"Good enough," she said, standing.

"And now a hat," Allie said.

"I actually have one in my room. I bought it in town a few days ago. Riley helped me pick it out."

Allie looked surprised. "Oh…that's great. So you just need one more thing." She pulled a band from her pocket and pointed to Nora's hair. "Can I help you do braids?"

Nora had already gone pretty far with the boots, jeans and hat. A braid seemed like too much.

"I'll be okay," she said.

"Okay." Allie handed her the hair band. "Tuck this in your pocket in case you change your mind."

CHAPTER ELEVEN

WHEN NORA WALKED out of the Lodge at ten minutes after eight—late for their meeting, which wasn't like her—Beck couldn't be annoyed. He was too astonished. He knew she'd purchased some Western wear in town several days ago, but he didn't expect her to look so…practical. She appeared to be ready to work. He wasn't going to risk saying it, but the jeans, boots and hat suited her. With a deeper tan and maybe some braids to tame her long hair, she could almost fit in on the ranch.

"Good morning," she said as if she strode out to a waiting horse every day.

Beck swung down from Hercules, feeling like a jerk for not giving Nora a heads-up about their mode of transportation ahead of time. He should have thought of it. As the professional she was, though, she was right on pace with him. He imagined she had to think on her feet, traveling around the world and walking into different resorts and different problems every few months.

He wondered if his Lodge project was more difficult than the usual places—and if *he* was more difficult that her usual clients.

"You're dressed for the day," he said.

"I was only partially dressed for riding horseback, but I saw you out the window and Allie helped me change."

"Is that what you bought at the boutique on Wednesday?" he asked.

Nora approached the horse cautiously and ran a hand down its nose.

"I got the boots from the closet filled with ranch wear that hotel guests can borrow," she said. "I didn't want to wear the fancy ones I bought in Remedy Creek. Not yet anyway."

Beck was ashamed to admit he didn't know there was such a closet. There were a lot of things he didn't know about the Lodge. He also didn't know what Nora meant by *not yet*. He wondered if she planned to wear the fancy boots for whatever event she was planning at the hotel. He'd tried to wrap his head around such a party, and concluded he wasn't standing in the way, but he wasn't attending it either.

"I…brought you a horse I thought you'd like," he said. "When you rode Daisy a few days ago, you probably noticed she was motivated by frequent stops for food, and she wasn't a great listener."

Nora face showed surprise. “I thought she just wasn’t listening to me. I thought I was the problem.”

Beck laughed. “You were some of the problem. But not all of it.”

“You could have told me,” she said. She sounded huffy but her smile gave her away.

Beck smiled, too. “It was more fun that way.”

“For you,” Nora said.

“You got me there.” Beck and Nora stood together between the two horses in the shadow of the Lodge, but he didn’t feel the tightness in his chest he usually got when he was anywhere near the place. Instead, he was thinking of how the jeans and boots suited her and how he planned to offer her a hoist into the saddle. It was the least he could do, help her up.

“What’s his name?” she asked.

“Her. This is Honey.”

“Is she named that because she’s sweet or because of her color?” Nora asked.

“Color. We didn’t know her personality when she was first born. Her parents are on the ranch, probably grandparents, too.”

“Do you have a lot of horses?”

“Dozens,” he said. “Of course, they’re way outnumbered by the cattle. Ready to saddle up?”

“Yes,” she said, but she looked at the horse whose saddle was eye level and didn’t budge.

"Let me help you."

"They showed me how to get on when I had a mini-lesson with Daisy in the stable. I mount from the left side and just sort of swing my leg over."

"Did you have a mounting block to step on?" he asked, already knowing the answer. There was a big difference between the controlled environment of the barn and being out on the range.

"I feel like you're calling me short," she said. "Which is unfair because compared to your impressive height, most people are short."

Beck smiled, strangely pleased that she appreciated how tall he was. It had been a sore spot when Bryan surpassed him by an inch, though no one had razzed him about his height in a long time. No one had teased him about anything in almost a year.

"Do you wear those high heels so you'll look taller?" he asked.

Nora glanced up and the breeze blew a chunk of hair across her face. She swatted it back and almost knocked her hat off. "I wear them because they are professional."

"Out here, this is professional attire," he said. He'd selected clean jeans and a fresh shirt, and he'd even shaved before riding over to the Lodge. He told himself it was because the meeting wasn't until eight, and he'd already been up for hours as usual. He'd had time. Judy had given him a once-over when he left his house as she was cleaning the kitchen, but she hadn't said anything.

Nora looked as if she wanted to make an argument about professional attire, but she didn't say anything.

"Do you have any suggestions on getting on this horse?" she asked.

He smiled. "Watch."

He moved to the left side of Hercules, put the reins in his left hand and a boot in the stirrup, and swung himself up in one smooth motion. Nora scrutinized him, lips parted.

"Will you do it again?" she asked. "Slowly."

He demonstrated, very aware of her watching his every move. "Your turn," he said.

She moved to the left side of her horse, took the reins with her left hand, and reached high to get her foot in the stirrup. She lost her balance twice before she got her foot in place and finally stood firmly on one leg. He wanted to help her with every muscle in his body, but he stood still, keeping a neutral expression. Were people inside the lobby watching? He didn't want them laughing at Nora.

"Now take a big hop with your right foot and when you get high enough, swing up into the saddle," he said.

Nora hopped and attempted a swing, but her

feet hit the ground with a thud and her hat fell into the dust. Beck picked it up and put it on his saddle.

"Let me try again," Nora said, her face flushed.

"Okay. But if you want, I could give you a boost," he offered.

"How?"

His hands itched to help her. "I could sort of, you know, lift you into the saddle. You'd be doing most of the work, of course."

"I can do this," Nora said.

She tried again and almost made it, and then again. Beck could tell she was working up a sweat, and their day hadn't even started yet.

"I've got a lot planned for today, and I know you'd get this with a few more tries, but I'd prefer you save some of your energy."

"What are we doing?" she asked, leaning on her horse and slowing down her breathing.

"We're going to ride over to the eastern part of the ranch and check the fences and the water. If I like what we see, I'll have my hands start to move the cattle there tomorrow."

"So, a scouting mission?" she asked.

"Yes, and it's easiest on horseback because of the terrain. Otherwise, I could have brought the truck."

"I don't mind this," Nora said. "I'll get it this time."

"I'm sure you will," he said.

She faced the horse and got ready, but then her shoulders relaxed as if she'd just made a decision. "Maybe you could give me that boost," she said. "I don't want to hold you up any longer."

Beck nodded. He respected her effort, but also the fact that she could ask for help. It was one of the hardest things to do, and he wasn't any good at it.

"I'll just put my hands on your waist and boost you that way. If that's okay," he said. It seemed like the safest way to touch Nora but also keep her at arm's length.

"Okay," she said.

He put his hands on her waist and steadied her while she got one foot in the stirrup, and then he asked, "Ready?"

"Ready," she confirmed.

She hopped and began the ascent, and he lifted her the rest of the way and seated her gently in the saddle. He held her just a moment longer to make sure she was steady, and he was sure his face was as flushed as hers. She was secure in her saddle, but he felt unsteady, even with both his cowboy boots on the ground.

NORA RODE ALONGSIDE BECK. They skirted some low hills and stayed on trails that were wide enough that Nora felt safe, though she recognized that they were climbing in altitude. She'd done enough traveling to know to trust local guides, but the local guides had always been on buses, trains or boats. One memorable time, she'd joined a bicycle tour of Amsterdam and cycled with a large pack, trying to see the sights while remaining upright. It had seemed challenging at the time, but there was no heat or dust and there were frequent snack and drink stops.

She should have brought a water bottle. "How much farther is it?" she asked, keeping her tone neutral so he wouldn't think she was complaining. And she wasn't. At least not totally. The scenery was beautiful, like a series of pictures that would make for fantastic social media. She considered getting some shots with her phone to use in advertising, but she didn't want to let go of the saddle horn to try to take pictures.

"We can take a break soon," Beck said. "If you can hang on for about ten more minutes."

"Of course I can," she said. Even though Honey was a larger horse than Daisy, she wasn't as wide, so Nora's knees weren't killing her as much as last week. Plus, the borrowed boots fit into the stirrups better than her sneakers, and her new hat cast a decent shadow over her face and neck.

"We'll follow the stream around this hill and see if there are any good pools for cattle. Once we move them to a new location, we have to keep a close eye so they don't eat all the grass and drain the water source."

"Do you have to move them a lot?"

"All the time," he said. "We… I…have twenty thousand acres, which sounds like a lot until you remember that we have thousands of cattle depending on it for their very lives. And my business depends on those cattle being fat and healthy."

"So you move cows around and make sure they eat and drink," Nora said.

Beck glanced at her and gave her a grin. "Is that what you pictured ranch work being like?"

She laughed. "Until quite recently, I never pictured ranch life at all."

"You weren't originally scheduled to come out here, were you? I remember seeing someone else's name on the contract my attorney showed me."

She'd wondered if he was ever going to bring that up. She didn't want to get into a whole explanation about how she'd clashed with the new management at the hotel on the Riviera and been pulled from that job. Beck might take it personally if he realized Remedy Mountain Lodge had been a bit of a punishment. At least that was how it had seemed to her.

"John ended up being reassigned elsewhere,"

she said. "It happens. There are fifteen or twenty people just like me working for the company, all of us going wherever we're needed."

"How did you feel about coming to Wyoming?" he asked.

There was no way she was going to insult Beck with the truth. That she'd written a scathing email to her boss, sat on it for a day, and then deleted it instead of sending it.

She needed a job. Especially since she had nowhere to go without one. No home, not even an apartment. Quitting was not an option. Failure was not an option.

"I felt the same way I do now. That there's a lot I don't know about Wyoming."

"Tell me what you want to know," Beck said.

The number one question—what happened to your brother and why can you hardly bring yourself to look at the Lodge—was not what she was going to ask today. It was clearly personal, and she didn't veer into personal territory with her clients. She wasn't usually even tempted.

"Describe for me a day in the life of a man who owns a giant ranch in Wyoming," she said, hoping he would talk for a long time and distract her from the heat and the blister forming on her hand from gripping the saddle horn like the newbie she was.

"Not possible," he said. "No day is like the one before it."

"I can relate," Nora said. "Hotel management sometimes means I'm talking to the pool company about expanding the hot tub and the next day I'm ordering new uniforms for the housekeepers. But still, I haven't helped manage a hotel property that's twenty thousand acres and I never needed a horse to get around."

"You were missing out," Beck commented with a smile.

"I did get to ride around in a golf cart at a huge resort in Mexico, and we had a water taxi at a place in the Caribbean. Does that count?"

They were silent a moment, the only sound the soft clop of the horses' hooves. There wasn't a person or building around for miles. Nora had seldom experienced such quiet and solitude. She breathed out and settled into the saddle, relaxing her grip on the pommel.

"There aren't any average days," Beck said. "And some are better than others. The fun days are the ones where we move cattle and they cooperate. There's nothing like the sight of hundreds of head of cattle moving ahead of you across land you own. Those days make up for the tough ones. Late nights during birthing season, long days when we vaccinate and brand the young ones."

"Do you do all those things yourself?" Nora asked.

He nodded, the motion exaggerated by his hat. "I do everything, but I have help doing it. There's no way one person can do some of the jobs, and I'm lucky to have a great team, even though I'm down an assistant manager right now."

"Did he…leave?"

"Mitch, Judy's son, is trying his hand at the rodeo over in Cody," Beck said. He paused for a beat. "He'll be back, hopefully in one piece."

"Is that a common thing, wanting to join the rodeo?"

"I guess," Beck said.

"You ever want to do that?"

"I never wanted to be anywhere but here. This place is enough. For me."

Those little words *for me* reminded Nora of what Allie had said about the brothers' differing ambitions.

They rode up to a small cabin between tall pines. The stream they'd been following murmured past, but it was almost a city block away from the cabin. If she were building a little house in the tough Wyoming terrain, she'd build it closer to the pretty, gurgling stream.

Beck stopped and dismounted. He looped the reins over a post in front of the cabin and then took the reins of Nora's horse and tied them to an adjacent post. “Need help?” he asked, holding his hands up.

“Getting down is easier than getting up,” Nora said. At least, she hoped so. She opened her own doors at hotels and of cars, not relying on her clients to do anything for her. She worked for them. Most of those clients were men who didn’t have any impact on her heart rate. They didn’t make her catch her breath.

But Beck did. Twice now, he’d held her waist as she mounted and dismounted a horse, and both times had imprinted the feeling of his strong, capable hands. A third time might be risky. Crossing any kind of a line between professional and personal was a risk she couldn’t take if she wanted to remain objective, do the job and get out of Wyoming.

“Okay,” Beck said. “If you’re sure.”

“I’m sure.”

Beck gave her one last look and then grabbed two buckets from the porch of the little cabin and headed for the stream. With his back turned and some distance between them, Nora decided to slide from the saddle. He wouldn’t be able to see it if she wasn’t graceful.

She stood in the stirrups, removed one foot and tried to swing it high over the saddle, but she hadn’t factored in how stiff her legs would be after an hour of riding. She twisted in midair and tried to jump clear of the saddle, but her other foot was caught. She reached out wildly with both hands, but there was nothing to grab.

Nora hit the ground flat on her back and all her breath whooshed out with an "oof" sound. To her horror, she couldn't breathe or move. She was completely frozen, the vast blue sky high above her. She struggled to get up, fearing the giant horse would step on her, but her body seemed to be in shock.

Beck's face came between her and the sky. "Nora. Say something."

She tried to draw breath and speak, but she couldn't. Her eyes were open, but all she could do was stare at Beck's handsome, panicked face. He ran his fingers over the sides of her head and palpated her skull gently. "Tell me what hurts," he said.

Mercifully, Nora could finally take a breath, although it hitched and prevented her from filling her lungs all the way. She struggled to sit up, but Beck put a hand on her sternum.

"No," he said. "Don't move. Not yet."

"I…think I'm okay."

He ran his fingers down both her arms and then squeezed her hands.

"Feel that?" he asked. His thumbs massaged her palms, and it was so soothing after the long ride. She closed her eyes, enjoying the feeling.

"Nora," he yelled.

She opened her eyes. "Just need a minute," she said.

Beck ran his hands down the outsides of her legs and then squeezed one of her feet.

"Feel that?"

"Just one," she said. Now she was starting to worry. Maybe she wasn't okay. Maybe she'd never walk away from this Wyoming job. The ranch life would kill her. She'd never see Barcelona. "Is that bad?" she asked in a whisper.

Beck's worried expression softened a bit. "You can only feel me squeezing one foot because you lost a boot when you fell off the horse."

"I did not fall off the horse," she said. She tried to sit up, and this time Beck supported her with an arm behind her shoulders. He cradled the back of her head with one hand, his touch strong but gentle.

"I didn't see it," he said, smiling. He was so close she could see the tiny wrinkles by his dark brown eyes. "But when I turned around, the horse was laughing and you were on the ground."

Her breath was back now, and she huffed at him. "Horses don't laugh." She paused and glanced up at Honey, who was watching them with a disinterested expression. "Do they?"

"I think Hercules laughs at me sometimes,"

Beck said. "But in all seriousness, does anything hurt?"

"No. I don't think so. I just couldn't breathe or move for a minute there."

"Got the wind knocked out of you," he said, nodding. "It happens."

It had never happened to Nora before, and now that the initial shock was over, she felt shaky. That feeling of falling when there was nothing she could do to stop it…had that been how her father felt in his last minutes as he fell off that apartment roof? Had he lain there for a moment, immobile, seeing only the blue Atlanta sky overhead? Her eyes stung and she realized with horror that she wanted to cry. She hadn't cried for her father since the days and months following his funeral. She'd cried for her mother and herself when they were turned out of the building, debt-ridden and homeless.

She squeezed her eyes shut, trying to hide her emotion. She felt Beck's arms slide under her shoulders and knees, and then she was off the hard ground, pressed against his hard chest instead. She heard his boots on the wooden porch floor and then felt the coolness on her face as he carried her into the cabin. A soft mattress underneath her surprised her, and she opened her eyes as Beck slid his arms out from under her and stood.

"I'm okay," she said. "You didn't need to do that."

"Why are you crying?" he asked, his tone so gentle that it almost made her wish he would take her in his arms and hold her so she could cry out that distant memory of her father.

"I was just...shocked, I think. Surprised, you know?" She sat up and swung her legs over the side of the bed. The room spun for just a minute, and then she forced it into focus.

Beck sat on the bed next to her. He put an arm around her shoulders. It felt good, comforting. Beck, with his quiet strength, felt like a safe harbor. A home. Nora didn't have a home and never sought out comfort or belonging with other people. She'd made her own world.

"Anything I can do?" he asked.

If he stayed there with his arm around her in that cozy cabin any longer, she was afraid she'd tell him everything. About the shock of her father's death, his depleted life insurance policy he'd been borrowing against, the sudden realization that she and her mother had no place to go.

"I bet Hercules and Honey would like some water," she said. "They're probably blaming me for creating a big drama when they're thirsty."

"I don't think horses experience blame or guilt," Beck said. "But you're right, they're likely to be thirsty. I'll be right back."

She expected him to be gone a few minutes, but he was back in a few seconds with her boot. He set it down next to her without a word and then left again.

While he was gone, Nora tugged on the boot, used her sleeve to dry her eyes, took deep calming breaths and focused on the interior of the cabin instead of the past. She'd assumed it was an abandoned cabin when they'd first ridden up to it, but it was clear that it was used occasionally. There was only one room, with a bed against one wall, a small table and two chairs, and a stove like one she'd seen pictures of in movies—black with a huge pipe that went out the roof.

She got up cautiously, but she felt steady. Nora suspected she'd have some bruises, but there seemed to be no actual damage done—except to her pride. There wasn't much to see in the cabin, and her self-tour was already over when she saw Beck through the door approaching the horses with a bucket in each hand. Nora glanced over a bookshelf with a glass front next to the door. Inside, protected from the elements, were dozens of books. She peered through the glass. Classics. A book of Shakespeare's plays, *The Iliad* and *The Odyssey*. There were four books by a famous naturalist and some Westerns. *The Count of Monte Cristo* sat next to a biography of Abraham Lincoln.

"We'll let the horses rest and drink up for a few minutes and then we'll head back," Beck said. Nora noticed that he stayed in the doorway and didn't come into the small cabin.

"But I thought you had fences and ponds to check on."

"Another day," he said.

"You don't have to baby me. I'm fine."

He didn't answer her, but he went out and got an insulated bag that had been tied to his saddle. He stood on the porch with the bag Nora hoped contained food and water for them, and she suspected he wanted her to come outside. Why didn't he want to be in the small cabin with her? Did he also feel a tug of attraction, or was the cabin personal to him, a space he didn't want to share with her?

She suspected those books were his, and she wondered if he used the cabin when he wanted to escape. She knew all about escaping.

"I hope there's lunch in that bag," she said.

He nodded.

"We could eat under the trees," she added. She pointed to a weathered bench. She started to step off the porch, but Beck reached for her hand.

"No railing," he said. "Watch your step."

She took his hand and navigated the two steps down, but then quickly released it as they walked to the bench.

"Tell me about this cabin," she said. "We're still on your land, right? What's it doing here?"

"My grandparents built it when they first came to Wyoming. They moved out here from Wisconsin because they'd heard about this magical town called Remedy Creek."

"The healing power," Nora said as she sat down and waited while Beck unzipped the bag. He handed her a sandwich and a bottle of water.

"Compliments of Judy, who always packs a good lunch for us when we know we might not be back to eat at the table," Beck said.

"Please thank her for me," Nora said. "Why were your grandparents so interested in the healing power of Remedy Creek? Were they ill?"

"My grandmother had rheumatoid arthritis since she was a little kid. They traveled out here, bought some land and built this cabin. They only visited the first few years, but something about the region made her feel better, so they eventually bought more and more land and then built the house I live in."

"Wow," Nora said. "Why do you think she felt better? Do you believe in the lore of Remedy Creek?"

Beck pointed toward the creek where he'd filled the horses' buckets. "I think you have to decide for yourself. It's clean enough to drink if you want to dip your bottle in it."

Nora wanted to ask him if he'd tried drinking the water or sitting quietly beside the creek, listening to its cheerful gurgle. Had Beck tried healing his own heart after his parents' deaths and his brother's? Was that why he kept this cabin?

Beck stretched his long legs out in front of him and crossed one booted foot over the other. Nora did the same as they picnicked under the trees, and she felt more peace than she had in a long time.

CHAPTER TWELVE

NORA SAT NEXT to Tristan, the teenage son of one of the housekeepers, who maintained the Lodge's website and kept the Wi-Fi alive for guests.

"Can you give me editing rights for the website and the passwords for our social media accounts?" Nora asked. She knew she should create an IT position and maybe hire a web developer, but right now, she needed to take control. Someone needed to.

"Yeah, sure," Tristan said. "No one ever asked before. Honestly, I'm just glad to be done with it. I'm starting eighth grade this year and I hear the homework's gonna be brutal."

Nora suppressed a sigh. If her bosses could see what she was up against here, they'd remember why she was so valuable to the company. How long would it take to erase her failure a few months ago and get her back in the top tier of consultants? The Barcelona job would be a reward, but she'd have to earn it.

She'd been in Remedy Creek ten days now. Of

course, she'd filled out the company reports documenting the action steps she had taken so far, but she'd also sugarcoated it a little bit, knowing Beck would have access to it. She hated to be too harsh about the truly astonishing lack of management at the Lodge, although she had been basically truthful. There was no discernable management, no plan, and it was a miracle the place was even open.

But the people who showed up daily really seemed to care, and the property itself was beautiful. The online reviews they had were positive—all seven of them.

"I'm sure you'll do great in the eighth grade," she said. "And thank you for keeping all the tech going since last fall."

"No problem. I can show you how to edit the web page," he said.

"Thanks."

Tristan waited while Nora got out a notebook so she could write down passwords and instructions. It would all go into a living document online that could be saved securely and passed on to the next manager.

Whoever that would be.

One of her first tasks in updating the website would be to add a Careers tab and begin posting the available jobs at the Lodge, along with job descriptions. Evaluations of current employees had been nonexistent, but that could wait. If she could hire an experienced general manager, that person would take on evaluations, and if she could get that position filled quickly, she wouldn't have to stay longer than the six planned weeks.

Nora glanced out the window where a view of the morning sun on the mountain reminded her of a postcard. Barcelona would have beautiful views, too, but it wouldn't come with horseback riding, a cozy cabin by a stream and a tough, handsome cowboy who had been so gentle with her when she fell off that horse.

"The site is dynamic. It's all connected, so if you update the website, the app shows it, too," Tristan said.

"Got it," Nora said. "Dynamic." She wrote that down and handed her notebook and pen to Tristan so he could write down the login information. Nora had some tech skills and had even navigated assisting with software in other countries and other languages. With a strong cup of tea in her room later that evening, she could figure it out enough to survive. She'd already added password protection to the file storage on Bryan's computer and contacted the company that wrote the software for the reservations system to purchase an extended service plan so the Lodge could get updates and begin using it again.

Little things. But they would add up quickly.

She could only imagine how far Bryan Duncan would have taken this gorgeous place if he had lived longer, but the more time she spent at the Lodge, the more she felt compelled to secure his legacy. For everyone. Including Beck. Maybe especially Beck, whether or not he wanted to be emotionally invested in it.

"Want me to help you make some changes while I'm here, just in case any questions come up?" Tristan asked.

"Thanks," she said, impressed by the offer and the boy's wisdom beyond his years. What thirteen-year-old thinks ahead like that? "Are you planning to go into IT one day?"

He shrugged. "Dunno. I don't want to leave Remedy Creek."

A week ago, her first question would have been "why not?" A bright young man like Tristan could find all kinds of opportunities out there in the world. But she was starting to see it had a certain appeal, and that appeal was probably magnified if a person grew up there.

Beck was devoted to his land, but it was clear he had split it with his brother. And then inherited it right back a few years later. No wonder the Lodge was a tender spot in his heart that he preferred not to touch.

"Let's add a Careers tab so people can find

available jobs at the Lodge and apply for them," Nora said.

"Do you want me to link it to a form so people can apply?" Tristan asked.

"Yes. Perfect."

By lunchtime, Nora had the start of an employment page, and she'd even linked it to social media with a catchy WE'RE HIRING graphic. She sent Tristan home with his mother so they could go back-to-school shopping, and then she did a walk-through of the entire building. The daily walk-through was a chance to see everything from a guest's perspective. Were there towels by the pool? Had the hallways been swept? Was the complimentary coffee in the lobby fresh?

Nora stepped onto the patio, straightened a cushion on one of the outdoor chairs, and then was surprised to see a familiar horse tied in front of the stable across the yard. Was it Hercules? She started over to the guest stable, picking her way across the dirt and stones in her work shoes and loose, flowing skirt. Despite Allie's suggestion, Nora was still dressing as if she could be working at any five-star city hotel. Hercules pricked up his ears when he saw her. Definitely Hercules—she could see the insulated lunch bag tied to the saddle.

"Hey," she said to the horse. "I know you. Where's your owner?"

"Right behind you."

Nora turned and saw Beck, jeans and boots as always, hat on head, and her breath caught. She'd thought he was a handsome cowboy the first time she saw him, but getting to know him over the past ten days had made it clear he was a lot more. She had no idea how he felt about her, but she certainly wouldn't be around to do anything about it anyway. A flirtation, no matter how innocent, could also cloud her judgment. She thought about that tepid report she'd completed where she downplayed the resort's downfalls. Brutal honesty was the only way to fix a broken hotel property, and she wasn't doing Beck any favors by not calling it what it was.

"I'm glad you're here," she said. "I have a great idea to bring in some local residents and entertain our guests at the same time."

"Is this the fancy dinner you were talking about?" he asked. His expression was cautious, skeptical.

"I changed my mind about the actual event. What do you think of 'An Evening by the Campfire'?" she asked, spreading her hands as if she was announcing something big.

"I've spent a lot of evenings by a campfire," Beck said.

"But this would be a special one. Here. We could use the patio, light some fires and have cowboy-themed food and drinks. We could even get a real live cowboy to show up and tell stories about ranch life and horses, things like that."

"Who's going to come to that?" he asked.

"Lots of people. We could do it on the full moon next week. Picture it—a crackling fire, the aroma of good food, the full moon overhead and Western lore."

"I don't know," Beck said. "How is that going to make guests want to make a reservation?"

"I'm starting locally, rebuilding interest, forging connections," Nora said. "It also gives us something to talk about on social media. We can post about the event leading up to it, and then we can roll out pictures for at least two or three days afterward. We ask guests to use a hashtag we create, and we start a little buzz."

"Is this the kind of thing you do at other resorts?"

"Yes," Nora said.

"All of them?"

"No. Each resort has different issues and problems. Some of them have plenty of guests, but they're still not making money. Some have issues with housekeeping, staff or food. A few have bad reputations I have to help them reverse."

"And the problem here?" Beck asked.

"It's too quiet," Nora said. "A lot of people

don't know about it, and the ones who do know about the Lodge can easily forget it."

She saw a shadow cross Beck's face, and she knew she'd trampled on a nerve. He'd tried to forget it, and she was there reminding him every day that the Lodge needed his attention.

"I'll make all the plans, but I need you to do one thing for me," she said.

"Okay," Beck said. He was already untying Hercules, and Nora could sense him tensing up for a fast getaway. They hadn't spoken in three days, not since their ride to the cabin.

"I need you to find me a handsome cowboy who will show up in full cowboy apparel, be charming and entertain our guests with stories."

He opened his mouth but then closed it again. He threw a leg over the saddle and mounted. "I'll see what I can do," he said. "But I can't make any promises."

"You have almost a week until the full moon," Nora said. "In the meantime, I'll be working through the checklist items on the document I sent you."

Beck nodded, glanced toward the horizon and then shifted his gaze back to Nora. "Thank you," he said, and then he trotted off.

BECK DROVE JUDY into Remedy Creek to do the weekly shopping. He didn't always go along.

Judy was a strong woman, easily capable of hauling groceries, but she had an appointment at the eye doctor and she didn't want to drive afterward. With her son Mitch over in Cody attempting to make inroads on the rodeo, Beck stepped up.

"I was at the Lodge for breakfast this morning," Judy said from the passenger seat. "Since you boys ate early at the ranch house, I went over and helped get something decent on the buffet for once."

"Isn't there always something decent on the buffet?"

"It's not what is there, it's what isn't. The muffins and coffee are fine if you're staying at a motel by the highway, but this is supposed to be a resort."

"Oh," Beck said. He knew the Lodge was falling short in plenty of ways. He'd read the report from Nora listing all the things that would make it a destination. Food service was near the top of the list and included the breakfast, lunch and dinner service in addition to room service and the cocktail bar that had been shuttered since last fall. "So, what was for breakfast today?"

Talking about food was better than talking about the Lodge or Nora. He'd had a hard enough time keeping her off his mind—and her request that he find a handsome cowboy to attend her evening event and entertain guests and anyone else she got to show up.

"Skillet breakfast like I make for the hands. Potatoes, eggs, onion, ham and cheese. The usual, but it's hearty. I don't know if it's fancy like Nora seems to think we need, but there wasn't any left to clean up."

"How many servings did you make?" he asked.

"Twenty. Enough for every guest in the hotel," Judy said.

Ouch. She wasn't wrong about the low occupancy, but it was still a jab to the gut. Judy was like an aunt to him, and he knew she was in his corner, but she was getting older. She couldn't continue to work at the ranch house and run over to the Lodge to help out. Nora had ideas about hiring a bunch of people, and maybe she was right.

"Is it okay if I drop you off at the clinic, do the shopping and pick you up when you're done?" he asked.

"I thought you might," Judy said. "I wrote out the list in order of the aisles in the store so you won't have to backtrack to find things. Unless they've moved something since last week, and I don't know why they would after forty years of keeping it the same."

Forty years. That was how long Judy had been working at the ranch. Since before he was born.

She'd seen him grow up—Bryan, too—and had been there when both his parents died. He suspected she'd been biting her tongue a lot in the past years. She'd only made one comment about the two brothers going in different directions on the same piece of land. It had been at the groundbreaking ceremony for the Lodge, and Beck had stomped around the house grumping about good grazing land being paved over. Judy had listened to him and then told him that she hadn't heard Bryan complaining about good resort land being used for a ranch.

He'd lain awake that night wondering if his brother would support his dream if their roles had been reversed.

"I talked to Nora after breakfast," Judy said. "I didn't have long, of course, because I had to get back so you could drive me into town."

She fell silent, and Beck suspected she was baiting him. He knew there was no winning.

"What did you and Nora talk about?" he asked.

"You," Judy said.

Beck sucked in a breath and concentrated on driving. It was another ten minutes to town, plenty of time for Judy to say what was on her mind.

"Mostly you," she corrected. "And the Lodge. We talked about how you're going to help her interview people for the jobs she has posted."

"I am?" Beck blurted out.

"Yes. She told me so. She said she was sure you'd want a hand in hiring people who will carry on the work at the resort after she goes on to her next hotel job. Who else would do it?" Judy asked.

Bryan had hired all the staff currently employed at the Lodge. Faithful people who hung on despite being left to drift most of the last ten months. They were all people Bryan and Beck knew or friends of friends. No strangers or acquaintances in the group.

"She also said she was waiting for your feedback on the ads she's putting online to bring hotel guests in from all over the country. I'm not sure she'll get people here in the winter, but she seems to think it can be done," Judy said.

"Winters are lonely around here, even at the wellness spa," Beck said.

"I tried to tell her, but she's got ideas and she's a big thinker."

Winter was months away. Was there enough time to get the Lodge back on its feet so it could stay afloat all winter? Beck's accountant, who shared an office with his attorney, had sent over some reports the day before that had a do-or-die theme. Get the place running profitably, or cut his losses by closing it or selling it, preferably selling it.

He hadn't told his accountant he was already planning to sell. Clearly it was the best choice, though.

"I might go visit my sister in Phoenix for a few weeks this winter," Judy said. "If you can figure out how to do without me."

"I'll try," Beck said.

"If you get the Lodge restaurant going, you can send the crew over there for their meals. They can eat in the kitchen. At least that's what Nora suggested when I told her my winter vacation plan."

"I thought you didn't have much time to talk to her."

"We had enough," Judy said. "Now I'm going to review some things on the grocery list with you while you drive. Pay attention. I put a star next to anything you can buy store brand, but I want name brands on the other things. And get the big sizes if they have them."

Beck listened to Judy read from her list. He tried to pay attention, but his mind kept drifting to the coming winter and how lonely it would be. He wondered where Nora would be when snow blanketed the Remedy Mountain Ranch and if she would miss Wyoming.

After he dropped Judy off at the clinic, Beck walked over to Riley's family's restaurant. He intended to just say a quick hello to Riley because his conscience had been chiding him lately.

"Hey, stranger," Riley said.

Beck gave her a hug and felt the familiar tug of guilt about the ring on his brother's dresser. She deserved to know, but would it just make it harder for her, especially now that so many months had passed? Maybe she'd processed her grief and learned to live with it. Why revive it? Knowing about the ring wouldn't bring Bryan back.

"How've you been?" he asked politely.

"Busy," she said. "A few tour groups have come through this week. Somehow our restaurant got on the map, and the buses have been stopping here before unloading again at Wellness Springs."

"That sounds like good news for business."

"Sure is. But I tried to spread the love around and tell some of the people about the winery and the bar, just in case they wanted a short walk or something different."

He wasn't surprised. Riley was generous in her thoughts and actions. Like his brother.

"How've you been?" Riley asked.

"Fine."

"You always say that. I think you'd say that if your pants were on fire or you were missing a limb," she said. She searched his face, and Beck was afraid she might read his thoughts. He was afraid of anyone reading his thoughts and being that close to his heart. He only kept himself together these days by balling everything up tight. No cracks.

"Like you, I'm busy. Moving cattle to late summer land. Got two horses sick and the vet coming out later. Down an assistant who's gone off to join the rodeo. Same old," Beck said.

Riley smiled wistfully. "Someday, we're actually going to talk to each other. Maybe we'll even go to the spa and indulge in some of that healing everyone's always talking about."

Beck held his breath, willing everything in him to stay still and strong. Even the lore of Remedy Creek couldn't help him get past losing his brother and carrying the full load of the ranch and the Lodge.

The bell rang over the door, and a group of diners came in. "But not today," Riley said, then turned to greet her new arrivals but looked back at him. "If you're meeting Nora, she's at a table in the back."

CHAPTER THIRTEEN

Nora believed in the power of business partnerships, which was why she'd just finished meeting the general manager of Wellness Springs for a late lunch. They had agreed to share promotions in social media and also collaborate on packages for visitors. Hal, the spa manager, acted like it was an innovative idea, but honestly, Nora couldn't believe it hadn't been done before. In a town that drew people in with the promise of healing, why wouldn't a local lodge with a luxury ranch vibe be the perfect partner for staying a few days in the region? The nearest nice hotel was thirty miles away.

She liked the cozy restaurant, so after the spa manager left, Nora remained at her table with her laptop, nibbling at a piece of cherry pie and reviewing applications for the jobs she'd posted online.

At least, she *intended* to dig in and review the applications. The problem was that there were only three, and the one she really needed to fill—

the general manager position—had exactly zero applications. She needed to cast the net wider and take advantage of the broad network of people she'd worked with for a decade. Surely someone with the right experience might want to move to Wyoming and work at the beautiful Lodge. Surely some people in the hospitality management business wanted to get away from cities and traffic and over-tourism and be able to breathe.

She considered it. That was how she would try to sell it anyway. Days out here were peaceful. The people were motivated but not in a hurry. They wanted to know you and care about you. And the scenery…well, it wasn't like the clear blue Caribbean or the Mediterranean. But when the sun laid shadows on the mountains—

"Hey," a soft voice said from way above her. Nora looked up from her bright laptop screen, but she already knew who it was without seeing him. She knew the voice, caught a hint of Beck's scent and felt his…well, presence. She noticed when he was nearby as if he had some magnetic pull.

She pulled her thoughts from the way she was going to describe Wyoming ranch life in the general manager's job posting, conjured up a friendly smile and nodded toward the chair recently vacated by Hal. There was still an empty coffee cup at his place.

"I don't want to interrupt," Beck said. "If you're here with someone."

"Not anymore," Nora said.

Beck took off his hat but stayed standing. He glanced at the empty coffee cup and then back at her.

Did he think she was on a date? If Beck only knew how few dates she'd actually been on in years. The only men she met were usually at the properties she served, and most of them were not available. The ones who were available were off-limits to her because she was working and because, as always, she was leaving when the work was done. "I had a meeting with Hal from Wellness Springs to talk about ways your business and his can work together. If I'd known you were going to be in town, I would have invited you to join us and give your stamp of approval on some of our ideas."

"Do I need to stamp my approval on anything?" he asked.

Nora pointed to the chair and pushed the coffee cup to the edge of the table. To her relief, Beck sat down and put his hat on the chair next to him. "Not necessarily," she said. "At least not to anything we talked about today. We're partnering up, but not financially, and there's no contract yet. Just what you might call a friendly agreement to cross-promote our businesses and offer packages at each place that come with discount codes for the other one. If someone stays at your hotel, we give them a coupon for fifteen percent off any treatment at the spa. Spa guests get a fifteen percent off coupon code to use on a stay at the Lodge."

"Okay," Beck said. "That sounds smart." He looked down. "Probably should have done that a long time ago."

"This is what you're paying me for," Nora said. "And plenty of other things."

Beck glanced up again and met her eyes. "Judy said you were waiting for me to approve the online ads you want to run."

"She works fast. We only talked about that this morning."

"I drove her into town for an appointment, and I'm waiting to drive her back."

"Is she okay?" Nora asked. She didn't get personally involved with anyone at the hotels she advised, but it was hard not to like the sweet older lady. And the other people she saw daily at the Lodge. She'd reasoned that she was starting to get to know them better than usual because there weren't many people working there. In cities and bustling tourist locations, there was always a sea of people.

"Eye appointment. She doesn't like to drive afterwards," Beck said.

"Can you take a minute to review the ads now?" Nora asked. She turned her laptop so he could see the screen.

"I'm supposed to do the grocery shopping while I wait."

The way he said it was funny, like a kid who'd received a to-do list from his mom and was afraid to disappoint. With both of his parents and his brother gone, was Judy like family to him? Who else did Beck really have? Her heart broke for a moment as she thought about his long days riding remote parts of his land, lonely evenings at the ranch house. No one to curl up with at night.

"I'll have you out of here in just a few minutes," Nora said. "I need someone who knows the area and ranch life to review the text on my ads so I don't say something stupid or unrealistic about cowboys and Wyoming."

Beck smiled. "I think I'm your man for that."

He certainly was.

Beck looked at her laptop screen. "'Come home to horses, mountains and sunsets right outside your door. Luxury accommodations with a Western vibe await you at Remedy Mountain Lodge under the wide Wyoming sky.'" Beck read the words in her ad in his deep, thoughtful voice. He read it all again, and it was mesmerizing. He looked up. "I like it, but it's a little long. We could use stronger imagery, maybe some cowboy vernacular."

Nora smiled. "Okay, cowboy. How would you put it?" She could have asked him why he hadn't bothered to advertise the Lodge before she came to Remedy Creek, but she didn't want to kill the tentative excitement he was showing about it.

He thought for a minute, tilting his head and flattening his lips so his square jaw was prominent in the shadowy restaurant booth.

"How about 'Wake up to a Wyoming sunrise from your luxury hotel room and then take a trail ride into the mountains surrounding Remedy Mountain Lodge,'" he said.

Nora made him repeat it while she typed the words into her document. "I like the 'Wake up to a Wyoming sunrise' part," she said.

"I always like the sunrise," Beck said. "Sunsets, too. I don't know which is more beautiful."

He smiled at her, and she felt a flopping sensation around her heart. She'd often had the same thoughts wherever she was in the world. Which was more beautiful? The day's beginning or end?

"I thought we were going for cowboy language," she said.

Beck smiled at her and then gestured at her half-empty dessert plate. "I would think better with pie."

Nora waved at Riley who was only two tables

away. "Will you bring a piece of pie for my friend here," she said with a grin.

Riley laughed and looked at Beck. "What kind?"

"Cherry if you have it."

"Coming right up."

"We could use the words *bunk down* somehow," Beck said.

Nora waited, surprised and strangely happy that Beck wanted to play along and be creative on something concerning the Lodge. Was the sore part of his heart healing a little so he could see the place more objectively?

"I love that. Keep going, you're on a roll," Nora said.

He toyed with a loose button on his shirtfront. A long thread hung from it.

"You should get someone to sew that on tight for you," Nora said.

"I'll do it later."

"You sew?" she asked.

He raised an eyebrow. "Out here, you have to do a lot of things for yourself if you want them to get done."

Riley put a piece of pie in front of Beck along with a napkin, fork and a glass of water. He nodded his thanks to Riley and then took a big bite of pie.

"See you tonight," Riley said to Nora before she walked away.

Beck glanced up, eyebrows raised. "Tonight?"

"Book club," Nora said. "A group of ladies have it once a month, and it was supposed to be at Sandy's house tonight, but her husband decided to renovate the downstairs bathroom without checking her calendar and her house is a mess. I offered to host at the Lodge."

"You're hosting a party?"

She nodded. "In my suite. Plenty of room for six women. We'll drink some wine and talk a lot, probably stay up too late. We won't bother anyone or be loud, though, so don't worry."

"You just…joined the local book club?"

She shrugged. "Why not? People are nice here. They make me feel at home."

Nora looked down at her pie plate and swirled her fork through the cherry filling. She'd jumped in and offered her suite when Riley told her about the club and the last-minute need to change the venue, but she'd thought it was just her hospitality instinct kicking in. Now that she thought about it, though, this was personal. Not related to her work at the Lodge. She wanted to get to know people in Remedy Creek, and it felt good being welcomed by them. She'd already considered how to arrange the couch and chairs in the living room of her suite and was planning to buy snacks and drinks before she left Remedy Creek.

She looked up and found Beck watching her. "Besides," she said cheerfully, "I've read the book already. It has a travel theme. Speaking of which, you're supposed to be helping me with the slogans."

He chewed, swallowed, and took a drink of water. He thought for a moment. "Wake up to a Wyoming sunrise, ride the trails and mountains, and bunk down in luxury at Remedy Mountain Lodge."

"Wow," Nora breathed out. "That's good. Say it again." She paused with her fingers on the keyboard.

Beck repeated the phrase, and she typed it into her ad copy.

"I don't think I could have said it better myself," she said. She remembered he'd said he'd majored in business. He was also hardworking and creative. Funny when he wanted to be. Tough when he needed to be. With all those attributes, she suspected he could have made the Lodge successful without her help, but she was glad he'd hired her company.

She hadn't breathed this deeply in a long time.

CHAPTER FOURTEEN

IT WASN'T HARD to avoid someone on 20,000 acres. Physically anyway. But avoiding thinking about Nora wasn't so easy. Almost a week had gone by since that piece of cherry pie downtown, and he couldn't stop smiling when he remembered that day. The way Nora had been impressed with his idea for the Lodge's advertisement… Well, no one had acted impressed by him or his ideas in a long time. Instead, he felt as if he'd been trudging along, doing his duty, and somehow disappointing people in the process anyway.

Wake up to a Wyoming sunrise, ride the trails and mountains, and bunk down in luxury at Remedy Mountain Lodge. It sounded like a vacation to him. He saw the sunrise every day, rode the trails and mountains, and bunked down utterly exhausted at night. But not in luxury. And there was no one to talk to after he brushed his teeth, no one to distract him from that empty bedroom down the hall from his.

Beck selected a plaid shirt from his closet with

silver snaps and decorations on the chest pockets. He pulled on clean but well-worn jeans. Put on a belt with a larger buckle than he typically wore. Got a bandanna from his dresser drawer and tied it around his neck, even though he wasn't riding the range and fending off dust today. He took a large, tan-colored cowboy hat from the top shelf of his closet.

He strode out to the living room where the late afternoon light filtered through the windows. He caught a glimpse of himself in the mirror over the fireplace. He looked like a man who was headed to Cody to try out for the rodeo.

Beck sat on the bench by the front door and pulled a pair of boots from under it. They were shiny black boots he only wore on special occasions, like a friend's wedding or a dance in town.

They hadn't been worn in a while. He swiped a thin layer of dust from the leather but then slid them back and got out his worn, brown boots with creases and wear marks. Boots that had spent a lot of time on his feet and in the stirrups.

It was only a ten-minute drive to the Lodge across ranch roads. Arriving on horseback might seem more authentic, but it would be dark soon. Beck put his hat on the seat of the truck and got behind the wheel. He was a modern cowboy, using a truck when convenient, or a side-by-side. He'd even been up in a helicopter with a rancher friend who had one, although Beck didn't fly or keep a helicopter himself.

If he had his preference, he'd always be on horseback, but 20,000 acres was a lot to cover.

His belly rumbled as he parked and walked around the Lodge to approach the back patio side. He smelled the campfire and the barbecue, heard voices of kids and adults and laughter. It felt as if there was life coming from a dead building, more life than he'd seen there in long time—not since the night of the grand opening.

Beck paused just around the corner from the patio and checked his watch. He'd promised Nora he'd produce an actual cowboy at six o'clock who would be willing to chat with hotel and local guests, join the campfire party, and tell tales of the surrounding region and cowboy life. He'd almost asked one of his ranch hands a dozen times, but it felt cowardly, sending someone else. He shouldn't care what anyone thought, shouldn't have to worry about bowing out of something he didn't want to do on his own land, but lying in his lonely bunk at night, he'd decided he needed to show up for the Lodge. Just this once.

He rounded the corner and strode toward the party just as he heard Nora announcing they were expecting a special guest. When she looked over and saw him, the surprise on her face was worth a dozen Wyoming sunsets. She stopped speaking but her mouth remained open. He heard a kid squeal, and another say something about a real cowboy. But all he saw was Nora Myers.

He stopped dead at the sight of her face lit by the campfire. His initial shock at the way she made him feel turned quickly into something else when she recovered from her surprise, smiled at him and beckoned him over.

He wasn't afraid of steep mountains, thunderstorms and wild animals, but he was afraid of the way Nora made him feel. He almost turned around and ran for the nearest horse.

But he'd told her he'd produce a cowboy for the party and there were a lot of people on the flagstone patio, all staring at him in anticipation. He tore his eyes from Nora and looked over the crowd. He knew about half of them by name or by sight, locals she'd lured in with the promise of a good time on an August night with food and a full moon. The rest of them had to be visitors, tourists, hotel guests—there for a vacation and to get a taste of ranch life.

He couldn't disappoint them. Or Nora.

"Here's our cowboy," Nora said. "Come on in and get some grub. There's a seat by the campfire for you."

He willed his legs to move and strode toward the small stage, which she'd created in the bed of a pickup truck stacked with bales of hay. Nora stood on the tailgate where the guests could see her. Did they all see how beautiful she was? He imagined her winning hearts all around the world and then breaking them when she left.

That wouldn't happen to him, of course. It would be a relief when she left because she'd stop asking tough questions and making him deal with the Lodge. He'd be free to sell it when she was done with it. And with him.

He smiled at the group, who had gone silent when he approached the tailgate of the truck someone had carefully backed onto the patio. He didn't step up into the truck. He didn't need to. With his height, the kids seated in a double ring about the campfire and the adults behind them could easily see him.

"Howdy," he said, remembering to play his part.

"Howdy," some of the kids shouted back.

"This is Cowboy Beck," Nora said. "It looks like you just came in from a hard day out on the range."

Beck wanted to laugh. He was sure she could tell he'd dressed up—no loose buttons on his shirt, no dust on his knees, a hat too expensive to get caught out in the rain with. He smiled and nodded to the group. What was he supposed to do now? He didn't know how to *act* like the person he actually was.

"Now that you're here, we can eat," Nora said. She pointed to long tables set up on the side of the patio with big warming trays on them. "But I'm going to take our special guest through the line first because I know he's hungry after roping calves, branding and herding cows."

She put a hand on his shoulder to step down from the tailgate, and he instinctively reached over and took her by the waist to swing her down. His face heated to oven temperature, and he was sure everyone in the audience saw it. Nora, too, looked flushed and surprised, but she quickly recovered and took his elbow to lead him to the food table.

He leaned close as they walked. "I was actually watching a webinar this afternoon on best practices with water management."

She glanced up and smiled. "Don't tell the kids."

A wisp of hair had escaped her braid and blew across her cheek, and he raised a hand to brush it back but quickly put his hand down when he saw Riley standing behind the food table. She wore an apron and a smile that was both questioning and knowing as she looked back and forth between him and Nora.

She was obviously getting the wrong impression—that there was something going on between him and Nora other than strictly the business of turning around the Lodge and making it profitable. If Riley thought that, probably lots of other people did, too.

And then it hit him. Riley was there. At a party at the Lodge. As far as he knew, it was the first time she'd been back since Bryan died. He'd dreaded this moment, feared the impact it would have on her. But she looked...okay. Even happy.

It was his first party, too, since the grand opening, and he'd just been smiling and joking with Nora. He felt sick. Was he dishonoring his brother's memory by playing the cheerful cowboy? If anyone should be there entertaining guests, it should be Bryan.

He wanted to run, but Nora handed him a plate and nudged him to go first down the food line where servers loaded him up with pulled pork, baked beans, corn on the cob and big, hearty rolls. He moved down the line with Nora behind him and the smell of the delicious food—he was certain Riley had something to do with that—mixed with the slight queasy feeling in his stomach.

"I have a seat reserved for you," Nora said as she followed him past the drinks set up at the end of the buffet line.

"Thank you."

"I'll sit with you and coach you on the plan for the evening," she added.

"Okay."

His plan for the evening was to keep his cowboy face on and not give anyone—locals or guests—any indication that he was struggling to keep himself together and not think too much about the last party he'd attended at the Lodge.

Nora had kept the hotel staff busy all day arranging chairs and tables on the patio and even bringing in extra tables and benches from the horse barn and other parts of the hotel property. She'd sold tickets online to locals and given hotel guests complimentary ones. The local newspaper was there for the Full Moon Campfire, and Nora had put Tristan in charge of taking pictures for social media in exchange for a free dinner.

The weather was perfect, and the perfect cowboy had shown up right on time. Beck had made a promise, and he'd come through. She just wished she had known he was going to play the role himself so she wasn't caught off guard by how handsome he looked. Or by the magnetic effect he'd had on her when he swung her down from the tailgate.

She didn't know how she was going to eat anything on her plate. She was supposed to be working, running a feel-good event to drum up local and regional interest in the Lodge that had been quiet for so long. Social media was going to be full of pictures and videos, and the event's success should be the first in a long line of them. As was what she did: promote, manage and strengthen hotel properties so they'd be fine without her when she left.

She balanced her plate carefully, even though her stomach dipped when she considered that she had less than one month left in Wyoming. The first weeks had flown by, but she had so much to accomplish still. On rare occasions, consultants like her remained longer than their original contract and rearranged future hotel jobs, but she'd have to offer a good reason for such a change, and she didn't want to hint at even a sliver of failure or delay.

Nora led Beck to the reserved table decorated with a lantern and some pine boughs. Allie met them there, wearing her usual Western attire from her front desk job. "Love the braid," she said, pointing at Nora's hair. "You fit right in."

"Thanks." Nora smiled and put her food on one side of the picnic table. She expected Beck to sit across from her, but he set his plate next to hers and then swung a leg over the bench seat and sat down.

"I didn't want my back to the crowd," he said when she hesitated before taking her seat beside him.

"Right," she said. "Good idea. I should keep

my eye on everything, too, even though we have some great hotel staff who agreed to work late tonight and help out."

His shirtsleeve tickled her elbow when he picked up his pulled pork sandwich. From the corner of her eye, she noticed he only took a small bite.

"I should give you the rundown on the evening so you can think about what you want to say," she said.

"I believe the job calls for telling cowboy tales and local lore. At least that's what you told me."

"Yes," she said. "Do you have any stories in mind? Do you want to talk through them?"

He shook his head. "You'll have to be surprised along with everyone else," he said.

Judy settled herself across from them. "I won't be surprised by anything this guy has to say about ranch life," she said. "I've known him since he was in diapers."

Beck coughed. "I hope you're not going to tell any of the party guests that I was once in diapers. It'll hurt my cowboy image."

"Your secret is safe with me," Judy said. She looked at Nora. "Nice party. Great to see some life around here."

"Thank you. I had a lot of help putting this together." She turned to Beck. "I kept detailed notes on everything from food to decor in case you want to make this an annual or even semi-annual thing, depending on how tonight goes."

Beck's expression went neutral for a moment, and Nora wondered if it was because he didn't think he could pull off such a party in the future…or he didn't want to. He'd slowly warmed up to the idea of helping her revive his hotel over the past few weeks, but she had serious doubts about her changes having staying power when she left—unless she worked very hard over the next month to build the staff and put systems in place. It would help if Beck showed some passion for the Lodge, but she couldn't make him fall in love with it.

Beck cleared his throat and moved some baked beans around on his plate. "So, give me my orders for the evening."

"Cowboy tales," Nora said. "I printed some from the internet just in case you need some inspiration."

Beck gave her a dubious look, so she dug a folded paper out of her shoulder bag and offered it to him. "I think these are technically tall tales, but I tried to find the ones that mentioned horses and cows. There are also some classic cowboy songs that came up when I googled campfire songs too."

Nora waited for him to take the papers, but he didn't.

"I'll be okay," he said. "I have plenty of stories."

"And songs," Judy said. "You heard the lady. Kids love singing songs by the fire—at least you and your brother did." Judy turned to Nora. "Beck has a nice singing voice. He'll never be on Broadway—"

"Which is personally devastating to me," Beck cut in, making Nora laugh.

"But he can carry a tune," Judy continued, ignoring his interruption.

"So," Beck said. "Everyone finishes eating, we gather around the fire, I tell some stories, we sing a few songs, and then we watch the moon come up."

"We'll roast marshmallows when it's almost dark," Nora said. She wasn't sure it was a Western thing, but she'd seen people doing it all over the country. "I have trays waiting in the kitchen with graham crackers and chocolate, too."

Beck laughed. "Very realistic snapshot of ranch life."

Nora smiled. "I don't think we'll get any complaints." She glanced at all the kids and adults sitting around in the beautiful, warm evening enjoying plates of food and talking. The Lodge rose behind them and reflected mountains in the tall glass windows. She could hardly remember a more perfect evening. "And who needs reality anyway?" she added. "People come to resorts to get away from it all."

Beck gave her a long look. "That sounds really nice," he said quietly, and Nora felt as if the words were meant only for her. What did Beck do when he wanted to get away? He'd told her about his vacations with his brother. Did he ever leave Wyoming now, go on vacation and take a break, clear his head?

Nora ate a few more bites but then surrendered her plate to the staff assigned to clear the tables. She walked among the guests who were finishing their food and eavesdropped on their chatter. One couple was discussing the view from their balcony and another talking about sitting in the hot tub after a long trail-riding lesson. Bookings were up for the following week, and when pictures from tonight's party hit social media, Nora hoped for another spike.

A few more locals had joined their staff in the past few days and were in training. She just wished there were applicants for the general manager position. With less than a month left, it would be tight timing, getting a person hired and trained.

When all the plates were carried off to the kitchen, two of the Lodge's maintenance men stoked the fire and helped guests move chairs into a circle. Nora helped position some chairs and found a cushion for Judy. Beck sat on the tailgate of the pickup truck, long legs dangling, a piece of shiny metal on his boots catching the firelight as he swung his feet. Nora watched from a few feet away, mesmerized by the rhythmic flash of light from his boots, like a little star winking or a distant planet sending a message through the dark night.

"I heard you wanted a story," Beck said to the crowd. "This one goes back to the days of my grandparents who owned this land." He proceeded to tell a long story about how his grandfather was befriended by a Native American man who lived on one of the mountains and taught him about the plants, trees and animals. "My grandpappy was a greenhorn, you see, someone who didn't know the first thing about ranching, horses and roping, but he'd been drawn to the area because Remedy Creek had a reputation for healing everything from a sore toe to a broken heart."

"Did he have a sore toe or a broken heart?" a kid asked.

"Neither that I know of, but everybody has something they need help with, and I've found that there's few problems I can't solve from the back of a horse. Especially when I have the smartest horse around. Good old Hercules is not only brave, but he's a good listener. One time, I was complaining about being really thirsty while we searched a canyon for a lost calf, and I swear Hercules understood me because he took me straight to a stream and stopped."

"Does he talk to you?" a little girl asked.

"Not in words, but a good cowboy and his horse don't need words, not when they spend all day together roping cows and riding alongside the herd."

"Is it boring?" a kid asked.

"No," Beck said. "And on days when the sun gets hot and you want to forget you're sitting on a big hot animal miles from home, there's one thing that always does the trick."

Nora listened, spellbound and surprised by Beck's storytelling and charisma. She wished he'd applied some of his creativity to making the Lodge successful. Certainly his brother had expended a lot of artistic effort and imagination. For the first time, she wondered if Beck felt he didn't have the right to make changes at the Lodge. She was still trying to sort through his complicated relation with the place and couldn't help feeling that she was missing something.

"You want to sing?" Beck asked the crowd. "I didn't bring my trusty guitar, so you're going to have to help. Okay, little cowpokes?"

He told them what their parts would be and helped them practice the refrain, and then Beck sang a story about a cowboy wandering the plains to find his lost love, and the kids joined in on the refrain. Nora stood a few feet away, just outside the firelight, and watched Beck swing his feet in time to the music while he sang campfire songs. The moon rose just over a low hill, and Nora knew that wherever she went in the world, she would never forget this night.

CHAPTER FIFTEEN

FAKE IT TILL you make it. Beck had a whole herd of experience with that. He'd never shown up to a campfire and played cowboy, telling stories and singing songs before, even though he'd spent plenty of time around a campfire. He listened to the kids singing the refrain, finishing the song, and suddenly his throat constricted and his chest felt so tight he wasn't sure he could breathe.

A memory of singing that song with his brother hit him like a charging horse. He could almost feel his brother's presence there with him, as he'd always been. It should have been Bryan here singing campfire songs at the perfect hotel he'd built. So many things should have been different. He swallowed and tried to push those thoughts away because dozens of people were staring at him. He almost succeeded, but then a vivid memory of last October's grand opening punched him from the other side. Maybe it was the lights emanating from the Lodge or the party itself, but suddenly Beck knew he had to get away.

He launched off the bed of the truck, his boots making a clomp as they hit the ground.

"This cowboy has to be up with the dawn, so I better bunk down for the night." He tipped his hat. "Happy trails."

Beck strode straight off the patio as if he was being chased and skirted the back corner of the Lodge. He tried to control his breathing as he practically ran for his truck. He thought he heard someone behind him, but he didn't slow down to find out. Instead, he got in his truck and slammed the door just seconds before a huge sob rose up from his chest and drowned him. He put his forehead on the steering wheel and fought a losing battle with his emotions. Everything he'd buried deep for ten months clawed its way aboveground.

He wiped his face with his shirtsleeve, but the tears would not stop. He could hardly catch his breath because his body was forcing him to ride the wave of deep, shuddering sobs. His only consolation was that there was no one around to see him like this.

He heard the passenger door open, and the interior light flicked on. His forehead was still pressed against the steering wheel, but he tilted his head enough to see Nora.

"Don't," he muttered.

Nora got in and closed the door, and Beck was thankful that the interior light went out but horrified when he felt her arms slide around him and hold him close. He hadn't cried in front of anyone in years. Hadn't cried with anyone when his brother died. That hadn't been his role. His job had been to be stoic and keep the ranch going. He counted his breaths, trying to restore order to his ragged breathing.

Nora wasn't saying anything. She'd scooted close to him on the bench seat of the truck and simply wrapped her arms around him. He couldn't believe she wasn't asking questions. He was trapped there in the confines of the truck, squeezed tight in her arms, but for once he didn't feel like running away. Didn't have the urge to jump on a horse and ride until the pain was far enough behind him.

The silence had been his enemy for ten long months, but right now, with Nora—a person who'd been a total stranger a few weeks ago—the silence didn't scare him. The crushing tightness in his chest relaxed enough that he could take an entire breath, and then another. He lifted his head from the steering wheel but didn't turn to look at Nora. He sat back and Nora withdrew her arms, but she slid her hand into his. Their shoulders touched and her hand felt as if it fit in his.

They sat in silence and watched the moon rise high over the mountain. Beck unrolled his window and the night sounds of crickets and birds filtered into the cab. They heard laughter from the party on the other side of the hotel. How much time had gone by? Ten minutes? Thirty? Beck didn't know. He felt as if he'd relived the past ten months and somehow gotten ahead of it for the first time.

Maybe it was coming back to the Lodge and facing a party, facing his memories of his brother. Maybe it was Nora's reassuring touch. He wondered how she'd known he was about to break when he took leave of the party guests. Had it shown on his face despite his practiced stoic look?

He turned to her and put a gentle hand on her cheek. There was more to Nora Myers than just a woman who swept in and fixed failing hotels, and he found himself wanting to know her better. She mirrored him, resting her hand on his cheek, too. She moved closer and tilted her mouth toward his. He waited for a second, every part of him wanting more of her touch, but then she made the decision for him and touched her lips to his in a soft, short kiss.

"Better?" she asked.

"I think so."

"Good."

"How did you know?" he asked, curious why she'd followed him.

She gave him a small smile. "I've been there."

"Do you want to talk about it?" he asked.

She looked at him for a moment, but then said, "Not tonight. You should get some rest, and I should get back to the party."

He caught her hand as she started to slide toward the passenger door.

"Thank you."

She squeezed his hand and gave him a look no one had given him in a long time. It felt like love.

NORA WALKED SLOWLY back to the party, full of thoughts about Beck, his brother, and her own father's tragic death. She never talked about it with anyone when she was on the road. The jobs were always about the hotels, not her. The few times a year when she visited her mother and her brothers, they didn't talk about it either. The fall from the apartment roof and the bad things that happened afterward were a dozen years in the past, but she could still remember the searing pain of loss.

For Beck, it was not even a year, and his brother's memory was embodied by the Lodge, like a monument to Bryan's dreams—but not Beck's. Did that make it harder for Beck, dividing the land they'd inherited into separate dreams?

She hadn't asked for details, didn't need him to tell her everything. Of all the men she'd met on the road with her job, there was seldom one who got past her professional veneer and made her want to care about him. Made her feel as if he could possibly care about her.

Do you want to talk about it?

His question had surprised her, but it also showed her the depth of his compassion and empathy. He was more than a tough cowboy taking care of thousands of acres and dozens of employees.

"I'm not going to ask you what happened," Judy said when Nora returned to the party where the number of guests had dwindled. It was getting late. Kids were off to bed, adults were driving back to town or visiting the hotel bar.

The fire had wound down to hot coals.

"I appreciate that," Nora said to Judy. She approached the check-in table where there had also been a stack of job applications. The pile was noticeably smaller.

"I forced some of those applications on people as they were leaving," Judy said. "I knew it was one of your goals, and if someone else fills in at breakfast instead of me, I'd be perfectly happy."

"I hope someone wants to be the general manager," Nora said. "That's the best-paying job, but it needs someone with experience and has the most responsibility, of course. I even put free housing in the ad I posted, but there have been no takers."

"The right person will come along."

Nora glanced up at the Lodge where lights shone from inside. "It has to be someone who really cares about this place. The Lodge deserves that." She didn't add that Bryan Duncan's memory deserved that. Judy had seen both Bryan and Beck grow up. She already knew that.

Judy started clearing away the papers on the registration table, and Nora helped her. They worked in silence for a moment as guests continued to call it a night and trail past them into the hotel.

"Was Bryan like his brother?" Nora asked. She didn't know why she was asking. It was none of her business, and all in the past.

Judy shuffled some papers into a pile and then finally looked up. "Very much. They looked alike, even though Beck liked to claim he was taller. Both handsome, sweet boys. Their only difference was that Bryan was more a dreamer. Always thinking of a new game to play or wanting to try something new for dinner. One time, he decided the horses might be tired of their usual stalls, so he rearranged all the nameplates and moved them."

"What happened?" Nora asked, imagining chaos in the barn at the ranch.

Judy shrugged. "Basically nothing. I think he was disappointed, like he thought he was going to rock their world by giving them different accommodations."

"Beck told me about their vacations and how visiting hotels in Europe and elsewhere had inspired Bryan."

"Did he?" Judy asked. "I'm surprised he talked about his brother. He's been closed up tight since the accident."

Nora knew she could ask Judy exactly what had happened that night, but she wanted to hear it from Beck. She sensed that he needed to tell it to someone. She wasn't a permanent fixture there; she'd be gone in a month. Maybe that made her a safe person for him to talk to.

That was probably why she'd kissed him.

CHAPTER SIXTEEN

Judy poured coffee for Beck as he sat at the breakfast table. The ranch hands had already left, and he was on his laptop reviewing documents. He glanced up, knowing Judy probably had something to say.

"I heard from Mitch early this morning," she said. She put the pot down and fidgeted with her hands.

"Everything okay?"

Beck had heard from Judy's son several times a week since he'd left almost a month ago. With his aptitude for riding and roping, Beck's former assistant manager had found himself a sweet spot in one of the traveling rodeo shows. Beck was happy for him, but also wished he'd just come home to Remedy Creek. Beck hadn't replaced him on the ranch, and he was starting to notice all the things that had been let go in his absence. Still, he wasn't going to stand in the way of anyone's dream.

He'd attempted to do that once with Bryan,

and a lifetime wouldn't be enough time to get over the regret.

"His show is on the road for the next three months, doing weeklong shows at various places in the west," Judy said.

"He texted me a few days ago and said as much," Beck said. He looked back down at his screen and saved the spreadsheet he was reviewing in case he accidentally exited and lost his recent data. He didn't have time for mistakes and do-overs.

"Unfortunately, one of their scheduled locations got on the wrong side of a wildfire, and it's not available, so they need someplace to go in two weeks. They're looking for a venue with plenty of space, decent roads and preferably a nearby hotel and restaurant," Judy said. "And I thought..."

Beck glanced back up at her. "Go on."

"Well, Nora is looking for ways to promote the Lodge, and this would bring in a whole week's worth of guests, plus the crew. It would be great for business."

"Have you mentioned this to Nora?"

"Just found out this morning," Judy said. "Thought I'd run it past you first."

"Why?" Beck asked. He tried to look disinterested because he really wanted people going to someone else with questions about the Lodge—

Nora or whoever she managed to hire as a manager before she left. However, he did like the sound of bringing in business and drumming up interest in the hotel. Maybe a buyer would be among the rodeo guests. As soon as the hotel got on its feet, he planned to get serious about selling the building and leasing the land it occupied. He just hadn't been able to bring himself to tell anyone yet.

Judy blew out an exasperated sigh. "Because it's your hotel, whether you want it or not, and it's your ranchland in the valley near the hotel where they'll set up grandstands and park their trailers and host the shows. I thought you'd care."

"I do care," he said on a long exhale. "If you want, I'll talk to Nora about it. Does Mitch have a contact person we should talk to at the rodeo?"

Judy smiled. "Mitch said he already told the managers all about the Lodge and they're waiting for him to make the connection. You can go through him after you talk to Nora. But the sooner the better. They're anxious to fill the hole in their schedule."

Beck closed his laptop. He hadn't talked to Nora in two days, not since that night in his truck when she'd seen him at his worst and somehow made him feel better. He'd gone about his daily business, but had felt a little lighter as if his boots had some spring to them and his hat didn't sit quite so heavy on his head.

"You can finish your coffee first if you want," Judy said. "Or I can make fresh for you when you come back."

Beck stood up, resigned to missing out on the tiny luxury of lingering over coffee. Most days, that was the only luxury he got.

"I'll head over there now."

Judy picked up his cup before he could change his mind, and Beck made a quick trip to his bathroom at the other end of the house. He brushed his teeth, even though he'd already done it when he got up, and changed his shirt instead of wearing the one with the loose button he'd told Nora he'd fix—but hadn't.

He drove straight to the Lodge but didn't feel the sense of doom he used to feel as he drove up to the place. Maybe he was just more accustomed to it because he'd been there so often lately, more times in the past few weeks than in the ten months that preceded them.

When he strode through the front doors, he saw a few people milling around in the lobby drinking coffee and chatting. A family with little kids walked past dragging their luggage. There was chatter down one of the hallways that used to be ghostly silent. At the front desk, Allie was a familiar sight, but he also found another woman he'd seen around town but didn't know. She wore a name tag and appeared to be helping a guest with a reservation.

"Good morning," he said to Allie. "Is Nora around?"

"Yes, but she's holding interviews in her office. You can go on back, though."

Beck hesitated. The private offices behind the front desk still had Bryan's name on the door. Beck hadn't been back there in a very long time.

"I can wait here," he said.

"Can I help you with something or do you need Nora?" Allie asked.

"I…need Nora," he said, the words sounding strange to him. Of course, he was only talking about the present situation. He needed her to turn around his hotel and unburden him. But he had also needed her arms around him a few nights ago and needed someone who seemed to understand even without saying anything. He never let himself need people, and it scared him. People he loved and needed could be gone at any moment. He'd been through that too many times. At least with Nora, he knew it was coming. It was part of the contract. But he would still be smart to keep his emotions out of his dealings with her.

"I'll text her to let her know I'm here when she's free," he said. He sat in one of the deep leather chairs in the lobby and just breathed for a moment. The Western paintings on the walls were a nice combination of realism but just enough impressionism to soften the realities of the tough terrain. He and Bryan had toured a few art museums in Europe, and Beck knew his brother had chosen the lobby art himself.

He'd chosen everything. Except leaving the hotel orphaned in the hands of a big brother who couldn't bring himself to care. Looking around the lobby now, though, it didn't seem like an orphaned building. There was a lot of life. Two women laughed together as they got coffee from the cart. A man pointed out the windows, gesturing at something to the little boy he held by the hand. An older woman rummaged through her purse and handed an eyeglass wipe to her husband who sat next to her on one of the sofas. The man proceeded to clean his glasses while his wife rested her hand on his knee.

People were comfortable. Happy. His brother had created this space.

Beck swallowed. If he sold it, would the new owner change the furniture? Put up blinds on the tall windows to save energy? Maybe swap out the Western art for something modern?

Quick movement caught his eye and he looked up to see Nora. She wore dark pants and a white blouse that were professional, but her long blond hair was braided as it had been two nights ago.

It was a minor change, but it made her seem as if she was being slowly absorbed into the life of the Lodge. She seemed to belong here more than he did.

"Would you like to hear good news?" she asked.

Beck smiled as she took the armchair next to him. "Does anyone say no to that?"

She laughed. "No. That's why it's a great conversation opener. It's nice never getting turned down."

Beck wondered if anyone ever turned down conversation with Nora. She was easy to talk to, understanding, and she had the prettiest smile. Whoever she talked to had to feel as if they were the only person in the room.

"Let's hear it."

"We're starting to fill out the staff with some good applicants, including a few who'd initially been interested in working here but then…well, their plans changed. But now they're back."

He didn't need her to tell him what had changed a lot of plans last fall.

"That's great news. Will you have time to train them all?"

"Working on it. I'm no stranger to putting together a quick staffing turnaround. It's often one of the challenges at the projects I manage. Of course, it would be a lot easier if there were a general manager here." She grimaced. "We have not had one single application for that job."

"Why not?"

A young couple sat on the couch across from them and Nora flicked her glance from the couple to Beck. "Would you like to go for a walk outside? It's a beautiful day and it might clear my head."

NORA POPPED INTO her office to change her shoes and then joined Beck under the front portico. He hadn't wanted to follow her to her office, and she knew it was the nameplate on the door that was stopping him. She'd actually considered removing that nameplate—she'd have to when she hired a new manager. The office was clearly intended by its size and location to be the general manager's office, and no one wanted to start a job with someone else's name on the door—especially if that someone was the deceased former owner, much beloved by the staff and missed.

No, the new general manager deserved a fighting chance to take over and make the place his or her own, and she doubted there would be any interference from the current owner. It was both a blessing and curse that Beck was hands-off with the Lodge. They walked toward the beginning of the path that led all around the resort and meandered around a stream and across a bridge, giving guests a two-mile round trip if they wanted it. As their feet crunched the soft ground underneath, she wondered if Beck would ever get to a place where he could see the Lodge as his instead of his brother's.

"So why doesn't anyone want the general manager job?" Beck asked.

"I wouldn't say no one wants it, it's just that no one has applied. Which means there likely isn't a local person who feels qualified, or my online ads have not reached far enough." She gave him a reassuring smile. "The right person will come along."

She hoped that was true. She always hoped her hotel assignments thrived when she left, and she did her best to leave them with talented, trained staff and a solid plan. But Remedy Mountain Lodge felt personal to her. Maybe it was using Bryan's office that made her feel as if she owed something to his memory. She glanced over at Beck's profile. He didn't have a hat on and his dark hair wasn't matted down in the places it usually was when he wore a hat. He hadn't been out on the range yet today. She was his first stop. He was also clean-shaven and wore a nice blue shirt that complemented his deep tan.

"There's something I need to ask you about," he said, meeting her glance.

For a moment, Nora believed they were going

to talk about the kiss. She'd certainly thought about it plenty.

Beck gestured to a bench tucked between two small pines alongside the trail, and they sat. It reminded her of their picnic by his grandfather's cabin after she'd ungracefully dismounted from that horse.

"My former assistant manager, Mitch—Judy's son—just started in with a rodeo group over in Cody, and his group does shows on the road. A week here, a week there, that sort of thing. Draws a big crowd. They need a place to be in two weeks because one of their booked venues was damaged by a wildfire."

"Do they want to come here?" Nora asked, excitement bubbling up her chest.

"If you can make that happen."

"How many rooms and what exactly would the Lodge be expected to provide?" she asked. She was already thinking of the incredible promotional benefits of such a group coming there. Social media, perhaps a future contract for another rodeo show. This was a gift.

"I don't know the details, but I'd assume it's a lot. They have dozens of crew members and performers, and these things sell out. I've been to a few myself," Beck said.

"And the rodeo show itself would be set up on our grounds?"

He nodded and pointed toward a large empty space in the valley adjacent to the hotel. "Probably right about there. Corrals, an arena, grandstands, tents, some vendors. It's a big deal."

"And this is okay with you?" Nora asked.

She expected him to deflect and say it was her choice since she was the manager there.

"I think it will be good for us," he said.

Nora paused, stuck on the word *us*. Was Beck finally seeing himself as a person with a vested interest in the Lodge? Little by little, he'd shown less trepidation about being involved. She was already using the tagline he'd created over that piece of pie. Was it desperation, was it the fact that she was doing a great job showing him the potential, or was he finally getting some healing—perhaps the work of Remedy Creek itself?

She hoped it was partly her, even though she knew she shouldn't. She'd be leaving and she always left hotel properties self-sufficient, able to go on without her. She'd only been back to the same hotel property once, and the little place on the Riviera had changed so much that she wasn't able to get her footing. Her personal attachment to the hotel had clouded her judgment, and she wasn't able to help them. She'd failed. Her company had pulled her from the job early.

She couldn't make the same mistake again.

"I think it will be very good for you," she said.

She didn't tell him all the reasons, but he met her eyes and took a breath as if he was thinking about saying something. He reached over and squeezed her hand.

"Thank you," he said. "I wouldn't even attempt something like this if you weren't here."

"That's my job," she said, even though she wanted to add that he would be fine without her. She would make sure of that.

Beck looked down. "I have a lot of people working for me, and the very best ones treat their work as if it's personal, more than a job. You're like that."

Nora swallowed, overcome by the profound but simple compliment. She had to get her mind on business, or she'd find herself kissing him again in daylight and plain sight. And that would be a huge mistake.

"If you have the contact information for the rodeo's manager, I'll call him this morning and start setting this up. My wheels are already spinning about filling rooms, stepping up our food orders, putting our maintenance staff in contact with their setup people to make sure we have the facilities and support they need. And parking, traffic. I'll get on that."

Beck reached over and put a hand over hers. "Slow down a minute. You don't have to do this if you don't want to. It's above and beyond what I contracted your services for."

Nora didn't withdraw her hand. It felt so nice under Beck's large, warm fingers. "You're paying my company to turn around this hotel, and I will do whatever it takes to make that happen for you."

His expression shadowed for a moment. Didn't he want her to do whatever it took for him to be successful? She'd thought he was coming around and feeling more ownership in the Lodge.

"I appreciate that," he said. "I've already gotten more than I deserved because I was lucky enough to have you as our consultant and not some guy named John as I'd originally expected."

"John is in Boston where he's probably hating traffic right now. Poor guy."

"Is it ever lonely, doing what you do?" Beck asked. "Traveling all the time, meeting new people and then leaving them behind?"

Nora held perfectly still. Somehow, he'd asked the question that had been keeping her awake lately. She'd never worried about getting too attached to people or places because moving on had been nonnegotiable, part of who she was. Wyoming was getting under her skin, though, and she wasn't sure if it was the wide blue sky, the scenery, the people, or one person in particular.

She would be sad to say goodbye to Beck. Not because he was the best client she'd ever had—there had been far more cooperative ones—but because she sensed that deep down he struggled in the same way she had. They had something in common.

"I'm sorry if that was too personal a question."

Nora withdrew her hand and leaned back on the bench. "I kissed you in your pickup truck. A question is hardly more personal than that."

"I'm sorry about that, too," he said.

Did he regret it or was he afraid he'd crossed a line professionally?

"I started it," Nora said. "I should be apologizing to you."

Beck smiled. "Okay, go ahead. I'll tell you in advance that I plan to accept your apology, and really, I'm not sorry at all. That was a nice kiss."

Nora laughed. "It was. But not to be repeated."

Beck hesitated for a full five seconds, then he slowly nodded and stood. "I'll walk you back. I know I just piled a lot more work on your shoulders."

CHAPTER SEVENTEEN

A FEW DAYS LATER, Nora had just closed her office door when her phone buzzed with a message. Seeing Beck's name on the screen gave her a little surge of adrenaline. He had that effect on her.

I promised to teach you more about ranch life, but I haven't made good on it. Are you free this evening?

Of course she remembered his promise to teach her some things she'd called ranchy. However, she'd gotten so busy hiring staff, building the resort's social media presence, and now planning for an upcoming rodeo on the property, she hadn't thought about that promise.

It had been a long day of training new staff, and she was ready to get takeout from the hotel restaurant and sit on her room's private balcony. She'd been doing that a lot, breathing in the fresh air and enjoying the peace of the Wyoming evenings. No sounds of cars, trains, traffic, sirens.

Just some birds and insects and the occasional call of an animal she couldn't quite identify.

Dinner is included.

She was surprised by the follow-up text. Was Beck hovering over his phone waiting for her answer? It was risky spending private time with him. She could feel herself slipping into liking him as a person, which would interfere with her professional judgment—she already didn't want to hurt his feelings when she pointed out issues with the Lodge. These jobs were never personal, which made it easier to be frank with hotel owners and also easier to leave. Tying her heart to a property as she had her own family's apartment building meant risking heartbreak when it was all taken away.

There's a very ranchy casserole involved.

Fine. Nora had to answer Beck or he was just going to keep texting.

Time? she texted back.

Any.

Thirty minutes. She reasoned that a quick change of clothing was all she needed.

Safe drive, he responded.

Well, she thought. They weren't exactly sending gushing messages to each other, so maybe there wasn't much risk of getting overly personal. She changed into jeans and the soft brown riding boots she'd borrowed from the hotel's loaner closet. Before she left in a few weeks, she'd make sure to clean them and return them to circulation, but while she was there, she liked seeing those boots in her suite's closet. She tamed her hair into a quick braid and left via a side entrance where the hotel's SUV usually sat idle.

Before she got in, she opened the internal app she'd instituted for the hotel to make sure no one else needed the SUV tonight. Satisfied that there were no airport arrivals to pick up, she put in the door code and found the ignition keys inside. If the hotel got busier, the miles would start adding up on the SUV, and that would be a good problem to have. They might even need a full-time driver to do the airport runs an hour away.

Dark clouds far in the distance didn't worry her. The weather forecast predicted rain after ten o'clock. She highly doubted she'd be busy learning ranchy things that late, and a few raindrops didn't bother her. She'd been through monsoon season in Singapore, rainy months in Seattle, and afternoon summer downpours in Orlando. As dry as it seemed in Wyoming most of the time, she doubted rain would even form puddles because it would be absorbed so fast.

Her stomach rumbled on the ten-minute drive to Beck's ranch house, and she hoped dinner would be first on the agenda. As she pulled up to the porch, though, Beck was outside holding the halters of two horses.

Okay, so horses first.

"Hello, Hercules," Nora said. "We meet again."

"Head on in and make yourself comfortable," he called. "I just turned off the oven so the casserole will stay hot while I rub these horses down and feed them. Then I'll be right in."

"I'll come with you," Nora said. "It's a learning opportunity."

Beck smiled, and Nora had the impression he'd been hoping she'd say that. She walked beside him as he led the two horses to the huge barn across a clearing from the house. Nora had been inside the riding stable at the Lodge, which was very guest-centered with a sitting and refreshment area, a changing room and restrooms. This, she realized as they walked inside and her eyes adjusted to the lower light after the sunshine outside, was a working barn. There were over a dozen horses, and although the space was clean and orderly, it was utilitarian. Not built for impressing anyone.

She was impressed anyway by the lofty ceiling, the hay stacked high in the loft space in the rafters, and saddles and bridles all lined up neatly. She inhaled the distinct smell of animals, but also hay. It was homey and comforting.

"We should get candles with this aroma to burn in the hotel lobby so people will get an authentic Western experience," she said.

Beck laughed. "I thought you wanted people to enjoy their visit and come back again."

"One thing I've learned in ten years of hotel management is that everyone has different tastes," Nora said.

Beck put one horse in a stall and began rubbing the other with a brush. "I hope your tastes run toward a ham and potato casserole I found in the freezer."

"That sounds delicious," Nora said. "Did Judy make it?"

He nodded. "She always makes extra and freezes batches in case of food emergency. She believes none of us would survive without her cooking."

Nora laughed. "Would you?"

Beck glanced over with a smile. "Probably not."

"Speaking of food, I know I mentioned asking Riley to consider a role at the Lodge, and I have something in mind."

Beck made long sweeping strokes with the

brush on the horse's side. "This removes dust and sweat and keeps the horse's coat healthy, and it also feels good to them, like a massage helps athletes recover after exertion."

"Makes sense," Nora said.

"Want to try it?" He held out the currycomb.

"Yes, but I want to watch a little longer while I tell you my food plans for the Lodge."

Beck exhaled and lowered his shoulders, and Nora took that as a sign to continue. "She works in her family's restaurant, and I wouldn't want to take her away entirely, but I could use Riley's help training our kitchen and waitstaff. I also need someone to help refine the menu so it has variety and sophistication but reflects the local community."

"The local community has its own variety and sophistication," Beck said.

"I know it does. I know it's not all ham and potato casseroles, even out here in the Wild West."

Beck looked up and smiled, and Nora couldn't help but think how handsome and sincere and intelligent he was. It was a wonder no woman had claimed his heart.

"So you want Riley to be an adviser of sorts," Beck said.

"Exactly."

"I can't think of anyone better, except maybe Judy, but she has a different method of feeding a crowd. She makes a big batch of food, and that's what you get. It's always good, but there are no menus to order from at the ranch house."

"So you think it's a good idea," Nora said.

Beck silently finished brushing the horse, put him in a stall and got the other one out. Nora sat on a bale of hay watching until he handed her the brush. "Your turn."

Nora approached the horse, which dwarfed her in size. "Hi, horse."

"Winnie," Beck said.

"Winnie," Nora repeated, running her hand along the horse's nose as she'd seen Beck do. The horse turned her head and gave Nora a sideways glance.

"She likes you," Beck said. "You seem to have that effect on people, too."

Nora was glad she was facing away so he couldn't see her blush. "It's necessary in my line of work. People have to know you value and respect what they've tried to do before they'll trust you to help them."

"Most hotels have had someone genuinely trying," Beck said. "I guess."

She knew what he meant. Of course it was apparent that the Lodge had been struggling with no leadership.

"Everyone has different circumstances, their

own reasons and challenges. All of them are valid."

She began brushing Winnie with strokes like Beck's, but it was much harder than he'd made it look. He was a lot taller and stronger than she was, so she took longer, but Winnie seemed patient.

"I worry about Riley," he said. "She was pretty invested in the Lodge along with Bryan. Not financially or anything, but they'd been dating all through the planning and design and construction. She probably feels she left a piece of her heart in that building. It might be too soon for her to be involved. She could still be healing."

Nora finished brushing and ran a soft hand down Winnie's face and then kissed her on the nose. "Healing is different for everyone," she said. "For some people, it's cooking for others, or taking care of them. For some, it's running away. For some, it's facing what hurts them most every day until it hurts a little less all the time."

She meant her words to be about Beck—especially the words about facing things. But her throat felt tight when she thought about her own past. She knew she'd been running, but it was her best means of protection.

"Sometimes they need a push," Beck said.

"I don't mean to push Riley, but she did well

helping with the campfire night and even seemed to like it. If she says no, I'll respect it."

She was still facing the horse, but she heard Beck get up and the soft swish of his boots on the wooden, hay-covered floor. She felt his heat when he stopped right behind her and reached up to unhook the lead attached to Winnie. He lingered for a moment and Nora fought the desire to turn around and raise her face to his. What would she see there? Was he almost ready to open up and talk about his brother?

"Dinner must be done by now," he said. He avoided touching her as he led the horse back to her stall. He gave both animals fresh water and forked hay into their stalls, then he strode toward the barn door, but turned and held out a hand. "Ready?"

Nora walked up to him but didn't take his hand. It was more a gesture than an invitation, wasn't it? She stopped when she saw the sky. The dark clouds that had been on the horizon seemed closer, larger and darker now. Beck looked up at the sky and took a deep breath.

"Rain," he said.

"I don't think so. I checked the forecast before I came over. It's not coming until late tonight."

"It's sooner than that," he said. He looked grim. Didn't ranchers like rain that made the grass grow and filled the streams for their cattle to drink from?

He put a light hand on Nora's shoulder. "Let's eat, and then you can tell me all about your rodeo plans."

"I thought you were going to teach me to rope and do ranch stuff after dinner."

He shook his head. "It's going to rain."

THE HOUSE WAS empty except for him and Nora. She was only one person but having her there made the entire spacious home a lot less lonely. Beck got the casserole from the oven while Nora went ahead and sliced bread without needing to ask where the knives and cutting board were. She'd done it once before. That was probably what made it seem like she fit in there.

Like she *fit* there.

"We don't have to sit at the table for a dozen ranch hands," he said. He scooped food onto plates. "There's a small nook off the side of the kitchen. It has a nice view of the mountains behind the house." He nodded toward the eating nook.

He carried their plates, and Nora carried their water glasses. The table by the window did offer a good view. Beck sat there with his coffee sometimes, looking out over the yard where his parents had a swing. His mom used to sit out there after dinner while his dad smoked and worked on his hobby—adding leather tooling to saddles and tack. There were reminders in the barn of his dad's craft, and sometimes Beck imagined the smell of his mother's cigarettes on evenings when he sat outside.

It wasn't an evening for sitting outside, not with those dark clouds. He didn't care what Nora's weather app said, there would be raindrops before they finished dinner.

Rain was a rancher's best friend, especially during fire season. Incredibly welcome to green up the pastures and fill the streams. But it could be a nightmare, too, when it came down so fast the water had nowhere to go, sluicing down roads that carried the volume like a heavy burden before giving up and washing out. Washing people out with it.

"You were right about the mountain view," Nora said. "Do all the mountains around here have names?"

He took a bite of casserole and nodded. "Official ones on the maps, and then there are the names everyone calls them."

"I bet there are good stories about how they got their names."

"I'm sure, but most of those stories are so old no one is around to remember them. Like that big one you see the top of in the vee between the two smaller ones in front." He gestured out the window. "That's called Silent Sam."

"Was there a very quiet man named Sam who lived on the mountain?" Nora asked.

He shrugged. "I've never found anyone who knew for sure. Whatever the story was, it died with someone a long time ago."

"That's kind of a shame."

He took a piece of bread but then forgot it was in his hand as he gazed out at the lawn. He remembered specific details about his parents, how they laughed, sounded, even smelled. Their favorite foods, the songs his mother taught him, his dad's way with animals. Those memories were comforting. They didn't hurt anymore.

His brother's memories, though, were sealed up tight. He'd pushed away the sounds of Bryan's favorite boots on the hardwood floors. The sound of him singing in the shower—so loud Beck could hear it out in the living room. The smell of the pine he loved tossing on the fire even though Beck thought it was too smoky. The way they'd argued about football teams.

Football season was just starting, but he hadn't turned on a game yet. Wasn't sure he could face Bryan's popcorn bowl that was on the top shelf in the pantry, collecting dust. Pain seized his heart like it was in the grip of a huge, unforgiving fist. He didn't think he'd survive it for a moment, but then he thought about football and the smell of pinewood burning and Bryan's singing. He didn't want those memories to die with his brother. Bryan had lived in this house for almost thirty years. It was wrong to block him out of it as if he'd never been there.

The pain around his heart eased and he took a slow breath. He'd crushed the bread in his hand, but he felt as if a weight was starting to lift.

"What is it?" Nora asked.

Beck had almost forgotten she was there, but the raw concern in her eyes told him how much she cared about him. Was she a catalyst for him to face the past? Was it her or the fact that she was bringing the Lodge back to life?

Beck swallowed and shook his head. A raindrop hit the window and then a lot of them, drawing Beck's and Nora's attention to the watery window.

"You were right about the rain," she said. She smiled, but there was still worry in her eyes. "I may delete the weather app and just call you next time."

"I can only predict what happens here," he said. "I won't do you much good when you're… gone."

He couldn't do anyone any good when they were gone. But he could do something about the people who were right here, depending on him. Caring about him.

Thunder rumbled outside and the room darkened. Beck got up and switched on the light, warming up the space.

"This is very good," Nora said. "If I give it a cool Western name, we can add it to the menu at the Lodge's restaurant. What's a fun name for a ham and potato casserole?"

Beck got a fresh piece of bread and dipped it into the cheesy food on his plate. The food was delicious, warm, filling. Had he even noticed the taste of anything he'd eaten lately, or was he merely surviving? The pie he'd had with Nora downtown had awakened his taste buds a little. He'd surprised himself by ordering anything that day, but it had been fun brainstorming a tagline for the Lodge's advertising.

"Let's see," he said. "This includes pigs, potatoes and cheese."

Nora smiled. "So, a pig, a potato and a dairy cow walk into a bar—"

Beck laughed. "No. Potatoes can't walk."

"But that's the joke," Nora said.

"For the description, you could say ham it up with cheesy potatoes," he suggested.

Nora laughed. "You are ridiculously good at taglines. Is that what you think about over all those miles in the saddle?"

He used to think and dream in the saddle. All his plans for improving the ranch. He'd poured his heart into it…except for the past ten months when his heart wasn't in anything. He'd just been existing.

Bryan would have socked him in the gut. Bryan who was a dreamer, a creator, a planner. He should have been the one making up fun names for casseroles or creating ad copy, but for the first time since his brother's passing, Beck felt as if he needed to honor his brother's memory by keeping it alive—no matter how painful the process of reviving it would be.

"If so, I'd love to come with you and try out that strategy," Nora continued. "Fresh ideas are a lot of work. Maybe we could ride after the rain stops?"

A month ago, Nora had never ridden a horse, but now she was suggesting it as an inspiring activity. He hadn't seen her red heels in a while or her suit jackets. A month could make a big difference.

"I'd love to," he said. "But not tonight. This rain isn't going to stop. In fact, it would be safer for you to get on the road soon before the ranch roads get too sloppy."

Her expression sobered. They'd been having fun, and now it looked as if he was rushing her through dinner and practically kicking her out.

She quickly recovered, though, and gave him her polite smile—the one that might convince a stranger, but not him. "Is that part of my ranch life education? Reading the weather and knowing when to skedaddle?"

"We don't actually use the word *skedaddle*. I'd call it a pragmatic exit."

"It sounds so romantic when you call it that, I think I'll add it to the brochures. Come to Wyoming, which is so beautiful you won't want to make a pragmatic exit." She opened her arms as if making a big proclamation, and Beck laughed.

"Fine. I don't want you to hurry up and skedaddle, but I don't want you driving after dark either."

They finished dinner and moved to the living room where they settled onto the leather couch. Beck got out his phone. "We can't go outside and try roping something, but I can show you videos."

"Are you in these videos?"

"Absolutely not. I try to keep my face off the internet."

"That's a shame," Nora said. "You make a handsome cowboy."

"Rancher," he corrected.

"That, too."

Beck felt his face heat. A beautiful woman was sitting close to him calling him handsome. They'd kissed once, and that the kiss had been at the front of his mind the past few days in the saddle. It was as if it had awakened him. Emotions had started to flood him lately and he wasn't sure he could turn them off as he had been doing.

He wasn't sure he wanted to. It was almost less painful to try healing than it was to keep living the way he was.

"The…uh…rodeo you'll see isn't exactly reality," he said. "It's an exhibition, meant to be entertainment rather than an actual portrayal of modern ranch life."

"I figured that out when I saw the videos of clowns."

"So you've watched some?"

"Research," Nora said. "I'm the girl from London, Milan, Zurich and Paris, you know."

Beck had put on a front for so long that he recognized one when he saw it. What was Nora running from? What was keeping her on the road to all those fancy places?

"I thought you were from Atlanta," he said quietly.

Her smile faded. "I was."

"The other night in my truck," he said. Her lips parted and her cheeks warmed. Was she thinking about that kiss that she'd already told him was not to be repeated? He moved back a few inches so she'd know he was respecting her boundaries. "When you…comforted me, you said you'd been there. What did you mean?"

She hesitated. He knew his question hit home with her, recognized the flash of vulnerability and then the wall that came down over it. He'd been doing the same thing, and he hadn't been ready to talk until recently. Until her. He owed her the same kindness. "You don't have to tell me," he said. He tried to smile. "But I've been there, too."

Her eyes glistened with tears, and she got up abruptly and moved to the window, which was dark and streaked with rain. The actual sunset was still an hour away, but nightfall came in with the clouds.

"I should go," she said. "You said I should get off the roads before dark."

Beck moved to the window and stood behind her. It was raining much harder than he'd realized. Temporary rivers crossed the ranch yard, and sheets of rain swooped off the edge of the barn roof. Just getting to the black SUV in the driveway would mean getting thoroughly soaked.

And the road on the way to the Lodge would have standing water. It might even wash out. Panic rolled through him and almost choked him.

"No," he said. "You can't go alone. I'll drive you."

Nora turned and put her hands on his shoulders. "Don't be silly. You'd get soaked for no reason. I'll be fine. I've gotten used to driving that SUV around the ranch. It's just rain."

CHAPTER EIGHTEEN

"ABSOLUTELY NOT," BECK SAID. "You're not driving anywhere in this storm."

Nora stepped back, arms dropping to her sides. There was something in his voice she recognized—fear. It was fear that brought that harsh note to his tone. He was afraid for her, and she suddenly put the pieces together about Bryan Duncan's accident last fall. Had it been raining that night?

"Okay," she said.

Thunder rumbled outside and lightning lit up Beck's face. He winced and closed his eyes.

"I'll drive you," he said again.

"No," she decided, suddenly resolved on a plan. "I'm not leaving tonight." She had no idea where she got the courage to invite herself to stay over at the ranch house, but she wasn't making Beck go out in a storm and she wasn't going to drive herself and put him through the pain of watching her go. "Unless the rain stops and the roads dry out."

He shook his head. "They won't be safe until morning."

Nora met his eyes. "You have a guest room, don't you?"

"Yes."

"And I'm no stranger to staying somewhere new. I've been doing it for a decade." He looked so serious, and Nora wanted to make him smile, but she also wanted him to talk, tell her everything. The man had a lot of baggage to unload. "I do have high standards for linens and pillows, though."

"I can try—"

"Just kidding," Nora said. "I can be happy with a blanket on the couch, even though I have gotten quite spoiled by 'bunking down in luxury' at the Lodge." She made air quotes when she used the phrase he'd come up with.

Beck attempted a smile, but worry still creased his forehead. "I'll make a fire." He turned abruptly and began expertly stacking logs and kindling in the massive stone fireplace. Nora leaned on the stones and watched.

"Have you made campfires out on the range?"

"Lots of times."

"I've never done it," she said.

Beck stopped. "Want to learn as part of your ranch life lesson?"

She laughed. "I'm happy watching you this

time. The rain cooled things off so much that I'm looking forward to a little heat from the fire."

"Coming right up."

Within minutes, a small flame became a crackling fire. It warmed Nora, and she lingered by the fireplace, watching the flames, while Beck sat in an armchair facing the hearth. A small coffee table separated his chair from the one next to it, and Nora wondered if anyone ever sat there with him. Had his brother when he was alive?

She turned and faced him. Behind Beck the windows were dark and streaked with rain. It wasn't stopping, and it was too late now. Beck was right about the dark ranch roads and the dangerous standing water. She was here for the night, and she had a choice to make. She could keep the conversation light and friendly, focused on the upcoming rodeo and future plans for the Lodge. They could discuss business like she would with any other client. But Beck wasn't just any client to her—a fact that unnerved her because she never got close to people on the road. However, she'd already kissed him and spent more time with him than was strictly necessary. She could risk one more night of seeing Beck as a man instead of just the owner of a hotel in need of rescuing.

He needed rescuing. And he made her want to share just a little of herself with him, though it was hard for her to unlock the things she kept private and separate from her work. Sometimes she felt as if no one really knew her.

"I used to like playing in the rain when I was a kid," she said. "Atlanta summers were so hot, and it was a treat to just go outside in your clothes and get soaked in the afternoon showers. My brothers and I would go barefoot in the small patch of grass near our apartment building." Nora hadn't thought about it in years, but the memory was a happy one. It was before everything fell apart.

"Where are your brothers now?" Beck asked.

"Still in the Atlanta area. My mom lives with one of them."

"Are they in the hotel business, too?"

"No. One is a teacher and the other is a loan officer for a bank."

Beck smiled and pointed to the chair next to him. Nora sat down.

"It sounds like your job is much more fun than theirs," Beck said.

Nora gave a little shrug. "We wanted different things." Her brothers were already out of the house when her father died, and it impacted them differently. They hadn't lost their home the way she had. In a way, the way they experienced the loss of their father was different, too. "Do you ever want to talk…about your brother?" she asked quietly.

Beck stared into the fire for a long time. "I always thought we wanted the same thing, Bryan and I."

Nora held her breath, afraid to move or say anything that would dissuade Beck from talking.

"We both loved the ranch, horses, the mountains, everything. When our parents died, I expected we'd keep on managing it together as we had been for several years. They were older when they had us, so we'd been taking more responsibility for quite some time."

"That's a lot," Nora commented when he was silent for a moment.

"We shared it, shared the labor. And it was working. But about a year after we inherited, Bryan came to me with a plan for the Lodge, and I…didn't react well."

"You were surprised," Nora said.

"Shocked was more like it. I couldn't believe he wanted to make part of his land a big hotel. It seemed like a waste of good grazing land, the wrong direction for both of us. I didn't like the idea from the start, and I really didn't like it when he sold off some of his half of the acreage to raise capital to build the Lodge."

"Oh," Nora said. "That must have been painful for you to see your parents' land divided."

"It was. We argued about it a lot, but I was being selfish. It wasn't about me. I shouldn't have made it that way. Bryan had the right to do what he did."

Beck got up and poked at the fire. "I didn't technically stand in his way, but I wasn't helpful either. Seeing that land sold off and watching construction crews coming and going for a year felt like watching part of a mountain crumble and knowing there was nothing you could do about it. The night of the grand opening…he was so happy. The place was perfect, a success, a testament to him as a dreamer and a planner."

"You were at the party," Nora said softly.

"For a while. I left early, told him one of us had to get up early and run the ranch. One of us had to honor the family legacy by keeping it going instead of playing around with fancy food and a riding stable for out-of-towners who had no idea what the reality of ranch life was."

Nora stayed silent, picturing the scene between the brothers.

"He told me he didn't have to live in the shadow of our parents and their dreams, but that I could keep on doing that if I wanted to. Those words cut deep. They play in my mind sometimes when I'm out working the land, sleeping in this house, riding the trails my grandparents cut. Looking back on it, I know he was right."

"You don't…want this life?" Nora asked.

He shook his head. "I do want this life, but that

doesn't mean he had to want the same thing. I wish I'd looked past my own pride or insecurity or whatever it was and stayed until the end of the party that night. Instead, I got in my truck and left."

Nora waited, relieved she was finally hearing the story but conscious of the pain it inflicted on Beck to tell it.

"The rain started halfway home and turned into a downpour by the time I got here. The party was still going when I left the Lodge, and I figured Bryan would stay until the last guest left."

Beck sat back down but didn't look at her.

"I waited up late, ready to give him a piece of my mind when he got in. When he didn't come home, I figured he'd stayed the night at the Lodge. There were a hundred rooms. He could have stayed. I wish to God he had stayed."

Nora watched his face as the firelight flickered on it. The rain pounded on the roof.

"One of my ranch hands found Bryan's truck in a gully early the next morning on his way to work," Beck said quietly. "It was washed off the road against a tree."

Nora reached over and put a hand on Beck's. "I'm so sorry."

"There isn't an hour that goes by that I don't regret leaving that party early. I should have stayed and celebrated his dream with him. I should have understood that we wanted different things. I should have driven him home."

"You can't blame yourself," she said.

"Sure can," he said. "My last words to him were bitter. I thought he was betraying our parents' and grandparents' memory."

Nora's heart broke for Beck, and she wanted to hug him, but she didn't move. He needed a chance to keep talking.

"But I'm the one about to dishonor Bryan's memory," Beck said.

Nora stiffened. Was he unhappy with her work? She'd spent the past month trying to bring the Lodge back to what Bryan had envisioned. They were making so much progress and—

"I'm the one who's going to sell the Lodge as soon as you finish bringing it back from the dead."

CHAPTER NINETEEN

NORA WOKE UP in the spare bedroom that had almost certainly belonged to Beck's parents. It wasn't Bryan's room. She sensed that was the closed door next to Beck's. She pulled aside the flowery curtains, and the sunlight hurt her eyes. No more rain, not a cloud—except for the one hanging over her now as she thought about the day ahead.

How was she going to keep doing her job professionally and cheerfully when she knew Beck was only planning to unload the Lodge as soon as her efforts made it successful enough to attract a buyer? He hadn't specifically asked her not to tell anyone his plan, but it was clearly a secret and would destroy morale and motivation at the Lodge. She was accustomed to being discreet at her jobs. But this was personal, and she wanted to kick herself for letting it get that way.

She dressed and splashed some water on her face in the adjoining bathroom before heading out to the living room where she'd left her boots by the door. The last thing she wanted was to run into Beck or anyone else.

"There's breakfast and coffee left over," Judy said. The older woman stood in the doorway leading from the dining room. "Everyone else is already gone."

"I'm fine," Nora said. "But thank you."

"That was quite a storm last night."

Nora nodded. She sat on the bench by the door and picked up a boot.

"Beck worries about storms," Judy said.

"I know."

"And I'm guessing you know why."

"He told me about it last night. About the night Bryan died," Nora said. "He didn't want me driving in the downpour, so we talked about the future of the Lodge and I slept in the guest room."

"He said as much before he left," Judy said.

Nora reached for her second boot. She wondered how much Judy knew about Beck's plans, but there was no safe way to pry for that information, and it was truly none of her business. Her job was to get the hotel on its feet, and its owner could do whatever he wanted after that.

Judy sat on the bench next to her and put an arm around her shoulders. The affectionate gesture caught Nora off guard. "You're a sweet lady, and you're doing a great job at the Lodge. I'd almost given up on that place until you came along." She sighed. "It's been a hard year. Bryan was like a son to me, and seeing Beck battle himself since his brother died has torn me up."

Nora had both boots on, but she didn't get up. The ranch house was silent around them. Peaceful. She'd felt a lot of peace since coming to Wyoming. Memories of her father and the difficult months after he died had surfaced as they often did, but then they smoothed out again. That tragedy had put her on the road for the last ten years, and Remedy Creek was the only place that had made her feel as if she could stop moving and find a home.

"I'll miss you when you leave," Judy said.

Nora felt her eyes sting. Had anyone said that to her at her other jobs? Maybe they'd miss her and her guidance professionally, but miss her as a person?

She turned on the bench and gave Judy a hug. "I'll miss you, too."

When she got in her car, Nora plugged her phone in. It had gone dead in the night without a charger, but she doubted anyone would worry about her. The staff at the Lodge wouldn't notice she hadn't come back. Her family was far away and accustomed to not hearing from her for weeks at a time. Judy's hug had reminded her of her own mother, and Nora started to punch in her mother's number so they could chat while she drove back to the Lodge, but a voicemail alert got her attention instead.

She hit the button to listen to the recording while she drove out of the ranch house's driveway.

It was the scheduler for Total Hospitality Management. *Hello, Nora. I'm calling to see how close you are to wrapping up the assignment in Wyoming. The Barcelona job we had penciled in for you went to someone else because they moved up the timetable, but I have another assignment starting in two weeks if you can swing it. I know you love the south of France, and this will be a fun one. Historic hotel, new owner who's struggling to play nice with the locals. We thought of you with this one because you're good at that. Call me.*

So they were thinking of her. And somehow, Nora hadn't actually been thinking of them very much. She'd gotten wrapped up in Remedy Creek, and while she'd filled out the daily and weekly progress updates for her company as required, she'd almost forgotten how upset she was when she first arrived in Wyoming.

Instead, she'd kept her mind and heart on the job, investing herself personally in it. She'd even learned to ride a horse. She thought about her braided hair and the borrowed brown riding boots on her feet.

She'd gotten invested. She'd played nice with the locals—something her company had apparently remembered they valued about her—but she'd also played with her heart. It was time to pull back, take off the cowboy boots and finish the job.

The Lodge assignment was going to go on her record as a success, and it didn't matter to her company what Beck did with it when she left. The France job offer proved the company still valued her and counted on her. Plus, it was a chance at redemption. She wouldn't be going back to the hotel on the Riviera where she'd struggled and been pulled out by her company, but it was in the same region and a chance to redeem herself. She was meant to be in nice hotels like that.

She could still smell last night's fire on her clothes, but as she drove the ranch roads lit by the morning sun, she could almost smell the good French coffee and crepes waiting for her around the world.

"HERCULES, WE'VE GOT a long day ahead," Beck said. He'd already driven the road to the Lodge and back as soon as the sun came up. The warmth between him and Nora had chilled fast last night, but no way was he letting her get on unsafe roads on her way out this morning. To his relief, the road had not washed out, and, aside from a few potholes that the Lodge SUV would survive, it was passable.

Nora had received his news about selling the Lodge with utter silence but then a curt nod and an assurance her company would do everything they could to increase the value of his property.

Her company.

He hadn't thought about Total Hospitality Management in weeks. He'd only considered Nora—her efforts, her enthusiasm, the way she fit in and treated the place as if she personally cared about its success. As if she valued his brother's dream stronger than he ever had. The place was shining again…but would it stay that way when Nora left?

"It doesn't matter. I'm selling it," he muttered to his horse. Saying the words aloud helped him get used to the idea. "I've got a right to sell it. It's legally mine."

Hercules ignored him and picked his way along the trail, which had already greened up after last night's rain. That was welcome despite the worry it had caused. That panic in his chest when Nora almost drove out in it had subsided, though. He'd survived it. He'd done the right thing this time, and talking with her about his brother had eased some of his burden, his guilt. There wasn't much harm in telling her everything because she'd leave in two more weeks when the job was done and he'd probably never see her again.

Never see those boots under the bench by his door or find a blond hair on the chair next to his at the fireplace. Never watch her plant a kiss on a horse's nose after giving the animal a rubdown.

"I'll survive," he said. He'd been surviving.

Hercules made a scoffing sound as if he'd been listening and thought Beck was full of cow manure.

Beck took his time, following the river for a while and checking its banks. The ground was soft under his horse's feet from last night's heavy rain. Satisfied that the rain had done more good than harm—nurturing the pasture grass instead of washing it out—he steered Hercules to a trail leading across a valley and up the side of a mountain. From there, he'd have a view of hundreds of acres.

In the distance, a rider approached. No dust kicked up from the horse's hooves, and Beck shaded his eyes, hoping to identify the rider. He was familiar, but none of Beck's men were planning to be in this area, a part of the ranch that partially bordered the Lodge's land. Beck called this part of the ranch the dividing line, marking the place where Bryan's inherited acres had been either sold off for capital or developed into his resort. The Lodge itself hadn't taken up all of

Bryan's land. Hundreds of acres had remained grazing land for the Remedy Mountain Ranch, and Bryan had been happy to share it with Beck.

There had been no reason to argue with his brother. Together, they had it all, and it could have stayed that way, even with the Lodge.

"I'm sorry, brother," he said aloud.

Hercules pointed his ears, but Beck didn't think it was in response to his words. There was no response to those words, no one to hear his apology. Instead, Hercules was watching the lone rider approach. It took Beck a moment, but recognition hit him.

Mitch. Beck had no idea he was back from Cody. Had he quit the rodeo, come to his senses and come home to help Beck manage the ranch? Beck pulled up under a shade tree to wait, knowing Mitch had seen him and would appreciate the shade, too.

"Welcome back," Beck said.

Mitch grinned and leaned forward in his saddle to shake Beck's hand. "Glad to be here, but only temporarily."

Beck hid his disappointment. The man had a right to do what made him happy.

"What's the occasion? I know it's not your mother's birthday."

Mitch laughed. "It's the rodeo road show. I'm performing in it, but they also sent me out here as their advance scout to make sure the setup goes well. We start setting up tomorrow, so I've got all day today to do some real work in the saddle instead of the stuff I do for the audience."

"I can find you some work," Beck said.

"No doubt. I already checked in at the Lodge and met Nora. She's a beauty, isn't she?" Mitch said.

Beck stiffened. Mitch wasn't wrong, Nora was beautiful, but Beck didn't want Mitch—or anyone—talking about her in that way. He wasn't jealous, of course. He just...well...he didn't like it.

"She's a very efficient hotel manager and she's turned the place around fast," Beck said. "I doubt we'd be able to host your rodeo show without her efforts."

"I'll have to thank her," Mitch said.

"I can do that for you."

Mitch tilted his head at Beck's tone but didn't say anything.

"How is everyone else?" Mitch asked, and Beck was glad to change the subject. The way he'd left things with Nora the previous night, she probably was unimpressed by him, to put it mildly. He deserved it. It was cowardly to keep his plan to sell the Lodge a secret for so long. He told himself he'd stayed mum to protect the place from gossip, but he knew the truth about himself—he didn't want to face uncomfortable questions. His attorney had already put him through the wringer a few days ago when he'd finally told him what he planned, asking questions and making suggestions about exactly how a sale would work—the Lodge building and business could be sold, but the land would remain under Beck's ownership and be leased to the Lodge's buyer.

Every conversation about his brother's property felt like a betrayal to Bryan, who should have still been there, making decisions about his own land.

"Fine, I guess. Busy. Got more people working at the Lodge, most of them you probably know or know of."

"Heard anything from Riley lately?" Mitch asked.

Beck studied his friend and former employee for a moment. Mitch was his age, and they'd grown up in a circle that included Riley and, of course, Bryan. When love had blossomed between Bryan and Riley, no one was surprised. They were all friends. With Bryan gone now, was Mitch watching out for Riley, just as Beck was?

"Some," Beck said. "Nora has asked her to take on some sort of advisory capacity at the Lodge, something to do with food and menus."

Mitch nodded. "She'll be good at that."

Beck was sure of it, but it wasn't going to matter much when the place was sold. New owner, new management. They could employ whoever they wanted, even though he was going to try to write something in the contract about keeping current employees for at least a year. His attorney had already warned him there would be no guarantees. When you sold something, you gave up control.

Giving up control had sounded great to him over a month ago when he settled on this plan, but the Lodge had started to feel more personal to him, and that was a problem. He needed to maintain his detachment if he was truly going to let it go.

The ranch took up all of his time. It was more than enough for him.

"I'm checking on the grasslands from up there," Beck said, gesturing toward the mountain. "Ride with me?"

Mitch nodded and his horse fell in step beside Hercules. They rode in comfortable silence, as they had hundreds of times over the years. Bryan had usually been in a saddle right beside them, too.

Things change, Beck thought to himself. He knew he had to let go of the past, but lately he'd realized that letting go might mean gaining something, too. Perspective, maybe, or was it peace?

You can't blame yourself, Nora had told him last night.

But he did. And soon everyone was going to blame him for spitting on his brother's grave by selling the beautiful thing Bryan had dreamed up and built.

CHAPTER TWENTY

NORA WAITED UNDER the front portico. She hated having all her eggs in one basket, but this single candidate for the general manager position showed solid promise on paper and he was willing to spend several days on-site for a paid working interview. Their online video chat had gone well, his references checked out, and now he was rolling up in a cloud of Wyoming dust.

It had been three days since Beck had dropped the bomb about selling the Lodge, and she had not said a word about it to anyone. Was it deceptive to interview and possibly hire this candidate when she had inside knowledge of a potential sale that could alter his employment? In her experience, hotel sales were a lengthy process, but she still felt dirty knowing something and not imparting it to anyone.

Of course, it wasn't her secret. It was Beck's. She was just a temporary employee, there to get the place back in the saddle so he could unload it.

The car pulled up and Nora greeted the man

who emerged from the back seat. Steven was a big man, tall, and his white shirt looked two sizes too small. Still, he presented a smile and held out his hand.

"I feel like I'm in a movie," he said.

Nora laughed. "This place is for real. Trust me."

"Should I be on the lookout for outlaws and wild horses?" he asked. He glanced around at the mountains and the wide-open sky. The man looked uncomfortable, a fish out of water, and Nora wondered if that was exactly how she'd looked to Beck on her first day, when she'd arrived in her suit and high heels.

She didn't want to think about Beck and how she'd grown to care for him. It made it that much harder to watch him do something she didn't believe was good for anyone—including him.

"Come inside," Nora said. "I'll give you a few minutes to settle into your room and catch your breath, then we'll do a property tour and I'll fill you in on the rodeo coming in just a few days. I'm afraid your working interview is going to be a trial by fire."

"I'm ready," Steven said. "And I'm sure this place is going to be heaven compared to the vineyard hotel in New York where I used to work. Everyone there knew everyone else. Out here, I feel like I can get away from it all."

Nora didn't have the heart to tell him that everyone here knew everyone else…and that was actually part of the charm. People had long-standing relationships here. They cared about each other. They'd kept the Lodge clean and operational for months on end with no leadership and very few guests, and then they'd welcomed her.

When she walked Steven through the front doors, she felt a surge of pride at the clean and orderly lobby, the short line at check-in that moved efficiently, and the aroma of fresh coffee. The tall, clean windows showed the morning sunshine and the mountains. Steven held up a hand against the glare and grimaced.

"Your room is this way," Nora said. "I've put you in a suite with a balcony, and your view is not just mountains but also the temporary arena for the rodeo."

"Oh," he said. "Well, you can't have everything."

Nora gave him a tight smile and reminded herself to be patient. He didn't have to be perfect to be a good candidate for the job. He was, by default, the best candidate she had. And she needed to replace herself so she could get back on the road. The sooner she decided on Steven's employment and trained him, the sooner she'd be heading to France—an assignment her company had hand-selected her for, which meant they hadn't forgotten her. She was getting a new chance to prove herself.

She stopped at a door and handed Steven a key card. "Take some time to refresh yourself and meet me at the front desk in about thirty minutes. We'll be walking a lot, both inside and outside, so feel free to change into something more comfortable."

As she walked away, she remembered those red high heels she'd shown up wearing. Since then, she'd adopted low heels most of the time. She'd also refined the front desk uniform to include a cotton shirt with Western details, snaps and red piping on the collar and sleeves. Most of the lobby staff wore black shoes or boots, and the resulting look was somewhere between business casual and Western evening out.

Even though she'd adapted to Remedy Creek in her daily apparel, she still had a closet full of clothes that would be considered professional. Those red shoes were gathering dust right now behind two pairs of Western boots—her fancy white ones and the utilitarian brown ones she'd borrowed—but she'd slip back into those impractical high heels when she got to France in as little as two or three weeks.

BECK HAD SEEN plenty of rodeos. He knew it was all about the showmanship and not the actual hard work that went into ranching. If it made people happy to watch cowboys wearing giant belt buckles and hats fancy-lassoing calves, it was no skin off his nose.

As he leaned on a temporary fence rail erected by the rodeo's advance team, it wasn't the pageantry of the rodeo that made him feel queasy. It was watching Nora—from a safe distance—showing the potential manager, Steven, the ropes. The man dressed as if he'd walked into a boring men's store in the mall and asked them for whatever was within a size or two of fitting him. By contrast, Nora had nailed the perfect combination of Western casual and hotel professional.

He blew out a breath. Nora had adapted quickly. Steven had only been there a few days, so he had to give him a chance. Not that Beck was looking for a long-term business relationship with him. The general manager's employment would be up to whoever bought the Remedy Mountain Lodge. With any luck, Beck would unload the whole place before the snow got too deep in the canyons.

He closed his eyes, picturing Nora's face that night he'd admitted he was only employing her to fix the hotel up so he could sell it, like fattening up calves for the market. He'd hardly choked down food for the past week because of the feeling in his gut that he was doing the wrong thing.

As far as he knew, Nora had kept his secret. He didn't have to face the disappointment and opinions of people he'd known his whole life—at least not yet. But Nora knew. Her opinion and disappointment meant a lot to him, but would she even remember him after she left for the next job?

Beck opened his eyes and couldn't resist a glance toward Nora across the arena. He was going to miss her, but his hands were tied and his plans were made. He couldn't run a hotel he never wanted, and she couldn't stick around. Her time was almost up. When the rodeo left town, Nora wouldn't be far behind it.

Unless he told her how he felt about her. The thought was like a tired horse sensing home and wanting to run toward it, even if it took his last ounce of energy. He cared about her, looked forward to talking to her, and had even opened up about his brother. She was special, and she'd made him feel as if he could heal and be whole again…someday.

It was that feeling of being an entire person and not half of a set of brothers torn apart that made him want Nora to stay. What would happen to him when she left?

He started toward her, determined to tell her that she meant something to him and was special and had opened his heart. He didn't know how anything was going to work, but didn't he deserve a chance to try?

After one step, Beck tensed. One of the performers from the rodeo was leaning on the gate, chatting with Nora and Steven. Nora was laughing, and Beck felt a twinge of jealousy. She looked happy, very unlike the last time he'd seen her face with its…was it disappointment? The rodeo guy was opening the gate, beckoning Nora in. She waved her hands at first as if to say *no thanks, cowboy*, but then she shrugged and gave in.

Nora was in the arena. Horses were running around, ropes were flying through the air, and yet there she was in her boots with a blond braid down her back. The cowboy held a horse for her and seemed to be inviting her to saddle up. What on earth? She was no rodeo performer. She was his manager, the person saving his hotel. She'd learned to ride just a month ago, and now this rodeo clown was—

Beck caught his breath. The man was lifting her into the saddle, his hands at her waist. She was smiling at him as she swung a leg over and adjusted her seat. Beck could not take his eyes off her. This was ridiculous. Who did that man think he was? Clearly, he saw a beautiful woman hanging around the fence and decided this was the way to her heart.

Beck's own heart thundered, and he worked his jaw but couldn't make a sound. The cowboy was on his horse next to Nora now, showing her a rope with a loop in the end. Was the man going to teach her how to lasso? That was Beck's job. He was the one who'd invited her to his house to teach her what she—adorably—called ranchy things. This guy…

No. Beck started to duck between the bars of the fence when movement caught his eye. One of the other rodeo performers was trying to coax Steven onto a horse too, but Steven was clearly not interested. He shook his head, took two steps away from the fence. Pointed to his city shoes. Beck was across the arena, but he was pretty sure Steven had gone pale at the idea of entering the arena and getting on a horse.

That guy wasn't going to make it out here. Sure he was new, but Nora had chased him down as he tried to escape her on horseback during her first thirty minutes at the place. She was brave. She had grit.

Steven turned and strode away, checking his phone as if he had something important to do other than learn and build a relationship with the traveling performers. Beck turned back to Nora and the unknown cowboy. She was now holding the end of a rope in one hand and swirling a lasso with the other while she listened intently to the young man on the horse next to her.

"Interesting lady."

Beck jumped at Mitch's voice. He hadn't even noticed his friend approaching.

"Easy, boss. Didn't mean to scare you."

"You didn't scare me," Beck grumbled.

Mitch leaned on the fence next to him. The temporary arena was large enough for riders to rehearse their show on one end but leave room for other performers to do the same. Nora and her companion moved to an open space where a wooden stand was built to mimic a cow, a practice block for performers to perfect their show.

Beck moved down the fence to get closer to Nora and Mitch followed. She didn't glance over, didn't even seem to notice him, because she was intent on swinging the lasso overhead and aiming it at the practice cow. He held his breath. Even experienced riders could lose their balance with a wild swing. He started to put a leg through the fence.

"I think she's got it," Mitch said. "I've seen worse beginners. Did she know how to ride before she came to Wyoming?"

"No."

"Well, then she's a quick learner. Must be in the air out here," Mitch said.

Beck wished he knew more about her life before she'd arrived in Remedy Creek. He'd opened his heart to her, but she kept her own thoughts guarded. Was it because she was there to do a job and she didn't want to mix personal things with business?

Of course that was sensible, and it probably contributed to her success at her job.

But he found himself wishing she'd given away a little more of herself to him. They'd bonded some. Kissed. And yet there was a whole missing piece—an important one that motivated her to keep moving on from place to place. Would she ever find a home? A place where she belonged? He thought of that leather chair by his fireplace that he could still picture her sitting in.

"Here she goes," Mitch said, clearly enjoying the beginner rodeo show Nora was putting on. Other people had found a spot on the fence rail and were watching, too.

Nora wound up her arm and tossed the rope, but she accidentally let go entirely. It glanced off the practice block and fell in the dust. She laughed, looking at her teacher for his reaction. He got off his horse and retrieved her rope and then handed it up to her. She smiled down at him and Beck felt as if he would burst with jealousy.

He had nothing against that guy except he wanted to shove him off a mountain and take his place.

"You're a good teacher," Mitch said. "Maybe you should go out there and help her."

"I'm not part of the rodeo. It's not my place."

Mitch laughed. "You own this whole place. If you want to teach a woman how to lasso something, no one's going to stop you—except Tommy who's clearly enjoying this."

"You know him?"

"Of course. We've been in the same show for weeks, and I've seen him do this at two other places. He finds a pretty lady, shows her some tricks, leaves her in the dust when we move on to the next rodeo."

"That's enough," Beck said. He went through the fence rails and stalked over to Nora's horse.

CHAPTER TWENTY-ONE

NORA RAISED HER arm to throw the rope, concentrating and lost in the moment. She knew she should be working with Steven, but when was the last time she'd had this much fun? When the cowboy had first invited her into the arena, she'd rationalized her *yes* in the name of building relationships with potential future clients for the Lodge.

"Nora."

The voice caught her off guard and she dropped the rope. Beck stood next to her horse looking…angry?

"I have time right now to review those reports," he said.

Nora was speechless. Beck wanted to talk about the progress reports she'd emailed him earlier in the day? He'd never wanted to do that before. And why was he flushed? It wasn't that hot, and she knew he hadn't just run up. He'd been over on the rail with Mitch, watching her.

Did he disapprove of her joining in the fun…or was it something else?

That spark between them had flickered, flared and then faded, which was all well and good, because it would make it easier to forget him. If she snuffed out her feelings when she thought of his smile and the way he made her feel like she could belong somewhere for the first time in a long time…well, letting it fade would make it easier for her to turn her back on Remedy Creek and move on, as she always did.

"If this is a good time," he added.

Nora almost wanted to laugh. In what world would this be a good time?

"Of course," she said. She *did* work for the man. "I would be happy to slide off this horse, dust off my hands and review a spreadsheet with you."

Tommy had backed off several steps. Nora assumed he either recognized Beck Duncan as the owner of this land or he noted the tone of Beck's voice, or he sensibly realized Beck had several inches and a lot of muscle over him.

Beck reached up with both hands, a silent invitation for her to let him help her down, just as they'd done before. This time felt different, though, as his hands circled her waist and he slowly set her on her feet. His movements were deliberate, as if he was handling a valuable possession.

She didn't belong to him or anyone, though, and moments like this, when their eyes met and she remembered every detail of the kiss she couldn't forget, well, these moments reminded her she needed to keep her head and heart clear or she'd…well, she'd get roped in. Give her heart away. Settle in knowing it could all be lost in the blink of an eye.

"My office," she said in as businesslike a tone as she could muster as they stood by the horse, Beck's hands still at her waist. *People were watching...*

"Okay," he said. He let go of her and instead put a hand at the small of her back as they left through a gate Mitch held open. Nora nodded at Mitch and smiled, and Mitch raised an eyebrow as if he was amused by something. She knew he went way back with Beck. Could he read his friend's thoughts? Not that it was difficult. It was obvious to Nora that Beck wanted her out of that rodeo arena and inside. With him.

It was temptingly attractive, being with him, reliving that kiss, feeling as if someone saw all the way through her and liked the view.

She forced her steps to remain steady as they went through a side door and entered the hallway that led to the offices behind the front desk.

People were all around because the hotel was well staffed now, preparing for a full house with the rodeo. Nora opened the door to her office, and they slipped inside before she considered the ramifications.

It was Bryan's office.

Beck stopped dead.

"Oh," Nora said, clearly realizing why Beck wasn't moving. "We can go somewhere else."

"It's okay," he said, but she saw his glance roving over items in the office—personal things and pictures his brother had left and she had not touched.

Nora could hardly believe Beck had finally stepped foot in his brother's office, but they were here. Together. Alone. She should keep it all business. It would be easier for him if they didn't talk about anything personal and got this over with fast so he could get out.

"I'm working hard to see if Steven will be a good fit for you and putting him through basically a working interview. He's catching on, he's—"

"I don't want to talk about Steven," Beck said.

"Oh," Nora paused. "I see. Since you're selling the place anyway, Steven may lose this job even if he gets it."

Maybe this was good. They should have an

honest conversation about what a sale would mean. Beck didn't respond.

"On that same subject, I'm worried about everyone who works here," she said. "So many good people who've been committed, dedicated."

"You're committed and dedicated," he said.

"But temporary. I'm not out of a job if you sell this place. I've already got my next assignment in Europe."

Beck leaned against the inside of the closed door, and the tension she'd seen in the arena seemed to melt out of him. He gave her a long look.

"Nora...do you ever get tired of running?"

NORA WALKED AROUND the other side of the desk, and Beck assumed she wanted to put space between them. Or between her and his question. He knew all about running and hiding. He hadn't physically left the ranch, but he'd found every avenue to avoid dealing with his brother's loss.

Until recently. He'd thought he'd found the one way he could face it—selling the Lodge. But Nora had reminded him almost daily that he still had a heart, even if he'd tried sealing it up tight. Breaking that seal had been painful, but every day the lid seemed to loosen.

He glanced away from Nora, who looked shocked by his question, and stared at the picture on the table by the window. He remembered the day of his college graduation as if it was last week, even though it had been ten years. His parents were on one side, smiling, but Beck had his arm around his brother on the other side.

It was a happy time. There had been a lot of happy times with his family. He hadn't let himself think about them in the past few years. He didn't want to be reminded of what he'd lost. But that picture reminded him of what he'd had. He wouldn't trade it, even though he wished he could go back in time and live it all again, even just for a day or an hour.

He swept his glance around the room, remembering the details. A lamp made by a local artisan, a polished cow skull he and Bryan had found along a trail once. A smaller-scale painting matching the Western art in the lobby. Beck had been in his brother's office plenty of times in the weeks before the hotel opened. It had been in this office that they'd had their final conversation. He hadn't been back since because he didn't think he could face it. He thought the office represented those last moments of bad blood between him and Bryan, the regret, the guilt.

But it didn't. It represented his brother whom he had loved and would always love.

"Beck?" Nora asked. "Are you okay?"

Now she was asking the questions.

"I…am," he said, surprising himself. He'd built up this moment in his mind as some insurmountable obstacle, a wall built by how much he had loved his brother and the pain of losing him. But it was also love that got him through the door just a moment ago.

Love. Nora had shown him love by listening to him, holding him when he'd grieved, and asking questions—no matter how hard they were to answer. She had shown him love and that he could love again. Did she have any idea how much that impacted him?

"Because of you," he said.

Nora opened a laptop screen and leaned over the desk to type. She avoided his glance.

"I mean it," he said. "You didn't intend it, but you got me in this office, which is more than anyone else has been able to do." Now that he recognized his feelings and opened his mouth, Beck was finding it hard to stop. "I'm glad it was you that your company sent out here."

Nora cleared her throat. "I'm glad, too. It's been a very interesting assignment so far, very good experience for me and I hope I've added value—"

"Stop, Nora. I don't want to talk about the Lodge."

"And you don't want to talk about Steven's role as general manager, either," she said. She finally looked up at him. "What do you want to talk about?"

"You," he said. He walked to the window, giving her space and a clear path to the door if she wanted to take it. He picked up a miniature red phone booth from a table by the window, remembering that day he and Bryan had visited London. There was also a picture of the two brothers on a ranch in Spain, astride horses and grinning. They'd had such fun that day, feeling at home in a place so far from here. Two such different feelings at the same time. Like aching for his brother but feeling close to him by being in the space he'd created for himself.

Nora abandoned the laptop and sat on the small couch by the window, taking one end of it, leaving space for him. Beck set the phone booth down carefully and then took the other end of the couch.

"Do you know why we've connected?" Beck asked.

"Have we…connected?"

"You know we have," he said quietly.

"Professionally, we've worked well together, and our goals—"

"Personally," Beck said. "You have grit and you work hard, and I'd like to think I have those same characteristics."

"You do."

"But you've also got something buried deep," he continued. "Mine was only buried for the last year or so." He swallowed, thinking of that family plot on the hillside. To his surprise, Nora reached over and rested her hand atop his. The warmth encouraged him to go on. "I don't know what you've got locked up inside, what keeps you on the road from hotel to hotel."

"It's my work. I love what I do."

"And no place has ever made you want to stay?" he asked.

Nora hesitated, and her professional mask slipped enough that he knew the answer to his question, no matter what she was going to say.

"If you get attached to a place, you lose your objectivity. You give yourself away too much."

"Is that bad, giving yourself away?"

"It is if you run the risk of losing everything," Nora said.

"Have you ever lost everything?"

Her expression changed and he knew he'd hit something. He was sorry to cause her pain, because it was something he knew a lot about. He also knew that healing started with ripping away an outer shell of protection.

"Just once."

"What happened?"

"We really shouldn't be talking about this," Nora said. "There's a lot to do to get ready for the influx of guests. Plus the extra food and beverage service the rodeo will need, and I really should find Steven."

Beck shrugged. "I still own this place, at least for now, and I think those things can wait."

"But you're my client, and I should look out for your best interests."

"I'm not just your client. Unless you go riding with all your clients, kiss them and make them open their hearts."

Nora's mouth opened and she stared at him for a moment. She withdrew her hand and crossed her arms over her chest. "I don't kiss my clients."

"Good."

"Or have personal conversations with them," she said.

Beck stood. He knew from experience there was no point forcing someone to talk about something they wanted to keep locked down. She'd have to come to it herself. But maybe he could show her how to do it. Give her something in return.

"Before you came here," he said, walking slowly to his brother's desk and keeping his back to her, "I didn't think I'd ever step foot in this office. I never even came to the Lodge. I guess I was just hoping it would disappear. I foolishly thought if I forgot about it, it would hurt less." He turned to face her and leaned on the desk—his brother's desk. "You asked too many questions and made me face the reality of the situation, which also opened up the wound as if it was fresh."

"Sorry," she said.

"Don't be. Five weeks ago, I was still running from what hurt." He crossed his feet at the ankles and settled his weight against the desk. "Look at me now."

She smiled. "I'm glad."

"I know about running, Nora. I know all about it. I guess that's why I thought you might feel safe telling me why you keep doing it." He gave a little shrug. "Kindred spirit and all."

Nora got up and looked out the window. He was sure she was going to make some excuse to leave, and he wasn't going to push her. He cared about her too much. She was so smart and good with people. Giving. Sweet. Caring. He smiled. And brave. What other greenhorn would enter a rodeo arena and try throwing a lasso from horseback? What other beginner rider would have gotten a horse from the stable to find him out on a trail, determined to meet him where he was?

"My parents owned and managed an apartment complex," she said at last. "It was where I grew up. We had a three-bedroom apartment on the first floor of the main building, and my brothers shared a room. I had my own. My dad used to say I was his princess, and I would inherit the kingdom someday."

Beck didn't say anything, but he pushed off the desk and stood next to Nora at the window. He ignored the rodeo and all the activity and instead raised his eyes to the mountains in the distance, just as Nora was doing.

"My dad loved that place. He'd inherited it from his parents and invested heavily in updating it. So many families lived there. It was like our own little bubble. I knew the other kids, played with them on a playground on the property, swam at the pool. I thought it was an ideal childhood. When I got older, I started working for my parents, doing odd jobs, helping with cleaning and maintenance. I was truly thinking of taking it over someday—my brothers were older and not interested, but I wanted to learn everything."

"Smart," Beck said.

"When I was eighteen, I went with my dad to the top floor and used the roof access. There was a leak in one of the apartments, near the outer edge. He wouldn't let me go out on the roof because it was too dangerous, but he wanted to see if he could locate the leak and maybe repair it himself, probably to save money."

Beck had a sick feeling about where this story was going. He wanted to reach for Nora, put an arm around her, but he sensed that would make her break and he wanted her to finish the story—both for herself and for him so he could understand her pain.

"He got to the edge and leaned over to look. I was so eager to know what was going on. I called out to him to ask, but there was no answer. That's when I heard screaming from below, and I knew."

Beck gave in and reached for Nora, pulling her close to his side. They both kept their eyes on the mountains, but he wanted to give her warmth and comfort.

"I crept to the edge of the roof and looked down. He was gone," she said. "Just like that."

"I'm sorry," Beck said.

He felt her shudder, and he turned and kissed her temple. She looked up at him with tears shining in her eyes. "After he…died, we discovered he was in pretty deep, debt-wise. The bank…well, we had to sell the place." She drew a deep breath. "And get out. Our home was gone. My future plans were gone. Everything was gone."

"Where did you go?"

"My mother and I stayed on for almost a year, working for the new owner and staying in a cramped bachelor apartment, but then his sympathy ran out and we had to leave. Mom went to live with one of my brothers, and I went to college, but I didn't have enough money to finish. I left after a few semesters and, once again, I was out of a home and a future."

"And then you started working in hospitality," Beck said.

"Yes. A hotel in Atlanta, where I got some good experience, and then for Total Hospitality where I've been for ten years now." She took a deep breath and crossed her arms over her chest again as if she was reassuring herself. "My homes are all temporary, depending on what property I'm helping, but at least I know that going in. I control the story, and I keep moving because, ironically, it's how I always have a place to call home."

Beck watched a bird soar past the window and out across the valley. He let Nora's words hang in the silent office for a moment, but he was afraid to let the opportunity totally go. He might not get another chance.

"What if you found a place that felt like home to you?" He turned and kissed Nora's forehead gently. He wanted to say so much more.

Nora looked up and met his eyes. "I'd be afraid to take a chance on it all being gone in a heartbeat."

"No matter how right it felt?" Beck asked. "If you really loved…that place?"

She shook her head. "If I really fell in love, it would make it that much harder when it all fell apart."

CHAPTER TWENTY-TWO

JUDY STRAIGHTENED UP and waved when Beck pulled up in front of the ranch house with Mitch in the passenger seat.

"I picked up a hitchhiker who was hungry for his mother's cooking," Beck said through the open window.

"He was just here last night," she said, smiling. Both men got out of the truck and Mitch dropped a kiss on the top of his mom's head. "Wash your hands. Dinner is about to come out of the oven."

Mitch went inside, and Beck lingered on the porch while Judy finished watering the potted plants.

"How is the rodeo setup going over at the Lodge?" she asked.

"Under control. Nora runs a tight operation."

"And the new manager trainee?"

Beck shrugged. That guy was never going to make it. He couldn't get the image out of his head of Steven declining to try a rodeo trick and backing away so fast he risked falling on his rump.

And Nora cheerfully accepting the challenge as if she was part of the show, part of everything there. Including his heart.

"I haven't seen enough of the guy to tell," Beck said. "But I'm sure not going to hire him as assistant ranch manager."

Judy laughed. "I was hoping you were keeping that job open for Mitch, in case he decides to come home and take up his old bunk again."

"But?" Beck asked.

"He seems happy. I think some travel is good for him, seeing new sights and meeting new people. Maybe he was getting in a rut, and this is what he's meant to be doing, and maybe he'll get it out of his system and come home happy to be here. Either way," she said, raising both hands, "I just want him to be happy."

"Can't argue with that," Beck agreed, even though he knew full well that he had argued with that very idea with his own brother. He'd thought he'd known what would make someone else happy and what path his life should have taken. It was easy to want to do that for people you truly loved.

"I'm glad his circuit brought him back home for a little while, though," she said. "It almost feels like closure, like a full circle." Beck sat on the porch railing and Judy put down her watering can and took the place next to him. "Loving someone is hard," she said. "You have to hand over a chunk of your own heart in the process and hope it comes back to you."

He thought of Nora and how hard it was for her to love after losing her father like that. And then he thought of Riley who had lost his brother. He and Riley shared that grief, but he'd hardly done anything about it because he was so roped in by his own feelings.

Maybe it was time.

After dinner with a dozen ranch hands—a dinner lively with Mitch's rodeo stories—Beck crept silently into his brother's room and picked up the small box from the top of his dresser. He pocketed it, got in his truck and headed for town.

Riley lived in an apartment over her family's restaurant. He texted her from the door at the bottom of her staircase and asked if she'd go for a walk with him. She joined him in just minutes.

"What's up?" she asked. "Did you have some questions about the menu I'm working on for the Lodge's grand reopening?"

Beck sucked in a breath. "Grand reopening?"

Riley attempted a smile. "Not officially, but that's pretty much what it is. With the rodeo and the full house, it's…well, it feels like a second chance for that place."

The box in his pocket felt heavy. Bryan would never get a second chance, and Beck would never get to tell his brother he loved him and believed in him. He didn't know how much Riley had healed from losing Bryan, but he did know she deserved to have the ring.

They crossed the street and started down the path that led through the healing forest attached to Wellness Springs. The walkway wound between pines whose fragrance mingled with the spring that fueled Remedy Creek's reputation for healing. He hadn't walked this way in a long time. Had he been avoiding it since Bryan died?

"It's nice out tonight," Riley said. "Not too hot, but not buggy either. I like evenings like this. Bryan and I used to walk here, you know?"

Beck nodded.

"I think it inspired the trails he had planned for the Lodge," Riley added. "Of course, he only got part of those done."

Beck paused near a bench and gestured to it. They sat in silence for a while. The sun was setting, its colored rays obscured by the pines around them—those same pines that made the trail feel safe, sheltered.

"There's something I should have told you a long time ago," Beck said. "I'm sorry I didn't. It was wrong, but I…well, I've been a mess."

Riley nodded. "Me, too."

"Lately, though, something has started to become clear to me. I know I'll never move on from what happened, but I think there's a way to move forward."

Riley met his glance. "One step at a time. That's what I've been telling myself. Some days, I think I'm gonna be all right, and some days, I'm right back to last October."

"Same," Beck said. "I'm sorry I haven't been a good brother to you."

"You're not, technically—"

"I would have been," he said, gently interrupting her. "That's what I wanted to tell you. Before he passed away, Bryan..." He swallowed and vowed to keep it together for Riley's sake. "Bought a ring."

Riley took in a quick breath and then let out a choked sob.

"He showed me the ring and said he was going to ask you to marry him as soon as the chaos of the grand opening was over with. It's been on his dresser ever since."

Tears flowed freely down Riley's cheeks, and she didn't bother to wipe them away. Beck hoped they were carrying her sorrow away with them. Was there any happiness mixed with her pain?

"Can I see it sometime?" she asked.

Beck fished the small box from his jeans pocket. He pressed it, still closed, into Riley's palm. She put one hand over the other and held the box as if it was a sacred object she was protecting. Beck waited quietly. He could almost feel his brother's presence, could almost hear his voice telling Riley to go ahead and open the box.

Riley sniffled, and he wished he had a handkerchief for her. He didn't know how to help her in her grief. He hadn't known how to help himself over the past year, but one thing he knew was that he'd only faced it when he was ready. And he'd had help. Nora had helped him. She'd opened his heart, even if she didn't want him to love her. He didn't want his feelings to remain closed in a box, forever on the top of a dresser, gathering dust.

Love had to be shared.

He put an arm around Riley's shoulders and hugged her close to him on the bench. "I think you should open it when you're ready," he said.

Riley nodded. "I'm just taking a minute to imagine it, to imagine Bryan going and picking it out and holding that secret in his heart. He knew the last time I kissed him at that party. He never got to ask me to marry him, but he knew he was going to. And he knew I was going to say yes. I'm sure of it."

Beck fought tears. Riley was so brave and loving, even at a moment like this.

She took a deep breath and opened her hands. She looked at the pink velvet box for a moment, and then slowly opened the lid. Inside was a diamond set in rose gold. A fresh wave of tears flowed, and Beck held her while she sobbed, but she finally calmed her breath and said, "Thank you for giving me this."

Beck shook his head. "I should have done it long ago."

Riley covered his hand with hers. "Sometimes I think about how much I loved him, and I let that hurt wash over me like a storm. It's so painful, but I feel a little better every time I let it happen, like love is slowly healing me."

He nodded, remembering that night he'd sobbed and Nora had held him. "I think I know what you mean."

NORA TUCKED HER tablet under her arm as she shook hands with the rodeo's publicity manager, Gary. He had just arrived from the airport and Nora was giving him the tour of the hotel property and amenities.

"I'll be posting throughout the day tomorrow," Nora said. "Mostly about the rodeo, but I'll also be featuring the Lodge, of course. I've talked to the performers and managers throughout the week while they've been setting up, and they shared with me the best potential events for good exposure."

"Not to make a joke at your expense," Gary said with a smile, "but this isn't my first rodeo."

Nora laughed. "It actually is my first, but I've been living and working here at the Lodge for over a month. I've learned the basics about riding and I can tell a cow from a bull."

"We'll have to recruit you for our rodeo management team," Gary said. He had salt-and-pepper hair and deep wrinkles, and Nora could tell he'd been in show business long enough to be a smooth talker.

"I've got a job waiting for me across the Atlantic when I finish my assignment here."

Gary smiled. "Your life is way more exciting than mine. I'm moving on to Idaho after this."

Nora wondered for a moment what Idaho was like. Were there beautiful mountains that changed colors with the sun throughout the day? Did elk and deer roam the open spaces? Were the people there a mix of tough but warm as she'd found the folk in Remedy Creek?

Beck was tough but warm. Smart but vulnerable. Kind but determined. She would miss him and Judy and Allie and a lot of other people, and she wondered how long it would be before they forgot about her. Considering that Beck would be selling the hotel, she expected her memory to disappear quickly, absorbed by the inevitable changes in management and staffing. Who knew if the new owners would keep the patio fire ring or the horses in the riding stable?

"We should talk about shared hashtags," Nora said, turning away from melancholy thoughts. "If we use the same ones, we'll help each other cross-promote."

"I usually use the name of the rodeo and some fun ones like #cowboylife, #notmyfirstrodeo and #rodeoclown in addition to tagging our performers. Some of them have quite a following."

Nora wrote down the hashtags and shared some of hers with Gary, most of them incorporating the name of the Lodge and Remedy Creek. She continued walking toward the patio area where she found Steven sitting with a cup of coffee, his back to the sunset. Nora felt a ripple of irritation. The man was technically there on an interview. Even though it was early evening, the hotel workday didn't end at five o'clock, especially if a person wanted to make a good impression and a massive rodeo had filled the premises.

Even if Steven was just taking a quick, well-deserved coffee break, why on earth was his back to the gorgeous sunset? She wanted to spin his chair around and show him what he was missing. There was nothing like a Wyoming sunset on the mountains behind the Lodge, not even the sunsets she'd seen on the Gulf Coast of Florida or in Hawaii. Steven had been there a few days; certainly that was long enough for him to notice the incredible natural beauty and its role as a huge selling point for the Lodge?

Still, he was the only candidate she had. "Steven," she said as she stood in front of him where at least *she* had a nice view of the sun on the mountain. "I'd like you to meet Gary who handles publicity for the rodeo. Gary, this is Steven. He's here interviewing for the general manager position for the Lodge. If all goes well, you two might be seeing more of each other in the future."

Nora observed their interaction and listened to their conversation for a few minutes. This was a working interview, and even off-the-cuff discussions added up and would be part of her hiring decision. Although Steven was professional and friendly, he gave one-word answers on anything pertaining to horses or his interest in the rodeo. Nora couldn't forget Steven's reaction the previous day when one of the performers, Tommy, had invited them both into the arena for a lesson.

She also couldn't forget what happened after that when Beck's strong arms had lifted her down from the saddle. She knew he was physically strong, but she was also surprised by his emotional strength when he'd faced his brother's office. Instead of dwelling on Bryan's loss, he'd asked about her. Probed her feelings. Refused to let her take the easy way out.

She'd done the same for him that night at his

house. It was the kind of thing a person did when they cared about someone else.

After Gary returned to the lobby where he had a meeting scheduled with the rodeo's manager, Nora walked Steven back to the arena.

"What do you think?" she asked. "Are we ready?"

"The hotel is ready. Half of the rooms are full tonight, and we have forty check-ins tomorrow. The staff seems competent, and the system is running. I checked with the housekeeping manager and food service."

"Good work," Nora said. "The managers are all locals and very dedicated. They're great to work with."

Steven nodded. "As long as they do their jobs and stay on budget."

"Department budgets aren't set in stone yet," Nora said. "The past year has not been what the original owner envisioned, and it's only been in the past month that we've started to build a set of metrics. The rodeo, a huge event, will throw off those metrics, so getting a sense of continuity and expectations will be part of the challenge for you if you become the new manager."

"That's one of my favorite parts of the job," Steven said.

Nora wondered for a moment if he was serious. Sitting in an office looking at reports and forecasting was the least favorite part of the job for her. She preferred scenery, people and food. Loved the click of her heels on a polished lobby floor, the ding of the elevators, or the feel of the trail under her cowboy boots.

Nora nodded politely and strode to the kitchen to see if there was a sandwich she could take up to her room for a quick bite before spending the evening double-checking everything for the next day. It was going to be a busy one with check-ins coming in during the first half of the day and an opening exhibition in the area during the evening.

"Hey," Riley said. "Dinner service is about to get busy in here for the hotel guests. We already set up the banquet room for the rodeo performers and staff. What can I do for you?"

Nora smiled at her friend. Riley had agreed to a few shifts during the busy rodeo in addition to redesigning the menu to reflect local flavors with a luxury twist. "I was hoping for a quick sandwich to take back to my room where I'm going to enjoy about thirty minutes of downtime before I dive back in."

"Busy times, but it's good that way," Riley said. She walked over and pulled a tray from a cooler. "Chicken salad okay?"

"Perfect. Thank you."

Riley slid a sandwich into a take-out box and

added some salad greens. She smiled as she worked, and Nora was glad to see her looking happy. She'd been worried about burdening Riley with work in addition to her full-time job at her family's restaurant. Not to mention the emotional impact of being back in the place her boyfriend had loved so much. Nora had not been back to the place where her father had died over ten years ago—not since she and her mom were turned out, grieving and homeless.

"I'm so grateful you're helping us," Nora said, tamping down her own memories. "Thank you."

"Honestly, it's my pleasure," Riley said.

And that was when Nora noticed it. A ring—a diamond ring—hung on a chain around Riley's neck. The kitchen light reflected off it, and Nora couldn't help staring.

Riley, clearly noticing Nora's attention, put a hand to her throat and toyed with the ring. She glanced around at the kitchen staff who were all working at a steady pace. It looked to Nora as if everything was under control.

"Do you have a minute?" Riley asked. She nodded toward a door leading outside.

"Of course," Nora said, though she was sure she knew what her friend wanted to tell her.

They stepped outside and stood under the overhang of the Lodge. That side of the building didn't offer a sunset view, but mountains were all around them with their steady presence.

"Beck came to see me yesterday," Riley said. "He said there was something he needed to tell me, and we went for a long walk." Her fingers were still curled around the ring.

So Beck had finally given his brother's ring to Riley. He had changed so much in the short time she'd known him. Nora was stunned.

Had she changed, too? She'd never gotten so comfortable somewhere and had tempting thoughts of staying put. Was it Wyoming or Beck?

"I can't believe it's been almost a year since the grand opening," Riley said. "The last time I saw Bryan."

"He must have been a wonderful man," Nora said.

Riley nodded. "He was. We'd been friends for years. I can't remember ever not being friends with him and Beck. We grew up together, and then it turned into love." Her eyes filled with tears. "It didn't happen all of a sudden like it does for some people, lightning out of the blue. For us, our feelings for each other just got stronger and stronger until we finally admitted we loved each other." Tears slid down her face, but she gave a little laugh. "He caved in first. Told me he loved me the day he broke ground on this place. For almost two years, I watched the Lodge get built while Bryan and I got closer and closer. We were always talking about building a life together."

Nora put an arm around Riley's shoulders and tilted her head to touch Riley's.

"I suspected he was going to pop the question, and I even thought it might be the night of the grand opening, but it was such a busy time. Maybe he didn't want his proposal to be overshadowed. Ever since he died… I've wondered about it. Until last night. Beck gave me closure. Finally. He said his brother did plan to ask me to marry him after the grand opening, and this ring was sitting in a little box on Bryan's dresser this whole time."

Nora felt Riley tremble, and she couldn't even imagine what Riley must be feeling. Did it double her sorrow to know Bryan never got the chance, or was it a consolation knowing that he'd loved her so much he bought a ring?

"Are you glad Beck gave you the ring?"

She felt Riley nod. "In a strange way, it feels like I can move on now. I don't know what I'm moving on to exactly, but I guess I can put some of my questions to rest and start the next phase of healing." She paused. "It's all phases, and I don't know when or if I'll ever be done. Beck said the same thing last night."

"It must have been good to talk with someone

who understands," Nora said. Tears stung her own eyes as she thought of the courage it would have taken for Beck to seek Riley out and give her the ring, completing the circle his brother wasn't able to. Just picturing it made Nora want to drive to Beck's house and put her arms around him, feel his stubble against her cheek and give him whatever comfort she could offer.

"Yeah. It was good for Beck, too. I didn't think he was ever going to be okay, but lately I've seen a change in him. You deserve a lot of credit for it, I think. Bringing the Lodge back to life has made Beck acknowledge the pain he buried last fall. You're good for him," Riley said. "He trusts you. And I think he needed you to come along in his life."

Nora fought her tears, but they slipped down her cheeks anyway.

"It took a lot of courage for him to come to me and give me this ring, and my wish for him is that he uses some of that courage on himself and finds what makes him happy."

Nora couldn't speak. Instead, she just kept her arm around the friend she'd made. She was going to miss Riley and all the people she'd met at Remedy Creek. They were more than notes in the logs she kept to document her work experiences. Remedy Creek was part of her heart now and had crashed through the barrier she'd kept up for more than ten years. Breaking that wall meant breaking her own heart when she left, but she couldn't stay.

Beck was going to sell the beautiful Lodge, and Nora didn't want to be part of that. Didn't want to see it sold off for the highest offer. Because she knew that it would ultimately break Beck's heart to make that mistake, and it would be too painful to watch him do it. Not when she cared about him so much that his pain felt like her own.

CHAPTER TWENTY-THREE

BECK PUT ON his hat and reminded himself not to be a grump about the rodeo. Sure, it was a silly depiction of what true ranch life was like, but people enjoyed it. Did ranchers really do fancy roping and tempt dangerous bulls to spear them? Absolutely not. But it wouldn't kill him to laugh a little and enjoy the show, especially when someone else was in charge.

Nora had it all under control. The Lodge was at capacity with guests, according to the reports he'd read before bed last night. The kitchen was running full steam. The grounds were under full utilization. If he rode Hercules on the nearby mountain and looked down, he wouldn't see a giant stain of asphalt mocking him with an empty parking lot, because there was a car in almost every space. The grounds around the hotel would be alive with performers, animals and spectators.

It was a far cry from the deafening silence of the past year, and he had one person to thank for it. If the hotel management company had sent someone else, it was possible that the hotel would be operating smoothly and the rodeo would be there. Those were business decisions. But someone else wouldn't have brought him what Nora had brought him. Peace. Healing. Love.

That tingle in his chest when he thought of her, the way her smile broke into his thoughts when he least expected it, the lightness in his step when she was around, and the way he wanted to wrap his arms around her to both shut out the rest of the world and keep her in his—he knew this was love, but he didn't know what to do about it.

It was still early when he got to the Lodge. The rodeo wouldn't really get going until later in the day, but there were mini-exhibitions starting midmorning with some cowboy talks for kids and roping clinics for adults and kids. Portable grandstands were set up on both sides of the arena, their silver benches gleaming in the morning sun. They were empty this early, except for one person.

Nora. She had a plate in her lap and a cup next to her, steam rising from it. She'd propped her feet on the bench in front of her, and he saw that she was wearing fancy white cowboy boots. Were they the ones she'd bought in town that he hadn't seen her wear yet? Maybe she thought it was now or never, with her time here growing short and an actual rodeo in town. She'd be gone in just over a week. He almost flinched when he thought about it, as if lightning had struck nearby. It both startled him and motivated him into action.

Beck didn't wait for an invitation. Instead, he strode up the grandstand steps, taking them two at a time with his long legs until he reached the top bench. He sat next to Nora.

"I'm pretty familiar with that hotel behind us these days," he said. "And I do know there are more comfortable places to have breakfast."

"Are you kidding me? That place is crowded, bursting at the seams." She smiled and held out her plate. "Want half?"

"I ate at the house. Judy outdid herself for breakfast because she won't be cooking dinner tonight. All the hands will be here for the show."

They sat in companionable silence for a moment. The sun was up, and the night's coolness was gone, though it lingered in the metal bench beneath him. He didn't mind it. Being with Nora was like having his own source of warmth. This place was going to be like a grave—again—when she left. Was it a good thing he was washing his hands of it for good? It would be too painful to walk through it without Nora's presence.

"Why are you eating out here?" he asked.

She shrugged and sipped her coffee. "Calm before the storm, I guess. I just wanted to soak it all in before too many people are around. It feels like—"

She stopped.

"Feels like what?" he asked.

She shook her head. "It's strange. It won't make sense to you."

"Try me."

"When I'm alone and walking around the Lodge, touching the leaves, feeling the wind from the mountain, it almost feels like…home."

Beck stilled.

"Of course it isn't my home, but I've put a lot of my heart into this place. I always care about the hotels I manage, but I never get attached and risk feeling like I don't want to leave."

He swallowed. "Do you not want to leave?"

Nora stood and put on her cowboy hat. "I have a job to do for the next few days here. With the rodeo on the premises, and hiring a manager. Then a new job's waiting for me in France." She picked up her plate and cup. "It doesn't matter what I want."

Beck stood. "Of course it does. If you like it here, maybe you could…stay and be the permanent manager."

Nora shook her head and her hat tilted almost comically, but there was nothing funny about this conversation. His feelings were so tied up, he felt as if he was one of the rodeo calves being lassoed for someone else's entertainment.

"No way can that work," Nora said. "First of all, my company depends on me. And secondly, once you sell this place, there's no guarantee they'll keep me or anyone else. It won't be the same and I don't want to be around to see it change."

He didn't want it to change either. When it had been empty and silent, he'd only thought of getting rid of it so he could stop feeling guilty. But Nora had brought it back to life and it was, once again, the place his brother had dreamed of. Would the buyer care about anyone's hopes and dreams?

"I thought updating hotels was your line of work," Beck said.

"It is, but I stay objective wherever I go. The one time I failed at that was at the place on the Riviera. I'm not sure if I told you, but that was my first job at THM. I loved that hotel. The owners sold it a few years later, and the new owners… they didn't do a great job. I got called back in since I was familiar with the place, but I couldn't handle seeing it so different that second time. I wasn't objective, and I failed at that assignment. That hotel closed. My punishment was getting pulled from that job and assigned here."

"Punishment," Beck said.

"But it hasn't been that for me," Nora said. "I've fallen in love, which is why I have to leave here, and the sooner the better. I'll be on my way as soon as the rodeo is finished."

Fallen in love. With him or the Lodge? Beck could hardly breathe, but Nora started to walk down the grandstand and he wanted to catch her attention, make her stay.

"What about the Lodge and the manager and..." He wanted to say *what about me*.

"Don't worry," Nora said. "I always leave hotels in good hands." She turned and continued down the steps. A blond braid swayed below her hat and her boots clicked on the metal. If he didn't do something, those images would flood him with regret long into the winter. The thought of Nora leaving had worried him for days, and now that it was on the horizon, it choked him like a dust storm.

"Nora, I don't want you to go," he said.

She paused but didn't turn around. An eternity of silence passed.

"I can't stay and risk getting my heart broken when you sell this place," she said.

She continued down the steps, and Beck let her go. He sat on the top row of the grandstand where the empty arena waited, silently, below him and the Lodge's windows caught the morning sun as if they were mirrors showing him what was in his heart.

When a hurricane had hit the Caribbean hotel where Nora was assigned, she remembered what a blessing it was to be so busy she didn't have time to think about how scared she was. As a girl who grew up in Atlanta, Georgia, a direct hurricane hit was a new experience. There had been days of warnings, and a solid hurricane plan was in existence. She remembered that time vividly—the anticipation, the unreal sense that the storm might not hit after all when the skies felt so calm in the hours before the first bands of wind. She'd mobilized everyone, called on the locals for their experience and expertise, and was thoroughly revved up on adrenaline and coffee by the time the rain started. She'd shoved a phone and a flashlight in the pockets of her raincoat and ridden out the storm on a wave of frightened exhilaration.

The cleanup afterward had been the nightmare. The heat returned after the storm, but not the power. They had no air-conditioning, and ruin was everywhere. People displaced, lives in tatters. She wished she'd been able to leave in the moments before the storm hit instead of weeks afterward when the smell of wet carpet and soggy possessions permeated everything.

As Nora walked through the lobby doors now to take up her post behind the front desk, she wished she was leaving today or tomorrow, before the rodeo packed up for its next stop, taking all the noise and excitement with it. There wouldn't be soaked piles of ruin left behind, but there would be a hotel property ripe for listing on the market.

"I have a few things to ask you about," Steven said. He stood behind the counter in the place she usually took. His presence there rankled, making her feel displaced for a moment, but she reminded herself that this was what she wanted—a replacement so she could leave without falling any deeper in love with Wyoming, the Lodge or Beck. It had taken every ounce of her courage to walk away from him in those grandstands. But she'd done it. He'd asked her to stay and manage the place. He was offering her a job, nothing more, and she already had a job.

"Of course," she said. "Let's go back to the office."

Inside, Nora pointed to the chair behind the desk to indicate Steven should sit there. She put her hat on the desk and then she chose a seat by the window where she could view the green and brown grasses, the small trees planted after construction a year ago, and the larger pines that had been there for perhaps a century, undisturbed by the Lodge. The hotel seemed as if it was meant to be there.

"Staffing for the restaurant may be too high

because the rodeo contracts with food trucks. They'll arrive and set up in the next few hours," Steven said.

Nora nodded. "Fair point, but we don't have any data to guide us. The rodeo has shared presale ticket numbers, but with the perfect weather, there could be a lot more people coming in for the day. Plus, it's hot out, which means some guests will prefer to come inside and eat in the air-conditioning."

Steven looked skeptical. "I can't believe there are that many people within a hundred miles. On the way from the airport, I passed way more cows than people, and cows aren't coming to an old-fashioned rodeo."

"You might be surprised by how many people show up," Nora said. "Either way, we don't want to disappoint anyone with slow service, so even if our staffing seems too high, it's still a safe choice."

"You're the boss," Steven said.

"Only until I find a new one." Nora smiled. She wanted to like Steven. He had a solid résumé and there was nothing wrong with his ideas. She sighed. This was the problem with letting her feelings get involved. She was making the business of hiring a general manager a personal decision, as if she owned the place.

There was also the matter of the inside knowledge Beck had shared about the sale. Was it unscrupulous of her to offer Steven a job that could be cut short in a matter of months with the property's sale?

"How am I doing?" Steven asked. He looked up from his laptop with eyebrows raised.

"You're doing fine," she said. "Have you ever done a working interview like this?"

He laughed. "With a rodeo?"

"Maybe not that." Nora chuckled. "Do you have any feedback for me on this interview process? Something I can use in the future? You can be honest. I'm going to recommend you to the owner if you're still interested in the job."

She had to. He was good enough, even if unimaginative.

Steven looked away for a moment. "I'm getting a good feel for the place, I think. Even if I didn't try getting on a horse and throwing a rope. I'm not sure I'll ever get there." He paused and gave a self-deprecating smile. "I guess I was expecting something more formal. Reviewing records, sitting down with heads of departments, that kind of thing."

"I understand," Nora said. "As you know, though, there isn't much historical data, and you're also here at a time when heads of departments are busy. I think you'll get a truer picture of the hotel when the rodeo packs up and leaves."

She would be sorry to see the rodeo go. She'd texted her mother a picture of last night's dress rehearsal and then her mother had called her. Nora didn't let it go to voicemail and call her back at a more convenient time like she often did. She'd taken the call on the second ring and chatted with her mother for an hour, telling her all about her assignment in Wyoming. Her mother had told her she sounded happy, and she'd also said the Lodge sounded like a place Nora's dad would have loved. It was the first time in a long time she and her mother had talked about her dad, and it didn't feel like a heavy weight in her heart as it usually did.

As she'd lain in bed last night, she'd reflected that her mother sounded happy, too. Maybe because Nora was. Love was like that. Nora loved Beck and seeing him heal and find a path toward happiness was her reward.

"I'm interested in finding out more about the career trajectory before I say yes for sure," Steven said.

Nora respected his measured statement, but in her heart she didn't understand it. How could the man not be in love with the Lodge and the mountains and the people? Was it really going to take much longer for him to be sure it was a great place to work? She'd been in the hotel business longer than he had, though. Maybe she was looking for something different than he was.

She looked out the window again. A tall rider on a golden brown horse passed by outside. There were dozens of horses and riders milling about, most of them with the traveling show, but she would know this particular rider anywhere. Beck did things to her stomach whenever she saw him.

She rose and went to the window. Beck rode to the edge of the arena and someone—Mitch, she believed—opened the gate. Once inside, Beck took a rope from his saddle and began swinging it in a circle, gracefully, as if he'd done it thousands of times. He was still talking to Mitch who stood next to his horse, but then he started to draw a crowd. Hotel guests who'd finished breakfast and moved outside gravitated toward the arena. The other rodeo performers who were there warming up and rehearsing moved aside, giving Beck space.

Was he putting on a show of his own? The arena wasn't far from the hotel, but Nora felt the need to get closer.

She grabbed her hat from the desk and started for the door.

"Are you leaving? I have more questions," Steven said.

"I have to…check on something. I'll see you later."

"But—" he began, but Nora was already through the door and heading for the hotel exit.

She strode toward the arena, mesmerized by the rhythmic circling of Beck's rope. He sat tall in the saddle, balanced, as if he'd been born on horseback. Would she ever achieve that grace in the saddle? The thought slowed her stride when she reflected that she might never get the chance.

Someone was clapping and whooping and Nora sped up her pace again, eager to see the show. Anxious to be closer to Beck, though she had no claim over him. Mitch was on horseback now, too, astride a gray horse. He also swirled a rope. The cheering got louder as Nora approached and she found a spot on the rail where she could watch.

CHAPTER TWENTY-FOUR

HE SHOULDN'T BE showing off. The real rodeo show was hours away, but Beck couldn't resist taking Mitch's challenge. And so he was attempting to out-rope Mitch—a man he'd worked with almost all his life.

This wasn't work, though; it was play. He and Bryan used to goof off and challenge each other to do riding tricks and make fancy lasso attempts. Sometimes Mitch had joined in. It had been too long since Beck had any fun, and he was probably past the age where he should care about impressing anyone.

There was only one person he wanted to impress anyway. But Beck doubted his skill in the rodeo ring was the way to Nora's heart. He'd tried asking her to stay, but he'd failed to say the one thing that might persuade her. He hadn't told her why he wanted her to stay. Why he needed her in his life. The thought hit him so hard he missed a calf by three feet. People gathered against the fence rails laughed and booed.

"Losing your touch, boss?" Mitch asked with a grin.

Beck was on the verge of dismounting and heading straight for the Lodge, unwilling to wait another minute to tell Nora he loved her. But as he started to swing his leg over the saddle, he saw Nora lined up along the fence. She was smiling at him, clapping. He settled back down on his horse.

"I'll give you that one since you were distracted," Mitch said in a low voice. "But you better make this one count."

Beck tipped his hat toward Nora and caught her gaze. She blushed at the attention at first, but then her expression turned serious, as if she could read something in his. Her lips parted and she put a hand over her heart as if she wanted to calm it. Everything stilled around them, and Beck felt as if the entire crowd was watching his interaction with Nora.

She backed away, and Beck lost sight of her as she was absorbed by the other people watching the rodeo warm-up. It felt like the sun going behind a cloud.

"You win," Beck said to Mitch. He swung down from the saddle and made his way to a gate at the edge of the arena, determined to find Nora and tell her the truth. He loved her and the thought of her leaving made him feel as if he was falling into a deep canyon. She had to want to stay, though. It had to be her choice, but he would never forgive himself if he didn't plead his case.

A big man stood in his way at the gate. "Beck Duncan, right? Just the man I was hoping to run into."

Beck had Hercules on a lead rope, and he reached for the gate latch with the other. Nora was partway around the arena the last time he'd seen her in the crowd, and he couldn't wait to get to her. Everything had become clear. She hadn't just brought the Lodge to life, she'd done the same for him. He could never have his brother back again, but he could love someone. For the first time in a long time, he knew loving someone was worth the risk.

Beck ignored the man and brushed past him.

"I'm August Camden. I own the rodeo, and we're looking for a new permanent location," the man said. "A little birdie told me this place might be for sale, and I thought we could sit down and—"

The crowd had gone silent in one of those odd synchronized moments that happen sometimes, and the man's words rang out loudly in the valley. There were out-of-towners and locals in the crowd. A few hotel employees. Some of his ranch hands. People who cared about the Lodge and had a stake just because it was there in the place they called home. The shocked silence was like a lead weight, and Beck knew for certain in that moment that he would never sell his brother's Lodge. *His* Lodge.

He stopped and turned toward the man, but his eyes were on the beautiful three-story building with its huge windows reflecting the mountains. *His* mountains. Was it just five weeks ago that he'd considered this part of his land an albatross around his neck? Everything had changed. It had started that night in his truck when he'd rested his head on the steering wheel and let his grief take over. Nora had been there. And then at his home where he'd told her about Bryan. And then about the ring he'd finally had the courage to give Bryan's beloved.

It had all been about love, the whole time. Nora had brought him that. He glanced around, hoping for a glimpse of her. He saw a white hat farther back in the crowd, but he couldn't be sure it was her.

"This ranch is my home," he said, loudly enough for everyone around him to hear. "This Lodge was my brother's dream." He didn't care that his voice hitched on that last sentence. "He wanted this to be a place where people could wake up to a Wyoming sunrise, ride the trails and mountains, and bunk down for the night. And it is. It's not for sale."

Beck was vaguely aware that Mitch was standing nearby along with dozens of other people, but the only person who needed to hear his words was Nora. He searched the crowd again and finally saw her blond braid swinging below her hat as she walked toward the riding stable.

"Everything's for sale," August Camden said with a chuckle. "For the right price. You haven't heard me out."

Beck handed his horse's lead rope to Mitch. "There's no price that would make me sell out on my brother's memory." Beck ducked his head to the side and caught a glimpse of Nora just as she entered the riding stable. The crowd felt thick around him, and he struggled to extricate himself.

"This place is exactly what we need for the rodeo—" August began.

Beck was already pushing through the people watching the rodeo warmup, but he heard Mitch's voice behind him.

"All due respect, Mr. Camden, but I don't think you're going to budge Beck Duncan on this."

Beck pressed past the people and got into the open just in time to see Nora on a horse. Riding away. There was no way he was letting her ride away alone. He turned and found Mitch, who handed over Hercules's reins with a wide grin.

"Good luck, boss," Mitch said.

SHE DIDN'T HAVE a plan. She'd wanted to see Beck perform in the arena, wanted to witness him at his best doing something he loved. It was a memory she could take with her when she followed the rodeo out of town. But then he'd turned and looked at her. Tipped his hat and held her gaze. And she knew. She loved him. She was in love with him. And forgetting him was going to take so much distance she wasn't sure she could get far enough away.

Still. If it had just been her heart involved, she could handle it. But that rodeo owner had asked about buying the Lodge, and she'd heard Beck's shocking reply. It had been a huge mistake letting things get personal between them. She'd never meant to hurt him or stand in the way of his plans, and all she could think of was getting away, just for a little while to clear her head.

Beck had decided not to sell the hotel and free himself of what he considered a burden. Something had made him change his mind, and she knew in her heart that it was her fault.

The trail ahead of her was familiar. It was the one she and Beck had taken a few weeks ago. How far was that quiet cabin by the gurgling stream? If she could just get there, she could compose herself and figure out how to leave Remedy Creek without leaving a mess.

Her horse—Bailey—was steady, and Nora had

gained some riding skills in the past month doing solo and small group lessons with the instructors at the Lodge's riding stable. The trail was also clear. If she braved a trot, maybe she could find that cabin in only thirty minutes or so. She could rest there, take one of the buckets from the porch and get water for Bailey, and in the silence she could figure out how she was going to say goodbye to Remedy Creek.

She pressed ahead, keeping close watch for loose stones or hazards on the trail. She remembered the day Beck had halted them because of a rattlesnake ahead. Would she see one if it was there? She took a hand off the pommel and touched the horse's neck. She didn't have the right to endanger a horse just because she needed a getaway. She'd already done enough damage in Remedy Creek.

"I'm sorry, Bailey," she said. "Maybe this is a bad idea. You could be munching hay in your stall right now."

She tugged gently on the reins and was amazed that Bailey came to a stop. She'd come a long way from that first ride. They were in a small clearing and now that she had stopped moving, Nora heard two things. One was a gurgling stream, and the other was approaching hoofbeats.

Nora turned in the saddle, but she hardly needed to confirm who was chasing her.

Beck's tall form on Hercules was unmistakable. He was approaching quickly, and she had just moments to figure out what to say to him. How to say goodbye.

Tears stung Nora's eyes, just thinking about leaving.

She waited in the saddle and kept her eyes on Beck's approaching figure. He slowed and soon she could see his face in the bright morning sunshine. He'd lost his hat. Had he ridden so fast it fell off somewhere along the trail? He looked exposed, vulnerable, and it made her heart ache.

Beck stopped Hercules just feet from Nora's horse. "What are you doing?" he asked, his voice low.

"I'm riding," she said.

"Why?"

"I wanted to clear my head." She paused, remembering that night at the campfire. "I think you were the one who said you solved problems on the back of a horse."

Beck dismounted and came over to her, hands in the air, a silent offer to help her down. She shook her head.

He dropped his hands but remained by her horse. "Am I a problem you have to solve?" he asked.

Hercules tossed his head and then walked over to the stream and dipped down for a drink.

"I have to go in a few days," Nora said. "Another job is waiting, and I want to leave you—leave the Lodge—in good shape, better than it was when I got here and ready for whatever you want to do with it."

Beck didn't answer but took the lead rope on Bailey and led him over to the stream with Nora still in the saddle. The horse took a long drink, and suddenly Nora felt ridiculous sitting up there on his back. She took a risk and swung a leg over the saddle. She bobbled on the way down, but planted her feet on the ground. Beck's hands flexed as if he wanted to help her, but he didn't touch her, and she was almost disappointed he hadn't. She would like to feel his strong hands around her waist one more time before she left.

"I'm not selling the Lodge," Beck said.

Nora took off her hat and put it on her saddle. "I heard you tell the rodeo owner you weren't."

"Did you hear everything I said?"

Remembering his words made her throat thick with emotion, so she nodded.

"I meant it," Beck said.

"What…changed your mind?"

"You did," he said.

Nora shook her head and crossed her arms. "No, that's not my role. I never intended to tell you what you should do with your own property.

If my actions changed your mind, then I overstepped. I apologize."

Beck caught her hands in his.

"Don't apologize. You never told me what to do. It wasn't anything you said."

Nora looked up at him and felt relief…and a glimmer of hope.

"It's who you are," Beck said. He lifted her hands to his lips and kissed her knuckles. "You made me feel alive again and somehow made me fall in love with the Lodge."

"That's…good, I guess," she said. "If that's what makes you happy." Maybe this wasn't so bad. Maybe she hadn't done permanent damage, and Beck could go on happily without her, running the Lodge. Then she could pack up her emotions and her heart and take them on to the next place, where she'd learn all over again how to bury herself in her work. She could do this.

Hercules snorted and bumped his nose against Beck's shoulder.

"I'm getting to it," Beck told his horse. He turned back to Nora, still holding both her hands in his. "You make me happy, Nora. I didn't just fall in love with the Lodge. I fell in love with you."

Nora gasped. "You can't have," she said. This was all wrong. She'd made the mistake of falling in love with Beck, but—

"I can," he said. "I am. I love you, Nora, and I'll do whatever it takes to keep you in my life."

"I can't stay," she said.

Beck took a deep breath and looked up at the sky. He swallowed. "When you rode away, where were you going?"

"I…didn't know for sure."

"You just wanted to run."

Nora opened her mouth but didn't say anything.

"You don't have to keep running," he said. "I know you're afraid to get too comfortable someplace because it can all be taken away in a heartbeat." His voice cracked. "Believe me, I know how that feels."

"You understand," she whispered.

"I do, but I'm not running anymore. It's painful to face the past, but it's even more painful to keep living that way." He paused. "I don't know if any of that old lore about Remedy Creek is real. If it is, it sure took a while and a kick start from you, but lately I feel like I'm becoming whole again. The only conclusion I can draw is…love."

Love. He said the word again. Was it possible?

She slipped her hands out of his and walked over to the creek. She bent and dipped her fingers in. The water sparkled in the Wyoming sun. It was peaceful, being there with Beck. It felt like home. Maybe it was time she found a home.

Maybe it was time she told Beck how she felt about him.

"You asked me where I was riding," she said. She turned and faced him. "I was heading for the cabin you showed me."

His face relaxed into a small smile. "My hide-out."

"I thought so," she said. "Those books are yours, aren't they?"

He nodded. "Why were you going there?"

She shrugged. "I liked it. I thought I could sort out my feelings there."

"Your feelings?" Beck asked.

Nora took a deep breath. "I should feel afraid. I always feel afraid when I even think about settling down anywhere for good, falling in love with a place and making it hard to leave. I always leave, not because it's hard but because it's the easy way out. The safe way."

"But you don't feel afraid now?" Beck asked.

"I…don't."

Bailey stamped a foot and whinnied, and Hercules munched the tall grass alongside the creek. Beck waited, his eyes on her for a long time. Finally, he looked down at the ground. "It's okay if you don't feel the same way about me," he said. "I know I haven't made your life easy since you got here, and—"

"I do," Nora said quickly. "I do feel the same way about you."

Beck's head came up, his eyes wide. "You do?"

Hercules came over and nudged her shoulder with his nose. Nora laughed. It felt so good to let go. "I love you, Beck."

Beck closed the distance between them in two long strides and wrapped his arms around Nora. He held her close, and she breathed in his scent of horses and leather and grass.

He pulled back and looked down at her. "Please tell me you'll stay."

Nora thought for a moment about all the places she'd been. None of them compared to being with Beck in the grassy clearing with the creek rambling past and the mountains around them. She smiled, feeling a rush of warmth in her heart. "I'm ready to wake up to Wyoming sunrises, ride the trails and mountains, and bunk down in luxury."

Beck laughed. "I can offer you that and more." He lowered his lips to hers. Nora kissed him, a kiss that went on and on until one of the horses grunted. She laughed and looked up at Beck. "I can't believe this is real."

He ran a hand over her hair and trailed his fingers along her braid. He kissed her forehead. "It's real."

She smiled up at him. "Do you think we should

get back to the Lodge? The rodeo crew may need something."

He shrugged. "Didn't you leave poor Steven in charge?"

"Poor Steven?" Nora asked.

"I hope he's not in love with the Lodge because I have a far better candidate in mind for running the place," Beck said. "If you'll take the job."

"I'd love to," she said, joy almost stealing her breath. "I have ideas."

Beck laughed. "I'm sure you do."

"And I'll put Steven in contact with some people I know. I think he'd be better suited for a hotel position in a city. Wyoming isn't for everyone."

"Is it for you?"

"Definitely," Nora said.

He pulled her close again and held her tightly. "I'm so glad your company sent you to me," he whispered against her hair.

Nora's heart swelled. "Me, too."

She felt Beck laugh and pulled back. "What?"

He smiled. "Remember that first day when I tried to run away from you and you chased me down in high heels?"

Nora laughed. "Vividly."

"I can't believe I ever wanted to escape you. I lost my hat chasing after you today, but it was worth it."

"Let's not run from each other anymore," Nora said.

"Agreed." Beck took her hat from her saddle, put it on her head and offered both hands to help her into the saddle.

"I can do it myself," she said. "I'm getting the hang of these ranchy things."

He grinned. "I know. But I like helping you."

Nora gave him one more kiss, and then she let him boost her onto her horse. As they rode side by side back toward the Lodge, which had become so special to her despite her best efforts, she realized that home was more than just a place—it could be anywhere as long as it was with Beck.

* * * * *